C000292587

Author

A Murder With A Twist

by

Richard Myerscough

Previous Works by Richard Myerscough

Bat Blood - The Devil's Claw
Bat Blood - Unshackled Demons
The Gilded Harvest

~

Copyright © Richard Myerscough 2020
published and produced by Fighting Roosters Press

All rights reserved

No part of this publication may be reproduced in any form, or by means
electronic, mechanical, including photocopying, scanning, recording or any
information browsing, storage, or retrieval systems, without permission in
writing from the publisher.

Distributed to the trade by The Ingram Book Company

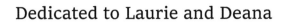
Dedicated to Laurie and Deana

Chapter One

Nancy smiled as she handed a short, middle aged lady a hard covered copy of 'Polar Diamonds'. As she let go of the book, she turned her head and stared at its strikingly, handsome author. Simon Black's jacket photo didn't do him justice.

Nancy watched the tall, chiselled author lean over the small, sparsely decorated table, and sign a book for the woman standing at the head of the line. Nancy sighed. He was more breathtaking than she had imagined.

He noticed the slender, twenty-one year old clerk's gaze. She resembled the provocative model on the cover of his previous book. He loved the way her long, red ponytail flicked from side to side as customers tried to distract her. His polite, pasted on smile grew into a wide grin as he handed the lady back her book.

Simon barely looked down as he signed another copy of his book, and handed it back to the thin man standing in front of him. The man turned and glanced at Nancy. "She is very alluring isn't she?"

"To bad she isn't a wee bit older."

Nancy's boss, Emily, stood behind the counter and worked the cash register. In front of it were stacks of Simon's new book. After inserting a customer's receipt next to the title page, she glanced at Nancy, grimaced and rocked her head back and forth.

The small, book store had barely opened. Inside, Simon's devoted fans were lined up from the back corner of the store to the door. Outside, the constantly growing line stretched to the end of the block. People were haphazardly parking their cars and racing to get in line. Vehicles with mostly out-of-province licence plates, lined the small, isolated community's main street along with the nearby side roads.

Nancy could hardly take her eyes away from the

world famous, forty-year-old author. The infatuated, young woman straightened the long, faded, red smock that Emily had forced her to wear. She wrapped the smock's tie straps around her slender waist and drew them in as snug as she could, in order to help show off her gentle curves.

She desperately wanted to take off the smock. Hidden beneath it was her favourite dress. The only visible part of the short, sleeveless, black dress was it's straps and the partially open back. She looked down at the smock and bit her lower lip. *'How could I impress anyone in this ugly thing.'* Then she smiled.

While making her way to the back of the store, Nancy squeezed past several customers. Ignoring their pleas for assistance, she slunk behind Simon as he opened yet another book awaiting his greatly, sought after signature.

Stretching out her right hand, she slowly glided her fingertips across his broad right shoulder. Her long, glossy, black fingernails almost matched his suit. They briefly disappeared under his shiny, well groomed, black hair at the back of his neck. His few grey hairs were barely noticeable. Her fingernails gradually reappeared as they slid down the contours of his left shoulder blade. Her shiny, black lips puffed out slightly as her smile widened.

After releasing a shallow sigh, she glanced at the counter. Some of the impatient customers that were standing in front of it were staring back at her. The hairs at the end of her long, dark red pony tail brushed against Simon's ear and cheek as she turned to go back to the counter.

Simon straightened his back a little and gazed at Nancy's long, fishnet covered legs, and the opening on the back of her dress, as she walked away. The fact that the attractive, young, willowy girl was almost half his age, only added to her appeal.

Looking forward, his grin relaxed into a polite smile. Before him stood a smiling, slightly curvy, but muscular woman in her early thirties, with short brown hair. Her well applied makeup tried its best to mask her tired, slightly weathered face. Despite the makeup, her puffy eyes indicated to Simon, that the woman had barely slept the night before.

In an excited voice, every part of the woman's body seemed to shiver as she blurted out, "I thought that I would never get a chance to meet you. This is the fifth time I've tried to get one of my books signed. I got to see you, but the lineups were so unreal. Last time, there were only a handful of people in front of me before you had to pack up and leave."

Without hesitation, Simon told her, "I have to agree, some of my book signings had gotten completely out of hand. My agent generally has me on a very tight and hectic schedule. I'm lucky if he factors in enough time for me to sign the first few hundred books."

"He has you run ragged. There were thousands at your Buffalo book signing last April. The arena was packed."

"Well, there is not enough room to do a reading and Q&A here. That gives me a little more time to spend with my fans." His smile slightly grew as he told her, "At least this time, you got here early." He released a gentle sigh before adding, "It's nice knowing that I don't have a plane waiting to whisk me away to another packed venue."

The woman tilted her head and stared into his dark brown eyes. "You are my all time favourite author. I have read all your books. I absolutely love them." Looking down at the book in her hand she quickly corrected herself. "Except for this one, but I am positive that I will love it too."

Simon looked at the nervous, fidgety woman as she tightly held a hardcovered copy of Polar Diamonds with both hands. Her closely clipped fingernails had fake diamonds imbedded in the red nail polish. The exposed ends of her fingertips had turned white from the pressure exerted on them. They came close to matching the sprawled diamonds pictured on the book's, blood red jacket.

Knowing that he had already spent too much time with her, and had to keep the line moving, Simon almost forced the book from her hands. "So I take it that you really like my books."

"Oh yes, I really love them." The woman stared at him with a huge, wide smile. "You know, your pictures don't do you justice. You are much better looking in real life."

Simon smiled, nodded and said, "Thank you." He used her receipt like a bookmark to open the book. With the tip of his pen hovering above the cover page, he asked her, "Now, who should I sign it to?"

The overly, excited woman almost started bouncing as she said, "Marion."

As he started to write one of his many pre-prepared lines in her book, he said, "Then Marion it is."

Marion was mesmerised by his smile as he scribbled his signature. As he handed the book back to her, she softly ran her fingers over the back of his hand and the large, gothic looking ring on his forefinger.

Not budging from the head of the line, she immediately opened her book and read the inscription. 'To Marion, one of my most devoted fans, Simon Black'. She slammed the book shut and glared at him. "One of? I am your most devoted fan, or at least I was 'til now."

She turned to the lady behind her. "That's the thanks I get. 'One of', I've been a lot more than just 'One of'."

Carrying the book in one hand, she erratically swung her arms as she stormed towards the exit. Simon looked at the stunningly, attractive lady that had been standing behind Marion. "I guess she has some issues."

The tall, chestnut brown haired woman smiled. Her subtle makeup, expensive jewellery and stylish, dark blue suit made her look out of place. In a calm voice, she tilted her head slightly and told him, "What was she thinking? Your eyes meet and you feel suddenly compelled to whisk her away on some exotic adventure. This isn't a scene from one of your novels. I tell you, some people are not quite grounded in reality."

A bit relieved with the alluring woman's calm, rational demeanor, Simon smiled and said "Very true."

She glanced over her shoulder and grinned as the frazzled woman stormed out of the store. "And I thought that I was your most devoted admirer." With a twisted, half smile on her face, she added, "I wonder what is worse, someone that is obsessed with books about love, betrayal, death and obsession, or those that live it."

The question stunned Simon. After a couple seconds, he smiled at the woman and said, "Those that live it have closure. Those obsessed by it don't."

The woman tilted her head and thought for a moment before responding, "You might be right."

As she started to turn away, Simon called out, "Didn't you want me to sign your book?"

The woman stopped, turned back around and politely smiled. "Of course. Of course I do." Her smile grew a bit wider as she added, "Make the dedication out to Cindy."

The book almost fell out of the woman's hand as she passed it to him. Despite her radiant beauty, the woman's strange question made Simon feel a bit uneasy. Fortunately for her, by the time his pen touched the cover page of her book, all he thought about was how pleasant she was compared to the frazzled woman before her.

As Cindy slowly walked away, she opened the book, stopped and read what he had written. 'To Cindy, the best fan any author could ever have, Simon Black'.

Simon watched as Cindy slowly closed the book and pressed it against her chest with both hands. Before leaving the book store she gracefully twirled around and dramatically blurted out, "Thank you. You have no idea what you and your books mean to me."

Simon turned to the man standing at the front of the line. The man raised his left hand and chuckled, "Hey, I really like your books, but I'm not crazy. You may be a good looking dude and all, but I'm not in love with you." The man shifted his eyes towards the door and softly added, "But, if you looked like her, I certainly might."

Cindy grinned and swayed her body back and forth as she exited the store. Simon released a cleansing sigh of relief and grinned. "Two in a row, that's enough for one day."

A few of the people standing in line started to chuckle. Others whispered to each other. Emily stood behind the counter and tried not to laugh as she rang in another sale of Polar Diamonds.

Outside of dodging numerous, flirtatious customers, Nancy found the rest of the morning and early afternoon frantic, but relatively uneventful. About three-thirty, Emily came up to her and said, "Things have calmed down a bit and I really need to step out for a while. Most of the people in line have already purchased their books. They seem to be behaving themselves. If you stay at the front of the store everything should be fine. I'll try not to be gone too long."

As Nancy went from one customer to another, an awkward looking man dressed in scruffy clothes vied for her attention. His clumsy but persistent demeanor made her feel uncomfortable. He repetitively interrupted her by asking questions about Simon Black. "Did he only come here to sign some books? Why was this store chosen? Who set it up? Does Simon have any other business in Blackett Hill? ...."

She tried to tune him out, but couldn't. Not knowing how to reply to his questions, she told him, "I don't know.", over and over again. Feeling bewildered, Nancy turned her back to the irritating man and tried to ignore him.

After Nancy dealt with a few more customers, she still felt uneasy. She stood on her toes in order to see over the aisles. Most of Simon's fans were standing in the line in front of him. She hardly saw anyone in the rest of the store. She relaxed her stance, closed her eyes, took a deep breath and smiled. The bothersome, awkward looking man was no where in sight.

The rest of the afternoon went smoothly. The long, slow moving line had made Simon's fans tired and sore. Some brought portable stools to sit on. Some stretched and ran-on-the-spot to help revive their aching arms, neck and legs. Others played games on their phones. However, most of them just stood in line, bought a book, read some of it, got it signed and left. Only a few strayed and browsed around the store.

At two minutes to five, Nancy went outside and asked the few dozen people that were patiently standing in line to come inside so she could shut the door. The door was barely closed before two smiling fans asked to leave.

A lady with a copy of Simon's book tucked under her arm, stood next to the counter and called out to her, "Miss, I know the store is technically closed, but can I still purchase a couple more items? It's going to be quite a while before I get to the front of the line."

Nancy looked at the woman and then at the unlocked door. "No problem. Some of these people haven't purchased their copies of Polar Diamonds yet."

Cupping her hands against the sides of her mouth like a megaphone, Nancy shouted out, "I need to lock the door for a couple minutes. If anyone needs to get out, please wait next to it so I can see you."

Before she got two steps away from the door, she heard someone knocking on it. She turned around and barely recognized Emily. The normally conservative, thirty-six year old woman had totally transformed herself into a socialite. Her face and hair were done up, and she was wearing gold, diamond imbedded jewellery, a short, thin strapped, black dress that greatly emphasised her cleavage, plus bright red lipstick and a pair of black pumps.

Emily waved her left hand at Nancy while she blurted out, "Go and help your customer, I'll let myself in." As she got out her keys, she added, "Sorry for being gone so long. I thought I'd be gone for only half an hour. I didn't mean to abandon you for this long."

As Nancy made her way to the counter, she said, "It's alright, I managed."

Emily saw a run in Nancy's stockings, her messy hair and a wide, dirty, triangular smudge across the back, lower part of her short dress. "I'm truly sorry. It will never happen again."

A couple of Simon's fans followed Emily into the store. As Emily started to zig-zag through the crowd towards Simon, Nancy asked her, "Should I lock the doors?"

"It's alright. With all the extra sales Simon has generated today, I think I can afford to pay you a little overtime."

Nancy raised her eyebrows and replied, "Time and a half, not just straight time?"

Emily stopped and waved her hand in the air. "No problem." After doing a rough head count of the people inside the store, she told her, "Get a roll of raffle tickets and start handing them out to the people in line. That way they can shop and not worry about losing their place in line."

Having spent hours in a slow moving line, the restless crowd dispersed throughout the store. Beforehand, not many of Simon's fans risked losing their place by getting out of line. After Nancy issued the tickets, they were everywhere. She was suddenly swarmed by needy customers.

She felt overwhelmed. She tried to tune out their voices, and focussed all her attention solely on one customer at a time. Some of the people vying for her attention became flustrated and began pacing in circles.

Their loud, desperate voices caught Emily's attention.

She left Simon's side and went over to the small group of annoying people. It didn't take long for her to discover the reason for their abrasive demeanor.

After whispering a few words to Simon, Emily wedged open the door to the back room. She used two footstools and a wide roll of red ribbon to help block off the section past the employees washroom. Several grateful, queasy fans shook her hand in gratitude as they formed a line in front of the washroom.

Luckily for Nancy, most of Simon's fans ended up grabbing a few books to peruse through and returned to the line. Many of them discretely rummaged through their backpacks and oversized purses for any remaining drinks, food and snacks that they brought with them. Wrappers and crumbs littered the shelves and retail floor.

Between customers, a needy, portly, middle aged woman repetitively asked Nancy for her opinion on various authors. She wanted to find someone that wrote adventurous thrillers, simular to Simon Black's novels.

Three quarters of a hour after the store was supposed to close, there was barely enough room for a person to squeeze down the aisles. More people had entered the store then left. Between serving customers, Nancy was constantly ringing in purchases and issuing tickets.

Looking around the store as she rang in a customer, she asked the lady, "How did you know we were still open?"

The lady smiled and told her, "It's all over the media. A lot of people got lost and thought it was over. There was a huge bunch of us at the truck stop when we found out that the store was still open." The lady reached out and shook Nancy's hand. "Thank you." She stared at Nancy for a moment, then added, "You look a lot younger than the photos people posted of you on the internet."

Nancy tried to force herself to smile. "I hope they were taken before I became such a mess."

"Don't worry, they were and you looked gorgeous." The lady took out her phone a showed her a few of the pictures. One picture showed her back. The apron covered her front, but had left the back of her dress available to public view. Nancy was shocked. She didn't realize how provocative the dress made her appear.

A soft drizzle created shiny beads and thin stripes on the windows. Soon afterwards, the doormat started to get soggy. Water dripped from the brims of people's hats onto the books and magazines they were looking at. Soiled footprints along with the growing amount of garbage, made the aisles look grossly unkept. The mere sight of them upset Nancy.

The frazzled, young clerk did her best to look after the customers at the front of the store. After shutting the door to the back room, Emily spent most of her time standing next to Simon. Occasionally, she would call out a number. "Does anyone here have the last three digits, 1, 1, 7. If so, can you please come to the head of the line with your book."

Nancy saw Emily bend down, tap Simon on the shoulder and whisper something in his ear. She knelt to retrieve a book from a bottom shelf. While looking between the legs of the people standing in line, she noticed Emily discretely stroking the side of his leg. Simon reached down, caressed Emily's hand and whispered something back to her.

As she started to stand up, Nancy noticed someone wearing dark blue pants go into the back room. She stood up, turned to the portly lady that she was helping, gave her the book and said, "Excuse me, I have to find out what is going on in the back room."

The lady smiled as she raised and jiggled her hand. "No Problem." She opened the book and added, "This author sounded pretty good. I might give her a go."

Nancy went to the back room and looked around. No one was there. She saw an open box of garbage bags and a pair of scissors sitting on a box next to the door. Several improvised raincoats were lying on the floor next to it. A small dented box was wedged between the bottom of the self-locking emergency door and the doorframe.

She opened the door and peered outside. She sighed as she saw all the discarded garbage and cigarette butts that had been spewed over the area. "Pigs, they are nothing but filthy pigs."

She picked up the mangled box. Inside of it was an expensive, specially ordered book about the Brazilian military, that had arrived on Friday. The edges of the hardcovered book, along with two corners were badly pushed in. As she took the book out of the box, a thin stream of water poured out of it. She spread the pages apart and stood it on a shelf to dry. "I hope it's not totally destroyed."

Behind her, she heard the employees' washroom door shut. She turned around just in time to see the door to the retail floor close. Feeling vexed, she marched back to the counter.

Despite the small store's meagre inventory, some of the shelves were nearly empty. *'Emily was right. Simon's fans must have felt obligated to buy more than they came in for.'*

The store was a mess. It was far beyond what Nancy could mentally handle. Something inside of her forced her to tie the corner of a garbage bag around her apron's strap. While picking up the garbage she tried to tidy up the shelves and baskets, and bring some degree of order to the store.

Nancy heard the door close and looked up at the clock. It was seven-fifty. The store was silent. She had been there for almost twelve hours with hardly any breaks. She was totally exhausted.

Nancy reached up, grabbed a shelf for support, and slowly got off her aching knees. She never saw Simon, Emily, or even the last few customers exit the store. Seeing no-one, she called out, "Is anyone here." There was no reply.

As she walked to the door, she stopped and gazed at her hazy reflection in the glass. Beyond her smeared makeup, she noticed her torn, twisted, bunched up stockings and how her scruffy pony tail was pointed almost sideways. The garbage bag dangling from her waist only added to her hideous appearance. Looking down, she saw how filthy her hands, forearms and knees were. "What was I thinking? I'm a complete mess."

Nancy untied her apron. The garbage bag fell to the floor. She took off her apron and dropped it on top of it. While staring at her reflection, she told herself, "He never saw how great I can look in this dress." She thought of the photo the lady showed her, then of Simon, and smiled. "However, something must've caught his attention."

Nancy couldn't stop herself from yawning. She could barely concentrate as she counted the cash in the till. After locking the register, she turned off the lights and yelled out, "I hope everyone is out, cause I'm locking the door."

Chapter Two

The next morning Nancy arrived at the store wearing no makeup, a warm, pink sweater and blue jeans. She yawned as she unlocked the door. Even the cool, brisk walk to work wasn't enough to fully awaken her. "Thank god it's Sunday. At least I got to sleep in for a wee bit longer."

Her apron and the bag of trash were still on the floor where she left them. She put on the apron and dragged the quarter full garbage bag behind the counter. After she got the cash register set up, she looked at the filthy floors and said, "I hope I have time to clean this mess before anyone sees it."

She went to the back room and retrieved the mop and bucket, a sponge, plus a couple dry rags. She stuffed the rags in one of her apron's front pockets. The bucket still had plenty of water in it from the day before. As she swished the mop around, she noticed some soapy bubbles begin to form. "That's probably good enough."

She quickly scrubbed the dried coffee, pop and stubborn juice stains off the floor. While looking back at the wet floor, she sighed, "Why do people insist on bringing drinks into a book store. I bet they don't spill this much at home."

As she used the sponge to scrub some sticky, juice stains off a bottom shelf, she looked back at where she had mopped. There were streaks all over the floor. "That water must have been absolutely filthy. I have to change it and mop the floor all over again."

Nancy wrapped her right arm around the mop and used it to help her push the bucket into the back room. After turning the washroom's doorknob with her left hand, she leaned her right shoulder against the door. It didn't budge.

She let go of the mop and pushed the door as hard as she could. As it started to give way, she heard a thump. Looking down she saw a man's hand flop out of the crack in the doorway. It was covered in flakes of dry blood.

Nancy knelt down and tried to pull the stiff arm out as far as she could. With only half of the man's forearm out, she rolled up the blood stained sleeve of his jacket. After she undid the damp cuff of his shirt sleeve, she tried to check for a pulse. There wasn't any. As she released the cold dangling arm, she recognized the large, oval, gold ring on the forefinger. It had a large emerald in the middle and five smaller, elongated ones that were mounted in the shape of a cross on a black onyx setting. The cross was encircled by a band of small diamonds.

She covered her face with her hands and started to cry. "Simon, how could this happen to you of all people. Why now?"

After weeping for what seemed like hours, but were actually only a few minutes, she wiped the tears from her eyes. That was when she noticed the blood on her hands. Her tears had rehydrated the flakes of dry blood that had rubbed off Simon's hand, wrist and arm. She stood up and went to a small mirror next to the door. Streaks of his diluted blood ran down her cheeks and across her eyes.

She went to her locker, grabbed a wad of tissues and tried to wipe it off. Looking at the small, magnetic mirror on her locker's door, she noticed the red smudges on her face. Dabbing the tip of the wad into the bucket to moisten it, seemed to make it worse. As she tried to get the blood off her face, diluted droplets fell on her sweater and apron. She ended up tossing the wad of tissue into the bucket. As the initial shock wore off, she realized, "I have to call the police."

Officer Kelly looked at Nancy through the glass door. She noticed the dark, pink blotches on Nancy's cheeks and neck, along with the off-colour smudges on the arms and neck line of her pink sweater, plus several more spots on her apron. "Are you the person who called the police?"

Nancy's hands were shaking as she unlocked the door. "Yes, I found Simon Black's dead body in the employees' washroom. I was trying to get inside to empty the water bucket, but the door was stuck." She started to cry. "His body was blocking it."

Officer Kelly took out her pen and notepad and started to jot everything down. "Can you show me his body."

"Sure." Nancy used her sleeve to wipe away some of her tears as she started to walk towards the backroom. "Watch your step, The floor is still wet. I just mopped it." The officer stopped to look around. "Why would you mop down a crime scene?"

Nancy shrugged her shoulders. "I didn't know anything about it at the time."

Officer Kelly saw the table at the back of the store. "What was going on in the store yesterday? I saw all the cars and the huge lineup in front of the store when I drove by it."

"Simon", Nancy stopped and took a couple cleansing breaths before continuing. "Simon Black was hosting the premiere book signing for his latest novel. We were very fortunate that he picked this store. Most successful authors launch their new books at one of the big book stores. If they plan on doing a reading, they usually rent halls, or small arenas."

The officer took out her pen and pad, and jotted down some notes. "So it was strange that he was even here at all?"

"Sure was. Blackett Hill is in the middle of nowhere. I'm surprised that so many of his fans were willing to drive so far to get here."

With a puzzled look on her face, Officer Kelly interrupted her. "How did they even find it? This place is only printed on a handful of local tourist maps."

Nancy sighed and shook her head. "Even out-of-towners know how to use a GPS. All it takes is one user to pin point a place, and voila, it's on their virtual map. My mother first noticed it on her GPS a couple weeks ago."

"Wouldn't that be about the same time as Simon

Black's book debut would've been announced?"

Nancy's eyebrows sank as she responded. "Yes."

The officer turned and looked out the window. "His fans didn't all just appear first thing Saturday morning. Do you have any idea when they start arriving? You must have talked to some of them."

"Apparently, a lot of them arrived on Friday. The hotel was booked solid, and so was the campground just off the highway. Some people even slept in their vehicles."

Officer Kelly nodded her head. "I was wondering why the town was so busy the last couple days. I drove into town yesterday, saw the long line up at the restaurant and decided that a cheeseburger just wasn't worth the wait."

Officer Kelly used Nancy's locker mirror to peer inside the washroom. Bloody hand and foot prints along with splattered blood covered most of the lower half of the tiny room. "His body is sprawled on the floor between the toilet, pedestal sink and the door. There isn't much room in there."

"I know." Nancy tried to peek inside but couldn't see past the blood covered pedestal sink. "There is barely enough room for a toilet, sink and mirror."

"Do you have a hammer and some screwdrivers?"

Nancy retrieved a small tool box and handed it to her. Working through the narrow crack in the door, it took the officer a few minutes to tap the pins out of the door hinges. As she removed the door, Simon's stiff body shifted sideways. The back of his head got wedged between the door frame and the sink's pedestal.

The two women stared at the body. His open eyes stared up at them. The first thing Officer Kelly noticed was the caked blood surrounding a small hole under the back, left side of his jaw. She turned to Nancy and said, "His killer must have struck a major vein to spew this much blood."

Outside of a funeral home, this was the first time Officer Kelly had seen a dead body, let alone a murder victim.

She turned slightly pale as she told the stunned clerk, "I'll have to seal off this store. Do me a favour and tape a large sign to the door saying that the store will be closed until further notice."

Standing just behind her, Nancy answered, "Sure, no problem. First, I need to call my manager and let her know not to come in this morning."

As Officer Kelly was talking to her superiors, Nancy went to the phone on the wall behind the counter and called her boss. "Hi, Emily, I'm sorry for calling you so early on a Sunday, but the police are sealing off the store."

"Why?"

"After opening up this morning, I discovered Simon's body in the washroom." Nancy wiped the tears away from her eyes. "It was horrible."

Emily rubbed her eyes and smeared even more mascara and eye makeup over her face. "What! What are you talking about?"

Nancy started to cry as she told her, "I saw him. He had a hole beneath his jaw. There was blood everywhere."

Emily sat up in bed and told her, "You just stay where you are. I'll be there in five minutes."

She stripped off the provocative black dress that she was still wearing. After grabbing a pair of jogging pants from under the bed, she put them on along with a sweater and the flip flops that she normally wore around the house. By the time Emily parked her car behind Officer Kelly's patrol car, the officer had finished taping off the entrance.

Emily's car windows didn't even have time to de-fog. She slammed her car door and ran towards Officer Kelly yelling, "Wait, wait, this is my store."

The officer raised her arm. "I'm sorry but this is now a crime scene."

Emily stopped directly in front of her. "At least tell me what happened."

"Your employee, Nancy Gamble, found a dead body in the washroom." Officer Kelly slowly rocked her head back and forth. "That is all I'm at liberty to tell you. I wouldn't have said that much, if it wasn't for the fact that I believe your employee had already told you everything that she knows."

"But I am responsible for everything that happens in that store."

The officer noticed Emily start to shiver. "Not now. How about you go home and warm up. This is now a police matter. I'll let you know when we are finished, and when you can reopen the store."

Chapter Three

A police van parked in front of the book store. A tall, thin, middle aged man, along with two shorter younger men, plus a small Asian woman with a camera case, got out of it and stretched. After talking to Officer Kelly, the crime scene technicians discussed what supplies they needed to bring into the store. The photographer took out her camera and immediately started to take pictures and videos of the outside of the store and the surrounding area.

The coroner pulled his car behind the van. The short, broad, grey haired man grabbed his bag and got out. While the three technicians started to unload some of their equipment, the coroner and the tall, lead technician went inside. After they put on all their crime scene, protective apparel, Officer Kelly led the two men into the back room.

Dr. Frank MacKay, English Lookout's only coroner, squatted down to assess the body. He examined the small, round hole beneath the back of Simon's jaw, and looked around the tiny room. Seeing the amount of blood on Simon's suit, along with all the splatter and bloody foot and hand prints, he figured that he had bled to death. As he stood up, he noticed a smashed phone in the toilet.

His vibrating cell phone redirected his attention. After removing his gloves, he took out his phone and read his messages. The coroner started typing his reply as he told the lead technician, "This guy is definitely dead. I don't think that there is nothing else I really need to see here."

The technician glanced at the body. "So it was definitely a murder?"

The doctor continued to type as he answered back, "I don't see anything here that could've caused that wound, so it wasn't self inflected. That makes it a murder."

The technician looked at the stiff twisted corpse and the size of the washroom, and said, "This is going to be fun."

The doctor stopped typing, turned to the technician

and told him, "There was a fatality at the highway construction near Hunter's Crossing. They got traffic blocked in both directions. Sorry to rush off, but I gotta go."

"What about the body?"

"Tell the detective that I can't make my final conclusions until after I get it back to the morgue. Get the photographer to take lots of pictures." Looking at the time, he added, "It will be at least another half an hour before they get here to remove the body."

Ten minutes later, Detective Douglas parked his car behind the police van. Officer Kelly held the door open for the stocky, slightly wrinkled, salt and pepper haired man. "You just missed the coroner."

"I know, he drove past me. I had to pull over in order to read his messages and email him back."

Jerking her head to one side, Officer Kelly directed the detective's attention to the young girl seated behind the counter. "That's Nancy Gamble. She's the one that found the body. Unfortunately, it was after she had mopped most of the retail floor. She even scrubbed a few of the shelves."

The detective looked around the store and noticed a camera in the corner. It had a wide lens, plus a clear view of both the checkout counter and the door. "Did you check the camera?"

The officer grinned. "This is a small town. In the three years I've been covering this part of the county, this is the first time the station had received a call from this town. I doubt that any of the cameras in this place have been properly maintained for years."

"So does the camera work or not?"

"Somewhat, but the pictures are too fuzzy to be used in court. The one that encompasses the rear exit is even worse."

"So the store has a back door?"

"There is a fire exit in the rear. Nancy informed me

that the battery inside the emergency release arm has been dead for ages. She also told me that a lot of people were going in and out of it yesterday. Just look outside. The ground is covered in cigarette butts and garbage."

"Isn't the exit hitched up to an alarm system?"

"The two doors are linked together. They are either both off, or both on." Officer Kelly glanced at a young technician as he bent over to open a large case of equipment. "Like I said, this is a small town. People don't even lock their doors at night."

Detective Douglas peered through the window at the front of the store. A small crowd was starting to form across the street. "Do you live around here?"

"Nope, I just patrol this area."

As they walked to the back of the store, the detective asked her, "No partner?"

"Why, the people here basically police themselves, along with the surrounding area. The pot holes in the local roads help govern everyone's driving habits. However, since they started resurfacing the highway, I have been issuing a lot more speeding tickets."

The detective arched his back, lowered his eyebrows and looked at her. "What do you mean by police themselves?"

Officer Kelly smiled. "If someone hits his wife or gets out of line, they had better be ready to move out of town. They won't be able to buy a loaf of bread or even a toothpick here. The people here take shunning to a new level."

"But no violence?"

Officer Kelly shook her head. "None, I've never seen a town like it."

"That sounds a bit creepy."

"Maybe, but it works both ways. If anyone needs help, or finds themself in trouble, the entire town is there to support them. For example, after a storm last fall, a bunch of town folk got together and repaired a local farmer's dairy barn. He wasn't even one of them."

Detective Douglas shrugged his shoulders. "So they believe in the good neighbour policy." Spotting the table at the back of the store, he asked her. "Do you know what that was used for?"

Officer Kelly glanced at the table. "Apparently, the dead man was a famous author. He had a book signing here yesterday. I don't read much, but I've heard of him."

The detective looked around the small store. "Someone famous in this cubbyhole? Why here?"

"I asked Nancy Gamble, but she doesn't seem to know much about it. She told me that Emily, the lady that runs the store, might know more about it."

As Detective Douglas bent down in front of the washroom door, the tall technician turned towards him and said, "I'm finding all kinds of prints in here."

Officer Kelly spoke up. "Apparently there was a huge crowd in the store yesterday."

"I can believe it."

Standing on the toilet, the petit photographer snapped another picture. The flash made the detective look away as he inquired, "Any places where you didn't find any prints?"

"Only the doorknobs." The tech pointed to the detached door that was leaning against the lockers across from the washroom. I only found one set of prints on the outside knob. I believe they are from the young girl sitting behind the counter. Officer Kelly informed me that she opened it a bit and found the body."

"Is it safe for me to come in and inspect the body?"

After the photographer placed a piece of plastic on the toilet tank, she sat on it and said, "Just give me a couple more seconds." She carefully leaned forward and took several more shots of the toilet bowl, as she told him, "I need to get a better shot of his cell phone." 'Click, click, click.' "Okay, done, I think I've got everything in here."

The detective lifted her off the toilet with ease, turned and put her down outside the doorway. "Don't go anywhere. I want you to take pictures of the entire retail floor, including the table in the back corner."

Flashing a quick smile, she said, "No problem."

The technician stepped out of the washroom to give the detective more room. Detective Douglas knelt to get a closer look at the body. He noticed red and black smudge marks on the side of Simon's neck. There wasn't any gunpowder residue around the hole under the back, left side of Simon's jaw. "He wasn't shot. It looks like he was stabbed by a long, pointed object, about the diameter of a pen or pencil."

Simon's hands and sleeves were covered in dry blood. The front of his shirt and jacket were still soaked. "He must have struggled with the killer. Whoever did it must have been covered in blood."

Officer Kelly spoke up, "They probably left through the back exit. Nobody could've exited through the front door with that much blood on them without drawing some attention."

At the bottom of the toilet bowl was a smashed cell phone. "The water had a very faint pink hue. They must have tried to flush it into the sewer."

Officer Kelly released a soft chuckle. "That's stupid. There is no way it would go through the hole, and certainly not the trap."

"Who said killers are smart." Wearing his latex gloves, the detective reached in and retrieved the phone. A crude circle the size of a quarter was crushed into its face, and hundreds of fractures radiated from it. Looking at the back of the phone, he saw deformed stress marks. "They must've tried to smash it apart. Someone really wanted to put this phone out of commission."

Looking at its face a little closer, he noticed some

fibres and other debris stuck between the cracks. The compartment holding the memory chip was slightly ajar. Using his pen knife, he carefully pried it open. The chip was missing. "The techs might still get something from it."

Bending down, he examined Simon's right hand. The tips of two of his fingers were severely scratched. "I guess he tried to call for help. Too bad his phone was broken."

Under large lamps, Dr. MacKay examined the large, naked, freshly washed corpse laying on the stainless steel table in front of him. He took pictures of every tattoo, bruise, and oddity on him, along with the interior of his ears and nose. By the time he was done, every square centimetre of Simon's body was digitally recorded in ultra high definition. "If I didn't know he wrote books for a living, I would've thought he was some kind of professional athlete."

Sitting on the doctor's desk chair, Detective Douglas looked at him and said, "He's a gym junky. He used his chiselled body and good looks to help him sell his books."

The doctor inserted a multi fingered, geared spreader into Simon's mouth and adjusted it so he could see inside. As he looked inside Simon's blue stained mouth, he casually asked the detective, "So when did he get the time to write them?"

"Maybe he didn't sleep."

As he looked under Simon's tongue, the doctor pointed to Simon's chest. "Did you notice the small cluster of small rectangular bruises on his chest?"

The detective walked over and looked at them. "Any guess on what caused them?"

"Not yet, but they are fresh."

Dr. MacKay used a wand with a small, adjustable camera at he end, to study the interior of Simon's mouth. The doctor's eyebrows almost came together, as he told Detective Douglas, "The murder weapon must have been quite long. It penetrated Mr. Black's neck, nicked an artery, then it was twisted upward and thrust through his tongue and upper mouth. I think it may have even reached his brain."

"That would mean a quick and sudden death."

"Not always. I believe most of the struggling was done after he was stabbed." The doctor pointed to the photos pinned to the cork board. "If he died instantly, there would be a large pool of blood instead of all the blood splatter. Depending how far it went in, it could've only affected his smell and speech. The killer was no brain surgeon."

"They seldom are."

The doctor did a stabbing action toward the detective's throat. "The killer went for Mr. Black's jugular. That is when he, or she, nicked his artery." Then the doctor placed his arm against his chest. "As Mr. Black was spurting out blood, they struggled. The killer probably got in too close." The doctor used his thumb to indicate a weapon and thrust it upwards. "That was when the weapon was twisted upward. The only thing the killer could do to finish the job, is push the weapon upward and hope to penetrate his brain."

"That makes sense. The washroom was quite small." The detective stared at the cork board. "Simon Black was a big man and that washroom was awfully small. If he thrashed about in there, the killer's body must be covered in bruises."

As the doctor took multiple swabs of every entrance and exit point the murder weapon made, he said, "That depends on how agile the killer was. Mr. Black wasn't expecting to be stabbed. If he wasn't a violent man by nature, his first instinct wouldn't be to fight back. He could've thrashed around in a feeble attempt to contain the bleeding."

"So you are telling me that he might've thought the stabbing was an accident, and hoped the killer would go out and seek help?"

"Exactly."

"That's the only explanation I can think of for there not being two bodies in that room. Look at the size of Mr. Black's hands. All he had to do is grab the killers neck and squeeze. He must have known, and trusted the killer."

"That sort of makes sense. They went into that tiny room together." The detective looked at the doctor. "What if the killer left and came back? That would've given Simon Black the opportunity to try to call for help."

"But why return?"

"To make sure he's dead, and destroy his phone."

"So this poor sap could've been waiting for help that was never going to arrive." While studying the debris on the swabs, the doctor told the detective, "I'd wait until we get some tests back, but right now, I think the killer stabbed him with some kind of pen. It was probably new and filled with some type of blue gel ink."

The doctor passed a tube containing a swab to the detective. "See that small semi-clear clump at the bottom of the tube?"

"Yeah."

The doctor turned to the detective. "Considering the ink I found inside his mouth, I believe it's the seal used to protect the tip of a new pen cartridge. I found it under his tongue."

While gazing at the small clump stuck to the swab, the detective replied, "You are sure it didn't come from something he ate?"

"Pretty sure." The doctor cracked a twisted smile. "I'm only surprised that the blood didn't wash it down his throat, or out of his mouth."

"It must've been an awfully long pen. It had to go all the way from bottom the left side of his jaw, through the back of his tongue and up to the right side of his brain. Figuring that the killer had to have something to grip onto, it must've been at least double the length of an ordinary pen."

The doctor looked at him and grinned. "He was killed in a book shop wasn't he? They must sell all sorts of novelty items there."

When Detective Douglas got back to his desk, he went on his computer and skimmed through the pictures of the retail floor. He isolated one that showed the novelty section of the store and sent them to the printer. "Sergeant, can you get the photo off the printer for me."

Sgt. Ryan coughed as he walked over to the printer. The sick, young sergeant glanced at the photo before handing it to the detective. "Here you go." Seeing an enlarged section of the same photo on the detective's computer monitor, the sergeant inquired, "What are you looking for?"

"A super long pen with blue gel ink." Looking up at him, the detective asked, "Do you feel up to going for a drive?"

The sergeant placed his arm in front of his mouth and coughed before answering, "Sure, where to?"

"To the middle of nowhere. A small town called Blackett Hill."

The leaves on the maple trees on the side of the highway were beginning to turn red. To break the silence, Sgt. Ryan turned to the detective and asked him, "So what team do you root for?"

"The Jets."

Sgt. Ryan snickered and then started to cough. After wiping his runny nose with a tissue, he replied, "I pegged you as a Leafs fan."

"I used to follow Toronto, but the media is all over them. I've found that the Winnipeg fans are a little more mellow. Now I get to enjoy a game without all the hype."

Knowing that the sergeant was sick and was not likely to be driving, Doctor MacKay sent him a message instead of the detective. Sgt. Ryan pulled out his phone and read the text out loud. "The smeared blotches on Simon Black's neck were two different types of lipstick. The lab is trying to narrow down the colours and manufacturers."

"Simon was a very, good looking man. He must have had women climbing all over him."

Sgt. Ryan looked at the detective. "You said women. Maybe that's what killed him?"

Sgt. Ryan threw his head back and coughed into his arm. The detective glanced over at him. "I hope you don't give me your cold. I can't afford any time off." Looking at the road, he added, "Apparently the victim's a real bigwig in the writing community. The press has already started pressuring the captain for information about the case."

"Well, they will just have to wait until we have something solid to give them."

There was only a wooden, handpainted sign at the turn off leading to Blackett Hill. Most of the two lane side road followed the edge of a steep ravine. As they looped around a 'U' shaped bend, they could see the river below. After the road straightened, Detective Douglas looked at the sergeant. "I wonder how many people died going around that curve. It must be treacherous during the winter."

After the fifty minute drive was over, Detective Douglas pulled up in front of the book store. Sgt. Ryan turned and looked at him. "Is this town even on the map?"

Detective Douglas snickered. "Sure it is. Someone marked it on the large wall map back at the station. Outside of that, I highly doubt it."

Before the detective stepped on the sidewalk, his phone began to vibrate. After reading the message he turned to the sergeant. "There were a lot of dead blood cells in the water bucket. Much more than a few tissues could have soaked up."

"According to Officer Kelly's report, Nancy Gamble had blood on her hands, face and clothes. Maybe she washed some of it off in the bucket."

Detective Douglas turned towards the sergeant and told him, "Maybe Nancy forgot to tell Officer Kelly a few things." Looking at the store's door, he added, "And didn't think to inform me either."

After entering the book shop, they both walked over to the small aisle that contained all of the miscellaneous novelty items. Detective Douglas picked up an oversized pen in the shape of a crossbow bolt. "That is certainly long enough to go all the way into a person's brain."

While looking at the tip, the sergeant shook his head. "It can't be the murder weapon. The barbs on the arrow head would have deformed the edges of the hole in Simon Black's neck. Plus they would make it very hard to extract."

Detective Douglas mumbled, "The only other pen here that is long enough is in the shape of a feather. It's made of some kind of rubber, and is too flimsy to be the murder weapon."

Sgt. Ryan rolled the tip of the bolt back and forth on one of the metal book shelves. "Maybe the tip was removed?" Even after he broke the plastic barbs off, he continued to roll it back and forth to see how smooth he could make it. After examining the results, he showed the detective the tip. "With a little more effort, I could easily smooth the edges some more."

"That would still leave a somewhat distorted edge. The wound was completely smooth. Besides, it would leave plastic residue behind." After looking at several tags, the detective concluded, "That can't be the murder weapon. They all contain red ink."

While gathering the pieces he broke off and placing them in a plastic collection bag, the sergeant said, "So we came all this way for nothing?"

"Not quite. We still have to interview the locals. Maybe they saw someone leave through the back door."

Sgt. Ryan spoke up, "And Nancy Gamble."

Detective Douglas looked at him. "You can interview her. She is more your age. Maybe you can get some straight answers from her."

From the different shops' posted hours, the detective found out that almost everything in town closes at five o'clock on Saturdays. The only exceptions were the restaurant and gas station at the far end of town. The murder happened long after that.

A lot of the locals refused to answer the door. Before Detective Douglas knocked, he would hear activity inside, afterward nothing. From those that did answer, he found out that almost everyone had gone home for supper. None of the people living above the shops admitted seeing anything useful to the case. Most just wanted to complain about the crowd and all of the vehicles that were parked everywhere. While looking around the rear of the book store, Detective Douglas noticed a couple houses with an open view of the shop's back door.

As he stood there studying their angle of view, a short, heavy set woman came out of one of the houses and began waddling towards him. In almost a whisper, he mumbled, "Well maybe we just caught a break."

The middle aged woman stopped next to the neatly trimmed, chest high, row of bushes that divided the two properties. "So, did you catch the killer yet?" Before the detective could reply, the woman put her hands on her hips and blared out, "You Johnny-come-latelies can't expect us to do all the work for you."

The detective rested his hands on top of a bush and stared at her. "We are aware of how isolated this town is. Despite that, we do our very best to police it."

"While your best is still next to nothing. Where were you yesterday? That guy had no business coming here. He disrupted the entire town. It could take us weeks to clean up all the litter those out-of-towners spewed everywhere."

Detective Douglas took a deep breath before saying, "Are you talking about the man that was murdered?"

"Of course I am." A grin formed on the angry woman's face as she added, "I guess he found out that karma's a real bitch."

The detective looked up at the sky and rolled his eyes. "Did you see anyone exiting the book shop's back door yesterday?"

"Sure, a whole bunch of them." The woman shook her head. "There was one smoking party after another outside of it yesterday. You are suppose to be a cop. Just look around this place, those pigs had tossed their garbage everywhere."

"When was the last time you saw anyone out here?"

"It must have been around seven. I was busy and wasn't paying attention to the time. A couple men were having a heated dispute. They were poking each other in the chest and everything. Out-of-towners are always poking each other, so I didn't pay them too much attention. I guess they went back inside."

Detective Douglas remembered the bruises on Simon Black's Chest. "Was one of them tall with a muscular build?"

"Maybe, like I said, I wasn't paying that much attention to them. I do remember that the one doing most of the poking was a bit shorter and skinnier than the other."

"So they were the last people you saw?"

The woman glared at the detective's face. "I told you, I was cleaning up their garbage. I was too busy, and too mad to pay those pigs any attention."

Detective Douglas handed the woman his card, and told her, "Well thanks for your help."

She stuffed the card into her back pocket. As the woman started to turn and walk away, "At least you didn't throw it on the ground like the other pigs."

Something about the woman's face looked familiar. "Have we met before?"

She stopped and told him, "Who knows, you cops all look alike to me."

Seeing her walk away, Detective Douglas yelled out, "I never got your name."

The woman turned and glared at him. "Why, what do you need that for?"

The detective took a step back. "My book work. Any information I find out has to include a source. Without it, it's just hearsay."

In a raised voice, the woman answered back, "Well consider it as hearsay."

"I know where you live and It won't take me long to find out your name."

The defiant woman waved her arm in the air and replied, "Good luck with that."

Within a few minutes the detective got a text back, 'No one is registered at that address or anywhere else in that local area, except for a Dr. Deathridge and a Mrs. Green. In fact, technically, the town itself doesn't actually exist.'

As he leaned against the back door of the book store, he shook his head. "What is going on with this place?"

Chapter Four

Sgt. Ryan knocked on Nancy's door. A very large, heavy set man opened it and gruffly said, "Who are you?"

"I'm Sgt. Ryan. I'm with the RCMP unit that is investigating the murder that occurred at the book store where your daughter works."

The large, stern, bearded man looked rather odd in his well tailored, casual suit. He looked the sergeant up and down twice before calling out, "Nancy, the police are here to question you some more."

Nancy came to the door and stood beside her father. Wearing no makeup, she looked quite a bit different than her pictures. Her red hair had turned to dark brown, and her fingernails were stripped of any sign of nail polish.

The sergeant looked at the images of her on his phone. "You have changed a wee bit since this morning, and a whole lot since yesterday."

Standing erect, she raised her head and said, "My parents thought that I had changed too much. I agreed with them and decided to revert back to my old self."

The sergeant told her, "I have a few questions that I would like to ask you." He glanced at her father before adding, "May I come in?"

Nancy quickly blurted out, "No, but we could go for a walk around the block together."

Her answer caught the sergeant off guard. He stared at her. "Sure, we can go for a walk."

"I just have to get my jacket first."

With her father defiantly standing in front of the door, the sergeant could barely see anything inside. He looked up at Nancy's father's face. His strong, ridged face and wide green eyes showed no sign of compromise. His brown, trimmed hair rubbed against the top of the doorframe.

Nancy ducked under her father's arm and stepped onto the porch. "So question away."

By the time Sgt. Ryan took out his pen and notepad, she was three steps ahead of him. He looked at her and yelled out, "Slow down. Give me a chance to catch up."

As she turned her head, a gust of wind caught her long hair and whipped it across her face. "This is the pace I walk. Remember, you get only one turn around the block to question me, and that is it."

"You know that I could haul you into custody and question you at the police station?'

Nancy stopped and turned to face him. "Then, all you will get is my name and my lawyer's phone number. I know how you cops like to pressure people and twist things around." She turned and continued to walk away from him. "You get one turn around the block or nothing at all."

Sgt. Ryan ran to catch up to her. Gasping for breath, he said, "Who taught you how to walk? A marathoner?"

"No, my mother. She always said that you should walk as if you actually want to get where you are going."

The sergeant quickened his pace. "Fine, now answer me this, you said that you tossed a wad of bloody tissues into the water bucket. The problem is that there was a lot of blood in that bucket. A lot more than from a few tissues. We need to know how it got there."

"How would I know? When I came into work this morning the bucket was full of water, so I used it." She tilted her head slightly as she turned a corner, and caught him staring at her. "I was really tired and needed to mop some coffee stains off the floor. I didn't see any sense in emptying, rinsing out and refilling the bucket for what I thought was going to be a quick mop."

Sgt. Ryan rocked his head back and forth a couple times before saying, "Sounds reasonable. Now, you sell pens in the store that look like short arrows. Did they only come with red ink?"

"No, they came in both blue and red ink. We ran out

of the blue ones sometime in the afternoon. I remember a customer asking if we had any in the back room."

"Did you sell many of them yesterday?"

"Oh yeah, tons of them. The assassin in Simon Black's last book used a crossbow. The bolt shaped pens were a real hit."

"All right. How about this? When did you last see Simon Black alive?"

"As I already told Officer Kelly, maybe ten, fifteen minutes before I locked the doors. I was peeking over the aisle as he was signing his last book of the day. Then he pulled out his phone and started to get flustered."

"So you didn't see him leave his table?"

"No, I looked an absolute fright. I was trying to avoid him. I didn't want that to be his last impression of me." Nancy's shook her head as she ran her fingers through her hair. She suddenly stopped, looked at the sergeant and barked out, "Is that everything?"

As she started walking again, the sergeant asked her, "No, one more. I am a bit curious. Why did you scrub your face and change yourself into someone that is almost opposite the person you were yesterday? I can't believe that your parents can simply suggest something, and you would blindly do their bidding."

"Well I wasn't always that person." After taking a long, deep breath, she added, "I was reminded that, that person wasn't who I was, nor someone I wanted to become."

"Who by, your parents?"

"That's another question, but I'll answer it anyways. By my parents and Susan, Dr. Susan Deathridge, the town doctor."

Detective Douglas and Sgt. Ryan compared notes in front of the medical clinic. Afterwards, they both entered the clinic and walked up to Dr. Susan Deathridge's secretary. The tall, muscular, male secretary stood up and asked, "Can I help you?"

The detective was the first to speak up. "I'm Detective Douglas and this is Sgt. Ryan from the RCMP. We need to talk to Dr. Susan Deathridge."

The secretary leaned forward and offered the detective his hand. "She has been expecting you. Unfortunately, she is presently with a client. Could you take a seat. She will be with you in a minute or two." With a polite smile on his face, he added, "Most of her consultations are quite short."

"Very well." The detective ignored the secretary's dangling hand. He turned and walked toward the long wooden bench across from the reception desk.

Sgt. Ryan quickly stretched out his arm and grabbed the receptionist's hand before it was retracted. "Sorry, he sometimes forgets his manners."

The receptionist forced a quick semi-smile. As he watched the detective sit down, he told the sergeant, "He should make an appointment. He definitely has problems."

As the sergeant released his hand, he noticed the scars and wide scratches on the back of it, plus across his wrist. "I take it that they are not from a cat?"

He looked at his hand. "No, I am not a cat person."

"You must have to handle some distraught clients."

The receptionist grinned and took a deep breath. "Unfortunately, not everyone has the self control needed to respectfully get along with others."

The sergeant looked around the small reception room. One bench, one coffee table, one coat rack, three scenic pictures on the wall and no magazines. Several neatly stacked piles of pamphlets were spread out on the coffee table. Turning to the receptionist, he said, "So I suspect that the doctor doesn't deal with many clients."

The secretary, slash receptionist, slash muscle, chuckled. "You are definitely not from around here.

Everyone in this community is one of her patients, including me. If you want to stay here, frequently scheduled checkups are absolutely mandatory."

As the short, defiant, heavy set woman left the doctor's office, the detective said, "So we meet again."

The woman glared at him. She scrunched up her face and shook her head. After a couple audible huffs, she turned and walked out of the clinic without uttering a word. The sturdy, mid-aged doctor stood in the doorway and told her secretary, "You can now inform everyone that I will resume scheduled appointments in about half an hour."

The doctor offered the detective her hand. Streaks of gray ran through her short, straight black hair. Her light brown skin and well defined cheek bones disclosed her aboriginal heritage. "Hi, I'm Dr. Susan Deathridge. The moment I heard about the murder in the book store, I knew the police would be wanting to talk to me. I even rearranged my schedule to prepare for it."

Detective Douglas looked back at the door. "What was the matter with her?"

The doctor smiled and told him, "Apparently you have a lingering effect on people."

Detective Douglas looked at her rough, muscular extended hand, and told her, "I don't shake hands." Looking up at her weathered face, he asked, "So what is going on in this town?"

The doctor strolled around her desk and sat down behind it. "First of all, as you have probably know, this is not actually a real town. It is more like a supportive commune for people that are often thought of as misfits. Second, there are only three people that actually reside on this property, me, Roger Blackett plus Mrs. Green, his secretary slash accountant. Mr. Blackett owns everything within a little over a dozen kilometre radius of this place. The rest of the people here are merely long term visitors. They can stay as long as they want, as long as they obey the rules."

Detective Douglas stared at her. "What rules?"

"Simple rules of common dignity and respect. If anyone demonstrates any signs of violence they are no longer welcome. If anyone fails to respect the other members of our community, they are also no longer welcome."

"So who decides who gets to stay here?"

"Roger has left that up to me."

Detective Douglas walked over and looked out the window. "So how many people live here?"

"I have tried to keep the total population to about one hundred. Small enough to manage, but large enough to form a functional community."

"Where did they come from?"

"Institutions mostly. A know a lot of psychologists. Many of them handle a lot of PTSD cases, extreme introverts and high risk of suicide clients. When they feel the system can't help them, they give me a call."

Detective Douglas turned away from the window and looked at her. "So these people are the worst of the lot?"

The doctor shook her head. "Not really. Some of their patients just can't cope with what you consider to be the real world. They need to be somewhere quiet, somewhere they can feel safe. Somewhere, where they won't be harassed or bullied about."

Sgt. Ryan spoke up. "So that explains why they don't want to talk to us."

"Why should they trust you? Your kind can't even imagine how their brains function. You call them rude, nonsensical names, and put labels on them to mask your own ignorance. You lock them up and say 'whatever', when one of them commit's suicide in one of your cells. Afterwards, you just wash your hands of the incident, and pretend it was unavoidable."

Detective Douglas turned and glared at the doctor.

"You still have not told me why this place exists. Sure, you want to give these people a place to live, but why here? There are a lot of good, government controlled institutions they could go to."

"But this place is much better." The doctor spread out the fingers of her hands and rested the tips of them on her desk. "You see, the owner of this property is one of my patients. Since he can't leave his property, he wanted me to set up shop here." She grinned at the two police officers. "Institutions are part of the problem, not the solution. Mr Blackett knows my patients' plight, and he has the financial means to step in and help them."

As the two men were about to exit, Sgt. Ryan turned back and asked the doctor, "So what was so wrong with Nancy Gamble, that you felt she needed to change?"

"She has trouble understanding her feelings. Before she found out about Simon Black coming here, she was more or less, the person you just interviewed." The doctor flashed him a quick smile before adding, "Her mother was worried about her. She also told me about your little chat."

The sergeant release a soft chuckle. "That was nice of her."

"Nancy is still young. The level of hormones in her body are almost triple that of most girls her age. That makes her a bit crazy and extremely vulnerable. Her family had moved here to protect her from predators." The doctor went silent for a few seconds before spewing out, "That book flogger had disrupted the entire community. He should never have come here."

Detective Douglas saw the fury in her eyes. "So where were you last night?"

The doctor stood up and leaned against her desk like a cat ready to pounce. "Ask my secretary. With all the commotion in town, I was booked solid. I was here until almost ten. Then I was busy doing house calls until well after midnight. The horde of out-of-towners that invaded this place yesterday, totally disrupted this entire community."

While getting into their car, Sgt. Ryan blew his nose then told the detective, "At least we now know why this town is not on the map."

Detective Douglas quietly sat behind the wheel and stared through the windshield. After almost half a minute of silence, he turned to the sergeant and told him, "We have an entire community full of nut cases and scaredy cats to deal with."

Sgt. Ryan bit his bottom lip and shook his head. "I guess that is what the doctor was trying to tell us. We are not properly trained to handle oddballs. We are taught that people are people. In a given incident, they all should basically act and react in a certain way."

"Well, I guess that doesn't hold true here."

Sgt Ryan looked at the detective. "What about Roger Blackett? He owns this entire place. Maybe we should have a long chat with him."

"That can wait a bit, first I think we should have another talk with Officer Kelly." As he started the motor Detective Douglas added, "If this is private property, why was she patrolling it?"

"The roads leading in and out of it are connected to the highway. Maybe she didn't know it was private property."

Glancing at the sergeant, the detective told him, "I still think that she knows more about the to so-called town than she has told us."

Sgt. Ryan's cell phone began to vibrate. He pulled it out and paraphrased the text message. "The lab has cleaned up some of the video that was taken in the back room of the store. Also they found traces of blood on the floor where Nancy mopped." He glanced at the detective and added, "Maybe she's telling us the truth."

"I thought that video was nothing but garbage."

"Apparently, the geek squad did a lot of enhancing."

Back at the station, the pair stood behind the technician and started to watch the fuzzy video on his computer monitor. The technician looked back at them and said, "Don't expect to see anything that you could use in court. The image is still awful."

Detective Douglas grinned and said, "As long as it points us to the killer."

The camera had been pointed at the door leading into the back room. Along the side of the frame was the washroom door. Fuzzy circled blobs came in and out of view.

"I highlighted a lot of bodies coming and going. The camera was motion activated and the video was time stamped. Lucky for us, Simon's physique made him easy to identify." The tech fast forwarded the video. "Here is some footage that I thought you might be interested in."

A woman with long hair came in and waited just inside the door. The hem of her dress seemed to flare out from her hips. A few minutes later, Simon appears and they both go into the washroom. A few minutes later, he comes out. Five minutes after that, the woman leaves.

The detective smiled. "I think I recognize that dress from the retail floor footage that me and the sergeant watched earlier. That's Emily White, the store manager."

The tech fast forwarded the recording a half a hour. Simon and a girl with a pony tail go into the back room. After a minute of passionate kissing and erotic fondling, they break apart. Then they pick up a couple stacks of books and leave.

The tech glanced at the two men. "There was a lot of people coming and going out of that room yesterday. The last person to enter it was Simon Black. Unfortunately, all I caught of the killer was a very crude outline as he or she left through the fire exit." As he showed them the recording, he added, "The sheer volume of the killer's hair indicates a woman. It is almost puffed out past the killers shoulders."

Detective Douglas rubbed the back of his neck. "Did you catch the killer entering the washroom?"

"Like I said, I am dealing with blobs. I caught the top corner of the washroom door as a bunch of blobs came in through the back door. The last blob snuck into the washroom. He must have waited for Simon to relieve himself before he left." The tech adjusted the recording and showed them the elongated, pulsating blob that entered through the exit and moved past the camera. "There were too many to separate. I had no clear edges to go by. In fact, even if the video was clear, we would only get the back of them."

"What about the killer leaving?"

"I'm still working on it. Right now, he or she is still a big, fuzzy blob."

"And the door leading to the retail floor is out of the other camera's range." Sergeant Ryan shook his head. "We don't even have any faces to go by."

"We may have a jealous, love triangle going on." Detective Douglas turned to Sgt. Ryan. "I need to question Emily White. How about you stay here and nurse your cold. I need you to find out everything you can about both Simon Black and Roger Blackett. At least you can't infect your computer with your cold."

Sgt. Ryan initially thought searching Simon Black's history would be easy. Instead, he found out that it was not even his real name. No records existed of him prior to his first novel. "He must be using a pseudonym."

Going through all the records and web pages he could find, the sergeant discovered the name of Simon's agent. "Bingo, now I'm getting somewhere."

The agency that Simon was working with was out of New York, and so was his publisher. The sergeant smiled. "Maybe I can wangle a free trip to the Big Apple."

He spent the next hour filling, filing and sending out

inter-departmental and international request forms.

Detective Douglas drove back to Blackett Hill and pulled up to Emily White's home. His car's headlights highlighted the crowd of spectators outside of it.

While pushing his way through the crowd, he got a glimpse of Dr. Susan Deathridge through the livingroom window. Holding his badge in front of him, he ordered Nancy Gamble's father to stand aside and let him in.

The doctor heard the detective and yelled out, "It's all right. Let him in."

The detective glanced at the doctor, "Thanks."

Emily White's shaking body was lying on the livingroom floor covered in a blanket. The doctor yelled out, "Get me some more blankets and another pillow."

A woman ran out the door as Detective Douglas knelt on one knee beside the doctor. "What happened?"

"She tore a couple bed sheets into strips, tied them together and attempted to commit suicide. Fortunately, her neighbours saw her and got here just in time." The doctor glared at the detective and loudly stated, "This is why these people moved here. They can't handle the emotional pressures of the outside world."

Detective Douglas looked around the room. The television and stereo were built into the walls. There were no wires or cords anywhere. Even the reading lamp was hard wired into the wall. Everything that a normal person would use to commit suicide had been removed. The hand torn bed sheet had been a feeble, badly thought out plan to commit suicide.

"Where were her parents?"

"They had to pick up some badly needed plumbing supplies in English Lookout."

As the detective started to leave, Nancy's father whispered into his ear. "If anyone dies because of you, or that outsider with you, you will find out that karma can be a real, unforgiving bitch."

Chapter Five

The detective drove to the small, eight room hotel that was situated next to a small restaurant at the far edge of Blackett Hill. After booking a room, he walked to the restaurant. It only had four booths and a half dozen stools at the counter. There wasn't a single customer inside it.

A mature, salt and peppered haired waitress, and her much younger, slightly chubby, brown haired co-worker, kept themselves busy polishing the dinnerware and cleaning everything in sight. Even though the place was spotless, they smiled and kept cleaning.

Through the service opening, he could see the constantly moving heads and shoulders of the two cooks. Unable to see what they were doing, he envisioned them scrubbing pans and anything else that was even slightly dirty.

Detective Douglas stepped forward and said, "Excuse me, can one of you take my order."

The two waitresses seemed a bit stunned. They both stood up straight and slightly off unison answered, "Can I help you."

The detective turned to the younger woman and said, "Am I too late? Are you closing up for the night?"

With a wide, child-like smile on her face, the waitress told him, "Oh no, we don't close for another two hours."

As she led him to the nearest booth, Detective Douglas asked her, "Are you alway this slow?"

The young woman froze. Her jaw dropped and her eyes seemed to pop out. Seeing her young colleague's face turned pale, the seasoned waitress screamed, "I don't care who you are, you can't just come in here and talk to people like that."

Detective Douglas suddenly realized what he had said. Waving his hands back and forth in front of him, he blurted out, "What I meant to say was, is the restaurant always this slow at this time of night, that's all."

The seasoned waitress wrapped her arms around her traumatised friend and glared at the detective. "If you really meant to say it, you would have said it."

One of the cooks burst out of the kitchen almost yelling, "Is everything alright?"

After she finished walking the young waitress over to the furthest booth away from the detective, and sitting her down, the waitress glared at the detective. "This outsider insulted her. He called her slow."

Detective Douglas turned to the cook. "I didn't mean to insult her. She took what I said the wrong way." Placing his open hands in front of him, he added, "I'm really sorry for the misunderstanding and any harm it may have caused."

The cook looked at the confused, apprehensive man. "You must be that cop that has been harassing everyone."

Detective Douglas lowered his hands and said, "I'm not here to harass anyone. I'm here to investigate a murder. In order to do that, I need to talk to as many potential witnesses as I can."

The cook raised his head and tilted it slightly back. Despite being the same height, with his jaw stuck out, his eyes looked down at the detective. After snorting a couple times, he forcefully said, "Sit down."

After taking a menu off the counter, he tossed it on the table. It bounced off the table and one of its corners struck the detective's chest. Seeing the detective cringe, the cook smiled and said, "When you figure out what you want, knock on the door. I'll personally come out to take your order."

As the cook turned around, the detective said, "I will just have a black coffee and what ever the special of the day happens to be."

Without turning around, the cook replied, "Then a cheeseburger and fries it is."

Detective Douglas looked down at the heavily

laminated, one page menu. There was no special. In fact, there was nothing on it that a half trained, sixteen year old couldn't make.

Staring at the door leading into the kitchen, it dawned on him, he wasn't in charge. As a police officer, he was the one that ordered people around and told them what to do. In this community he felt shackled. Even a word out of place could lead to a fatality that he could be held accountable for.

He looked at the two huddled waitresses sitting in the far booth, and softly muttered, "This whole place is insane. I'm going to be glad when this case is wrapped up."

Within a few minutes, the cook returned with his order. After placing the to-go-bag on the table, he told the detective, "I'll put your coffee in a travelling cup. If you ever come back here, you better watch your mouth. If you don't, you will find out just how bad of an unforgiving bitch karma can really be."

That was the third time he heard that expression since he started the investigation. After placing a twenty dollar bill on the table he picked up the bag and took the coffee from the cook. "Again, I am sorry about the misunderstanding. I promise, it won't happen again."

The words, "It better not." Rattled in his ears as he walked out of the restaurant.

Seeing the cook pour the coffee made him feel that it was safe to drink. He sat on the edge of the bed and took a sip. The intoxicating aroma from the cheeseburger filled his olfactory system and made his stomach rumble. Ignoring his hunger pangs, he grabbed the bag and tossed it into the garbage. "God I'm going to regret that."

While laying on the bed, he took out his cell phone and called his wife. As the call was transferred to the answering machine he looked at the time. "She was probably watching some sappy movie and fell asleep." After the beep he simply said, "Honey, I'm spending the night at a hotel in a place called Blackett Hill. Hopefully I'll see you sometime tomorrow."

He looked at his notes and thought about everything that happened that day. Shaking his head, he mumbled, "Everyone here is either crazy, suicidal or a total sociopath. I may need to have a shrink with me, just to talk to them."

The next morning Detective Douglas asked the lady standing at the hotel counter, "Is there anywhere besides the restaurant next door, that I could get something to eat."

"I guess I could make you some toast, and maybe poach you a couple eggs in the microwave."

The detective smiled at her. "Right now even a coffee and a bowl of cereal would do. I'm famished."

The lady guided the detective into the narrow room behind the counter. In it was a kitchen counter with shelves above it, a small table and four chairs. The detective pulled out a chair, sat at the table and looked around. The doors leading into her modest bedroom and bathroom were wide open. Out of politeness more than curiosity, the detective asked her, "So, how do you like living here?"

"It's nice here. It's nothing like the outside world." As she placed the bread into the counter mounted toaster, she informed him, "I've been here for a little over five years now and I can't even imagine a better place to live."

He looked around as he sipped some coffee from a plastic mug, he noticed some stark similarities to Emily's home. There were no cords and nothing made from glass. Plastic everything. Even the knife she used to butter the toast was plastic.

As she cut his toast into two, the tip and part of the edge of the knife broke off. Seeing the remaining, sharp jagged point, the frazzled woman immediately tossed both pieces of it into a hole in the top of the kitchen counter. "There, now we are safe again."

When Detective Douglas finished eating, he pulled out

his wallet. The lady was aghast. "I offered to fix you breakfast because I felt you were a bit out of sorts. I didn't do it for the money."

Not wanting to cause another scene, he slowly put his wallet back into his pocket and nodded his head. "It was very much appreciated. Thank you."

As he went outside and walked down the street, he finally realized that the town was completely void of children. There were no schools, playgrounds or anything related to children anywhere.

There was a long line in front of the doctor's office. He stood and watched the receptionist escort the young waitress to the front of the line, and then inside. "Maybe I should have made an appointment."

While standing on the sidewalk, he phoned the sergeant. "Hello, are you at the station?"

"Yes and the Captain isn't happy. He feels that you are dogging it up there. He's been hounding me on why you haven't been able to make any headway in the case."

"Tell him to come up here and see what I'm dealing with." The detective noticed that some of the people in line were starting to stare at him. He didn't realized how quiet the street was. Turning to face the road, he lowered his voice so it wouldn't carry as far, and continued, "Any luck on finding out who arranged Simon Black's book signing at the store?"

"No, and the literary agency that oversees him, hasn't got back to me yet. I was planning on giving them another half hour before calling them back."

"I wish this town had a few more working cameras. The ones I've checked so far are more or less just wall ornaments. We have no idea who was in Blackett Hill at the time of the murder, or who was in the book store when it happened."

After coughing and wiping his nose, Sgt. Ryan told

Detective Douglas, "I thought I saw a camera at the gas station at the far end of town." Viewing a map of the area on his computer, he added, "Plus there is a truck stop on the highway on the way there. Maybe we can get the technicians to compare their videos to the book store's."

Detective Douglas lowered his head. "I'll check them out. If we are lucky, we might even be able to connect some licence plate numbers to the people at the book signing."

As he turned and faced the lineup he told the sergeant, "In the mean time, see what you can dig up about this place and the people living here. By the looks of the line in front of the doctor's office, I think she has her hands full. Maybe you should check to see if we have any shrinks that might be available to help us out."

"Sure, but all the shrinks that I know prefer seeing their clients in a clinical environment. They like to have complete control over their subjects during an examination."

"Just explain the situation here. If they are any good at their job, they should be able to assess people in their own environment. If they can't, maybe they are in the wrong profession."

"I think I should ask them a little more nicely than that. I don't want to call any shrink inept. They may want to psychoanalyse me."

Detective Douglas laughed. "If they do, keep my name out of it."

"I'll try my best, but no promises."

The detective walked to the gas station at the end of town. He glanced down every side street. With all the lots being roughly the same size, it was easy for him to figure out the total number of houses in the community. On the main road there was a gas station, hotel, grocery store, restaurant, book shop, medical clinic, clothing store, odds and ends store, a repair shop, a barn full of building supplies, a recreational building, and a meeting hall. On the side streets there were fifty-two houses, two of which were unoccupied.

As he passed each shop, he tried to count how many were employed there. For every job that he figured would normally require only one worker, there were two or three people. Seeing hardly any customers in any of them, he concluded, '*They are mostly keep busy jobs, maybe some kind of work therapy.*' The detective froze as it suddenly dawned on him, '*If that was the case, the book store was grossly understaffed on the day of the book signing.*'

Outside of the gas station, Detective Douglas noticed a pair of up-to-date cameras tucked beneath decorative hoods on the corners of the building. "How did I miss them."

Inside, shielded behind a plexiglass wall, the thin, awkward looking gas station attendant was very accommodating. The detective was only there five minutes before the attendant's co-worker walked out of a back room and slipped a memory stick through a small opening in the plexiglass next to the cash register. "I copied everything we got from Friday night 'til now." With a pasted on smile, the overweight, mid aged man asked, "Is there anything else we can help you with. A drink, chips, chocolate bar, we sell more than just gas here. We have a little bit of everything."

"No, the surveillance video is good enough for now."

"You are welcome, come again."

As the detective turned and went out the door, he heard, "Rude, not even a thank-you. What a typical outsider."

Passing the hotel, he remembered that Nancy had said it was full the night before the signing, and so was the camp ground outside of town. "How stupid of me. This place isn't even on the map. Anyone that really wanted to be at the book signing wouldn't want to risk getting lost. They would want to get here well ahead of time."

For the rest of the morning, he drove around collecting all the surveillance recordings and data he could find. The hotel was booked solid Thursday, Friday and even

Saturday night. The camp ground owner told him that he had a couple remote, unserviced, hike-in campsites that were still available.

Detective Douglas knew that most of the recordings from the local stores would be of poor quality. However, he figured that the more information he gathered the better.

On the way back to the police station in English Lookout, he stopped at the truck stop. Their high quality recordings covered both the gas bar and the restaurant.

After the long drive back, he walked into the police station and placed all of the CDs and data sticks that he had collected on Sgt. Ryan's desk. "I hope you are feeling a lot better because we have a lot of video to go over."

After exaggerating a loud cough, the sergeant replied, "I'll be fine."

A preliminary viewing showed that most of the video was indeed unusable. Some of their grainy images lacked the detail required to identify anyone. In others, it was like watching water ripples on a sandy beach.

The gas station, truck stop and the campground had kept all of their cameras in good condition. All three had cameras mounted to record their customers' licence plates plus the people sitting in the front of the vehicle.

The hotel's cameras were mediocre at best. They had cameras mounted above the stairwell doors at the end of each hallway and one in the lobby. The video from the lobby camera was slightly better than the book store's. Most of the other videos were too fuzzy to properly identify the faces of individuals. However they were still useful.

Seeing this, the detective told the sergeant, "Start by comparing the plates from the campground to the plates from the gas station in town. Get one of the techs to compare the images from the book store's to that of the hotel's and campground's. Hopefully, they can find some faces that we can identify. We need to find out who was in Blackett Hill when the murder occurred."

As he looked at the captain's office door, he took in a deep breath. "Any luck finding out who actually arranged and booked the signing in the first place?"

The Sergeant plugged a stick into his computer before swivelling his chair to face him. "Not yet. Simon Black's agent didn't show up at his office today."

"Is that normal for him?"

"Apparently it happens a few times each month. He travels out of town a lot to deal with his more lucrative, and up and coming clients."

Detective Douglas put his hand on Sgt. Ryan's shoulder. "You need to locate him."

"Yes sir" The sergeant looked at the detective's hand. "And what will you be doing?"

"Seeing a shrink." The detective glanced at the sergeant's computer monitor. On it was a black and white image of a sleek, attractive woman wearing a wide brimmed hat, sitting behind a steering wheel. "Try to find out as much as you can about that crazy, so-called town."

When the detective got back to Blackett Hill he noticed that there was no lineup outside the doctor's office. After parking his car outside of the hotel, he walked to the clinic. There were only three people in the reception room. Before he could sit down, a man left the doctor's office and the secretary immediately escorted a woman in.

As the secretary returned, he went over to the detective. As the tall, muscular man looked down at him, he said, "You will have to wait your turn. It will probably be about fifteen minutes, no more then half an hour."

The detective released a sigh of disapproval before looking up at him. "I can wait."

The lady sitting at the far end of the bench looked at him. As he looked back at her, she straightened up and folded her arms in front of her. The man sitting between them turned and told him, "You shouldn't be so gruff. Your attitude won't change anything. That dead guy will still be dead, and you will still be a rude, obnoxious outsider."

The detective released a small huff. He desperately wanted to tell the man off, but knew he couldn't. Feeling his right hand beginning to clench, he tucked it under his leg and sat on it. The secretary saw what had transpired and quickly stood up. The detective gazed at him and then looked away.

The only reading material in the room were the stacks of pamphlets on the coffee table. Two of them seemed to stand out, 'Understanding Abusive Behaviour', and 'Escaping an Abusive Relationship'.

After impatiently sitting there for twenty minutes, the secretary approached him and said, "Now it is your turn. Now, the doctor will see you."

The detective bit his lower lip and stood up. "About time."

As he entered the doctor's office he glanced at the secretary's wide, defiant eyes. It was as if he absolutely despised him. After the door was shut, the detective turned to the doctor. "Does he have anger issues?"

The doctor looked at him. "You just seem to bring out the worst in people."

Detective Douglas clenched his hands together in front of him. "It's my job. I need to get people to reveal their true selves. I need to find out who is guilty and who isn't."

The doctor placed both hands on her desk. "In this community, that won't work. Everyone in this town is paranoid of the outside world. If you try to push them, they will either clam up or push back. Either is an admission of guilt, and you will lose. You lose their trust, their respect and most of all you will end up getting nowhere."

Detective Douglas crossed his arms and defiantly told the doctor, "My methods have always worked for me."

"These are not your run-of-the-mill so-called average

citizens. They are not thugs. Most of them have seen how the police treat different and emotionally disturbed people first hand. It isn't nice. In fact, most of them think of the police, the same way as a young child thinks of the boogie man. They are scary, horrifying monsters. Some of them believe that the police even seek them out just to harass, imprison, hurt and even torture them."

Detective Douglas spread his arms in front of him, grinned and almost jokingly said, "Come on, we are not monsters. Our job is to enforce the peace."

"Enforce the peace. What an oxymoron." Doctor Deathridge pointed to the window. "You try to tell that to the people out there." She gave out a chuckle. "You can barely open your mouth without offending someone."

Detective Douglas squeezed his hands together until his finger tips turned white. He slowly walked over to one of the chairs in front of the doctor's desk and sat down. After a long few seconds, he gazed at her. "So how do you expect me to find the killer?"

"Look elsewhere. I know everyone in this community. It wasn't one of my patients that killed Simon Black."

"So it was bad karma was it?"

The doctor took in a couple deep breaths and glared at him. "Karma had nothing to do with his death."

The detective saw the wild gleam in the doctor's eyes and sat back in his chair. "All right, who do you think killed him?"

"I don't know, but it wasn't one of my patients."

Detective Douglas glared back at her. "I can't rule anyone out, and until I can, I have to treat everyone as a suspect." Leaning forward, he added, "I'll need to see your files. I can't rule out anyone here until I do."

The doctor shook her head. "You know that as a doctor, I can't do that. I can not and will not betray their trust. You will need a court order."

"Then I'll get one. As you said before, Simon Black's appearance here disrupted the entire community. Sometimes it doesn't take much for an unstable mind to snap. I can't see any judge having a problem issuing me a court order for me to see your files."

"If you do, there will be deaths, and they will be on your's and whatever judge you dupe into signing the orders shoulders." The doctor glared at him. "And if that happens, I will file criminal charges against both of you. Then you will find out how much of a bitch karma can really be."

Before the detective could say a word, the doctor stood up and blurted out, "And by the way, I tape all my sessions including this one, or did you forget to read the sign on the door. I have solid proof that I warned you."

Detective Douglas glanced back at the door. The secretary must have blocked his view of the red and white sign. After shaking his head, he sat back in the chair and slapped his thighs. "I still need to know if there is anyone here that is capable of killing Simon Black. I can not just take your word for it. Without seeing those files, a killer could be walking around free. I don't care if I have to uproot this entire community."

The doctor cut him off. "Not while I'm alive."

The detective lowered his voice and told her, "Listen, we both know that the quicker I catch the killer and leave this place, the better it will be for everyone."

The doctor slammed her fist against the top of her desk so hard it echoed. "That we can agree on, but I can't show you any files. We both know that under the right circumstance anyone is capable of killing someone. Psychopaths excluded, in a killer's mind, they see killing as an act of self defence. That's how they can self justify it. Even those who kill during a robbery, see it as a way to escape justice and remain free. Again, a self defence mechanism had taken over. Simon Black was going to be here for only one day, and then leave. Where's the motive?"

Detective Douglas grinned and defiantly told her, "People kill for many reasons. Some of them don't make any sense at all."

"Maybe to you, but not to them." The doctor slowly sat back in her chair. "Say a man starts slaughtering babies in front of the pope. If it went on long enough, do you think the pope wouldn't try to stop him, even if it meant killing the man." The doctor smiled. "Would you have expected him to be a killer."

"That's far fetched. So what are you telling me?"

"There were hundreds of obsessed people here on Saturday. People that actually knew Simon Black. Any one of them could have been the killer." The doctor started to rock her head back and forth. "Stop looking for easy targets to bully into a false confession and manipulate in court. That could get you into some very serious trouble, especially here."

The detective gave out a couple snorts. After wiping his nose with the back of his hand, he cocked his head and looked at the weathered doctor. After a period of silence, he calmly asked the doctor, "Doing what you do has taken a toll on you, hasn't it?"

The doctor nodded, "Yes it has. I've been given a lot of responsibility and I take my job very seriously."

The detective interlocked his fingers in front of him and tilted his head. "The murder happened here. Some of your patients had to have witnessed things connected to it. It is my job to find out what they were. I have to interview them. Maybe you can come with me as a moderator?"

Dr. Deathridge looked down at her desk. After a few seconds, she looked up at him and replied, "Fine, but I'll be there solely for my patient's welfare, not for you."

Detective Douglas's cell phone started to vibrate. He pulled it out and read Sgt. Ryan's text. The detective looked at the doctor. "I'm going to read you the text I just got.

'None of the locals gave us their real names. They are all using aliases.'" Looking straight into the doctor's eyes, he said, "How do you expect me to solve a murder when I don't even know anyone's real name?"

"You shouldn't need an innocent person's name to investigate a crime. What kind of cop are you?"

"The kind that collects and sorts through all the facts until he finds the right answer."

"You mean dug up all the dirt you can find and dump it on someone who's profile fits. That's garbage policing. All you care about is putting someone behind bars. You don't really care if they are actually guilty or not." The doctor looked out the window and then back at the detective. "Like I said, that will not happen here. I won't allow it."

Detective Douglas wiggled his finger at the doctor and burst out, "Listen, I'm a good police officer." As he was about to continue his rant, he saw the wide sadistic grin on the doctor's face as she sat back on her chair. "What, what just happened?"

The doctor's began to chuckle as she told him, "Anger management. Why don't you just go back to your comfortable office in the city and not come back until you have an actual lead. You are not going to solve your case by hassassing my patients."

It took the detective a while before he could respond. "But if I have to question any of the locals, you will come with me, right?"

The doctor leaned forward and handed him one of her cards. "I said I would didn't I? Just phone my secretary first so I can clear my schedule." Then the doctor glared into his eyes. "But only if you have a valid reason to question them."

"I will." Detective Douglas bit his bottom lip, cocked his head and looked at her. "I've walked around town and seen how the rest of the stores were grossly, over staffed. So why was the bookstore under staffed on Saturday?"

The doctor shook her head and glanced out the window. "I couldn't get anyone to work there. They knew that Simon Black would bring in hordes of out-of-towners. They also knew that while standing in line, they would want to chit-chat. Even the waitresses at the restaurant are not required to converse with strangers. No one here is."

"What about Nancy."

"Nancy's problems are different. She can handle most strangers, as long as they are passive. It's when they get aggressive that she has problems."

"What kind of problems?"

"In her mind, aggression and sexual desire are the same thing. Like I already told you, her hormones are way out of wack." Dr. Deathridge smiled. "Overall, I thought she did a remarkable job on Saturday. I was very proud of her. Even Emily had to find a way to escape dealing with the huge crowd."

"You mean her infatuation with Simon Black."

"An entire section of the store was devoted to Simon Black. It even included reference books detailing facts behind some of his novels." The doctor looked down at her desk. "When she heard he was coming to town, she was ecstatic." In almost a whisper, she added, "She had channelled all her emotions towards him, and that helped blackout all the chaos that was going on around her."

"When did you find out about this channelling?"

The doctor meshed her fingers together and took her time answering him. "Some of it I knew beforehand. Emily was one of my last patients Saturday night. She was upset and I gave her a couple pills to help her wind down and get some sleep. Unfortunately, I didn't know the full extent of her infatuation with Simon until Sunday."

"I see. I guess that's enough for now." As he began to turn towards the door, he asked, "By the way, how is Emily White doing? When will I be able to talk to her?"

Dr. Deathridge walked around her desk to see him out. "Definitely not today, maybe tomorrow, we'll see. I gave her some sedatives." With her hand on the edge of the door, she glared at him. "Like all my patients, she's very fragile. You can't treat her like some thug off the street. Cause if you do, you will answer to karma."

Detective Douglas looked at her and shook his head. "In my lifetime, I haven't seen any proof that karma exists."

The doctor grinned. "If you keep up acting the way you are, you soon will."

When the detective left the doctor's office, he walked around town looking down at his cell phone. At every opportunity, he covertly snapped photos of as many locals as he could.

In the restaurant, the cook saw what he was doing. He ran out of the kitchen and snatched the detective's phone. By the time Detective Douglas could react, the cook smashed the phone against the counter. "That's invasion of privacy. You have no right taking a person's picture without their consent."

Detective Douglas defiantly glared into his eyes. "I could have you arrested for impeding a police investigation, and assaulting an officer of the law."

"I see, one set of laws for cops and nothing for the rest of us." As the detective tried to grab his phone, the cook slid it off the counter and onto the floor. Before the detective could bend over to pick it up, the cook's right heel stomped on it. "Woops, my foot slipped."

The detective's face turned red as he fought back the urge to retaliate. After picking up his broken phone he stormed all the way to his car, got in and slammed the door. Through the nearby windows he saw over a dozen locals staring at him.

"Have your laugh while you can." As he opened up the back of his cell phone and took out the memory chip, he smiled, "Cause when I return it's going to be a different story."

Chapter Six

As Detective Douglas drove into English Lookout, he looked at all the 'For Sale' signs and thought about how it had deteriorated. It was barely holding onto city status. The closing of a nickel mine, along with the devastating, and fatal fire at a locally owned tannery and leather garment company, had made living there very difficult. Tourism had become the town's main industry.

The outline of the tannery's walls were still visible above the weeds, bushes and small trees. The detective recalled seeing the fire from his front yard. By the time he got there, the roof of mostly wooden structure was starting to collapse. The security guard's charred bones were all the coroner had to work with.

With the guard being a retired RCMP officer, the investigation of the fire was quick. There was still some lingering smoke coming from the ashes, when Detective Douglas made his first arrest as a detective. Obtaining a full confession from a homeless vagrant, there wasn't even a trail.

At the police station, Detective Douglas went straight to his desk, picked up the phone and started to call his wife. While the phone rang, he sat on the corner of his desk. Across from him, his captain stood next to Sgt. Ryan's desk and cleared his throat. Detective Douglas put down the phone, looked at him and asked, "Any new developments? My phone got smashed and I've been out of the loop?"

Sgt. Ryan looked at him. "Yes, apparently Simon Black's agent is in Canada. We flagged his passport. He entered the country last Thursday and hasn't left."

The detective walked over to the sergeant and asked him, "How many Canadian clients does he have?"

"Only three, Simon Black, one in Nova Scotia, and another one in Toronto. His plane landed in Toronto. He would have flown into Halifax if he was heading east. His other client in Toronto is presently on a two week vacation in

France and won't be back until Saturday."

The captain glared at Detective Douglas. "Tread carefully. We are dealing with someone with connections. We don't want to become some hack's best selling spoof. I don't want anyone in this department being portrayed as a keystone cop."

The detective looked at him and straightened his stance. "Always, this is not my first high profile case."

As the captain left, Detective Douglas turned to Sgt. Ryan. "Have you been able to locate where his agent is staying?"

"Yes, he is right here in English Lookout. He used his credit card to book a room at the hotel just down the street from the station."

"So he could have been at the book store on Saturday."

"Easily." Sgt. Ryan glanced at his computer screen. "The Toronto police are still looking into places where he could've rented a car. They haven't found anything yet."

"Maybe he got someone to pick him up at the airport?" Detective Douglas rubbed his chin. "Have you contacted the hotel to make sure that he is still there?"

The sergeant swivelled his chair to face the detective. "Yes, and I told them to call me if he stepped out. I was waiting for you to show up. I thought you would want to be there so we could both question him."

The detective nodded his head. "Good, you did the correct thing."

The hotel was only a few blocks from the police station. As the sergeant started to walk there, Detective Douglas yelled out and waved his arm, "Where are you going, the car's this way?"

The sergeant yelled back, "But I can see the hotel from here."

"I don't care. We're taking the car."

The sergeant placed his hands on his hips. "By the time we walk to the car, park it and walk to the hotel's entrance, we will be walking about the same distance."

Detective Douglas shook his head. "What if there is a call that we have to respond to?"

"Then I'll run back and get the car."

"How about you get the car now, drop me off in front of the hotel and park it. Then at least one of us won't have to do all that walking."

The detective went over to the bench in front of the station and sat down. The sergeant begrudgingly started to walk toward the parking lot on the far side of the station. As he passed his superior, he muttered, "When is your next physical coming up?"

"I passed mine last month."

The sergeant shook his head and mumbled, "How?"

After a short, silent ride, the detective got out of the car and walked into the quaint hotel lobby. The slim, fit, middle-aged woman behind the counter watched him enter and piped up, "Can I help you."

"I hope so." He pulled out his badge and showed it to her. "I'm investigating an incident up north a ways, and I was hoping you could help me."

"We have been expecting you." As the lady smiled the wrinkles on her face seemed to disappear. Looking five to ten years younger, she cocked her head a little and said, "I will assist you any way I can."

Her girlish smile forced Detective Douglas to smile back. "Do you have a Robert Swayze booked here?"

After a brief glance at the registry, she told him, "Yes, he is in room 412. Is there anything else I can help you with?"

The detective pulled out his notepad and began to scribble in it as he coldly said, "Yes, can I get a copy of the hotel's security footage from the lobby's camera, from the time he first entered the hotel until now."

The woman's radiant smile disappeared. "I'll have to get the manager. I'll only be a sec."

As the sergeant entered the lobby, the woman came back with a middle-aged man. His hand stroked the small of her back as he circled around her to get to the counter. Standing at the end of the counter, the receptionist looked the detective over from head to toe. After a brief pause, she saw Sgt Ryan walk up to the detective. "I take it he is with you?"

Seeing her pupils focussed on the detective's face, Sergeant Ryan said, "Unfortunately, but sometimes I wonder which one of us is in charge."

She released a small chuckle before turning to the sergeant. "He doesn't seem that bad to me."

The hotel manager cleared his throat, to redirect their attention. "It will take me a few minutes to download the video you requested. I'll leave it with my receptionist when I'm done."

Detective Douglas smiled at him and said, "That would be great. I'll get it when we come down."

The detective motioned for the sergeant to follow him. On their way to the elevator, they could hear the hotel manager harshly whispering something to the receptionist.

Once inside the elevator, the sergeant turned to Detective Douglas, and told him, "That receptionist seemed to think that you are not as out of shape as I thought you were."

The detective snapped back, "It's her job to flirt with everyone that comes through the hotel lobby."

The sergeant chuckled. "You didn't see the way she was looking at you when your back was turned."

With a scowl, he barked back, "I'm married."

The sergeant kept smiling. "So are the majority of the men going into this hotel. Think about it, I'm younger and far better looking, and she barely gave me the time of day."

"You are way too young for her. A woman like that

isn't looking for someone to babysit."

The sergeant looked down and almost incomprehensibly mumbled, "You are closer to needing your diapers changed then I am."

The detective stood outside of room 412 for a few seconds and gathered his thoughts. With his badge in his hand, he knocked on the door. He heard some scraping like furniture being moved and the clambering of footsteps, before a male voice answered, "Who is it?"

"Detective Douglas of the RCMP. We need to talk to Robert Swayze."

"Just a minute."

The detective heard some more shuffling and footsteps. After several seconds, the door opened a crack and a man said, "Can I see your badge?"

Detective Douglas quickly flashed his badge in front of him. "Are you Robert Swayze?"

"Yes."

"I need to ask you a few questions."

With a slight slur to his speech, Robert said, "How about you letting me actually see your badges first. Before I open my door, I like to know who I'm letting in."

Both officers held up their badges in front of the crack and the man's only visible eye. After a few seconds, Robert said, "They seem real." As he unlocked the chain and let them in, he said, "I suppose this is about Simon Black's untimely demise."

Detective Douglas studied the tall, small framed, middle-aged man's, unshaven face. His blonde hair was a mess. His stylish, square famed glasses couldn't hide the dark bags under is eyes. With a long red robe wrapped around him, the man went over to the office chair next to the desk that the hotel had provided, and sat down.

While looking around the room, the detective sauntered over to him and asked, "Our information indicates that you were Simon Black's literary agent. Is that correct?"

Robert said, "Yes, that is correct."

As they talked, Sgt. Ryan walked around the modest two bed, hotel room. The sheets on one bed were only slightly messy. In contrast, the blankets on the other bed were twisted completely sideways and draped over both sides, concealing everything beneath it. Next to the bed he saw unusual skid marks in the nap of the carpet.

The detective asked Robert, "Did you see Simon Black at the book store in Blackett Hill on Saturday?"

Robert poured a golden colour liquid from a tiny clear bottle into a glass, and took a sip. "Yes, but only for a few minutes." After taking another sip, he added, "The alarm on my phone went off. I had totally forgot about a meeting I had to go to in Hunters' Crossing. The meeting was with, what I hoped was going to be, a new best selling author. Unfortunately she was a no show."

Passing the detective his phone, he told him, "Here, check my text messages. I'm telling you the truth. I've got nothing to hide. I was no where near that book store when Simon was killed."

"How do you know when he was killed?"

"Well, the store closes at five. It must have happened shortly after that. If it happened during his book signing, it would be all over the internet." Robert glanced at the sergeant as he walked around the room. "As I told you, I was in Hunters' Crossing when it happened. I left Blackett hill around three-thirty."

Sgt. Ryan listened to them review and identify the sources of Robert's various text messages. Every once and a while he got the whiff of a strange but unique odour. Bending down at the head of the messy bed, he could smell Robert's cologne along with some kind of herbal hair conditioner. As he stepped between the two double beds, he smelt a faint but subtle and much more feminine perfume. "Did you have a woman in your room?"

Robert looked at him. "Only the housekeeper. She came in and tidied up a bit while I had breakfast."

The sergeant shot back, "Did you go back to bed afterwards?"

"Yeah, what of it? My top client died. I ate, drank some tequila and went back to bed." Robert shook his head and glared at him. "Do you have any idea of how much money I just lost? I'm paid by commission and Simon was my top client. I just lost over a quarter of my gross income."

Detective Douglas watched as Robert crossed his arms. As Robert's face lost some of its colour, the detective asked him, "Are you the one that set up the book signing in Blackett Hill?"

"No, it wasn't me. I had already booked a store in Toronto. I even paid for non-refundable, pre-arranged ads in the local media, the works. I had to cancel everything. That shouldn't be hard for you to check out. The whole Blackett Hill thing took me by surprise."

The detective looked at the sergeant and bit his lower lip. Turning back to Robert he asked, "Do you know anyone with a reason to kill Simon?"

Robert shrugged his shoulders. "I don't know. Maybe it was a jealous husband. Simon had hordes of women pining over him. Maybe his womanising finally caught up to him."

"Maybe."

Pointing his finger into the air, Robert said, "Wait, I have proof that I was in Hunters' Crossing at the time. While I was waiting at the coffee shop I got a parking ticket."

"We had the Toronto police check all the car rental outfits at the airport. Neither your, or your company's name appeared on any list. So, who's car were you driving?"

"A friend met me at the airport. She was driving to Simon Black's book signing and had to pass through Toronto anyway. We arrived at the hotel on Friday, and I rented a car from a lot on the other side of town Saturday morning."

Robert opened up his briefcase and pulled out his rental agreement, plus the parking ticket he had received. As he handed them to the detective, he said, "I'm telling you the truth. I got nothing to hide."

Detective Douglas looked at the date and time of the ticket. "That only proves that the car was there."

"Wait, I used my credit card to get some fuel when I got there. The station probably has cameras that can prove it was me." After finding the receipt, he told the detective, "That should prove that I was there."

"We still don't know how long you stayed there after the ticket was issued."

"Do the math. The ticket was issued at 4:23. Blackett Hill is almost three-quarters of an hour away from there. The store closes at five, so why would I drive all the way back there?"

"Maybe to catch him before he left. The sergeant here has done some research and found out that Mr. Black's book signing's had a tendency to run late. On Saturday, the store didn't actually close until almost eight."

"Now, how could I've known that the store would actually still stay open that late. That doesn't make sense."

The detective studied the flustrated man's face as he said, "I may have some more questions to ask you. Are you planning on staying at the hotel for a while?"

"Yes, I have rescheduled my meeting for Thursday. It depends on how well that meeting goes, as to how long I'll be sticking around."

As the detective passed him his card, he said, "I will probably be in touch before then. If you think of anything that could help this case, please give me a call."

As Sgt. Ryan followed the detective out of the room, he looked back at Robert's unfinished glass. *'That small bottle of tequila is sure lasting a long time for someone trying to drink away his sorrows.'*

Turning to Detective Douglas, he asked, "What now?"

"Lets see if Emily White is well enough to be questioned." As they walked to the stairs, the detective told him, "While we are in Blackett Hill, maybe we should see if we can find any holes in Nancy Gamble's story."

The sergeant tapped his fingers against his thigh. "Before we go, maybe we should check to see if there was anything Officer Kelly forgot to tell us. Maybe she remembered something that she thought was trivial that might actually help us out?"

"That wouldn't hurt."

Cindy MacDonald waited a few seconds before she crawled out from beneath the messy bed. "I thought they would never leave."

Robert went over to her, bent down and gave her a hug. As he gently kissed the top of her forehead, he told her, "Everything is fine. Those clowns will eventually find someone to pin the murder on, and will be out of our way. Soon we will be free to start our own happy, and very profitable venture."

While he brushed his fingers through her hair, Cindy stood up and gazed into his eyes. Smiling from ear to ear, her radiant face seemed to glow. "I just wish we could start our new life now."

"I wish we could too, but we can't. Not now." Robert tugged the shoulder of Cindy's robe. As it slipped down her side, he slid his hand down her bare back and cupped her left butt cheek. While giving it a gentle squeeze, he whispered in her ear, "Until then, we will just have to enjoy each other's company the best we can."

Chapter Seven

While Sgt. Ryan drove, Detective Douglas phoned Dr. Susan Deathridge's office. Her receptionist answered in a calm, relaxing voice, "Dr. Deathridge's office, how can I be of assistance?"

"This is Detective Douglas. I was wondering if the doctor is available?"

The receptionist's upbeat voice turned cold. "She is with her last patient of the day right now. I guess I could ask her to call you when she is done."

"That would be greatly appreciated."

The Sergeant glanced at the detective. "The truck stop is just ahead. Maybe we could grab a bite to eat before we get to Blackett Hill?"

The incident at the restaurant flashed in Detective Douglas's mind. "Sure, why not. We might be in for a long night."

As they pulled into the truck stop, the detective's phone rang. The detective looked at the caller's name. *'Private number'.* "I hope this is not another telemarketer." After two more rings, he finally answered, "Detective Douglas."

"Hi, this is Dr. Deathridge. You called my office. How can I assist you detective?"

Feeling a bit of relief, the detective grinned. "First of all, I was wanting to check up on Emily White's condition."

The doctor sat back on her chair and looked up at the ceiling. "Her condition hasn't improved much. It could be quite a while before I could allow you to question her."

"What if you acted as a mediator, a kind of go between? We could even arrange the interview in such a way that I don't even have to be in the room with you."

"And how would that work?"

"We could equip you with a tiny microphone and a receiver you can insert into your ear. Most women clip the microphone to their bra. That way we can hear what is going on, and relay the questions that we want you to ask her."

The doctor slouched over her desk and thought for a few seconds. "That might work. However, I would have to re-word your questions. You can be kind of coarse."

"I can live with that. So, when do you think we would be able to set up an interview?"

"How about meeting me at my office around six-thirty?"

As Sgt. Ryan shut off the car, the detective glanced at him and said, "Great, we'll be there."

The sergeant looked at him. "We are almost a half hour away."

"We can grab something to go. I'll eat in the car. You can eat while I'm prepping the doctor for the interview."

Leaving Sgt. Ryan in the car to eat, the detective walked into the doctor's office. The doctor stopped pacing the floor and glared at him. "You are late."

The detective spread his fingers in front of him. "Are you sure about that?"

The doctor pointed to the clock above the bench in the waiting room. It read six-thirty-five. The detective looked at it and then looked at his phone. "That clock is almost ten minutes fast. Maybe you should change the battery in it."

The doctor froze for a second. "I'm Sorry, this whole interview thing has me rattled."

As the doctor pinned the microphone to her bra strap and readjusted her sweater, she told him, "Emily is staying with Nancy Gamble and her parents. Both of you will be staying in your car while conduct the interview, right? I don't want to upset Emily, Nancy or her parents anymore than is absolutely necessary."

Detective Douglas deeply sighed before saying, "No problem. That is why we are conducting the interview the way we are."

As the doctor inserted the receiver in her ear, the detective asked, "You had already told me that you saw Emily Saturday night. Did you see her between the time she found out about the murder and her attempted suicide?

"She had phoned to set up an appointment, but my receptionist said that she didn't sound overly stressed out or anything. He is normally an excellent judge at reading people's voices. If he thought there was anything wrong, I'm sure that he would have told me. If I had known she was suicidal, I would've dropped everything and rushed right to her house."

"So he booked her an appointment?"

"Yes, it was scheduled for first thing Monday morning. Derrick knew that I had already given her some sedatives and something for her to get to sleep. Maybe he thought it was the drugs kicking in, making her feel a little off when she phoned the clinic."

The detective started to pace the floor. "So if he is such a good judge of a person's emotional state, do you have any idea what happened between that phone call and her suicide attempt?"

The doctor shook her head. "Nothing comes to mind. Maybe he had just judged her wrong. After all, he isn't a licenced psychologist."

"Or maybe he has been lucky up til now."

As they pulled their cars up to the house, the sergeant parked on the street behind the doctor's car. The doctor knocked on the door and Nancy's father let her in. Spotting the two officers in their car, he whispered to her, "They are not coming in here are they?"

The doctor cupped her right hand around the side of her mouth and whispered back, "No, I arranged things so they won't have to set foot inside this house."

Nancy's face turned pale as she hugged her mother and watched the doctor enter the room where Emily was staying. Her father peered out of the long, narrow window next to the door. Neither officer had left their car.

The doctor closed the bedroom door behind her. She pulled a kitchen chair next to Emily's bed, sat down and gently held her hand. After seeing her pale skin, clammy forehead and lifeless eyes, she softly asked, "How are you feeling?" She tried to keep her calming voice just above a whisper. "Do you need anything?"

Emily turned her head and stared at her. "I'm fine."

"You are not fine. In fact you are far from being fine." The doctor waited for a response, but none came. "Do you think you can answer a few brief questions?

Emily blinked and emotionlessly said, "What about?"

"What happened in the store."

"Simon died."

"I know, but I need to know what happened between you and Simon?"

Emily blinked again. "We were in love."

The doctor began massaging Emily's arm as she asked her, "Did you arrange for him to come to the store?"

Emily's face showed no emotion what-so-ever. "No, it was ordained. We were meant to be together."

"Is that why you tried to kill yourself?"

Emily's head started to twitch as she looked into the doctor's eyes. "I don't know. Maybe. Everything went blurry. It was surreal, like I was watching myself in a movie."

"So you didn't really want to commit suicide?"

Grabbing the doctor's arm, she cried out, "I don't know."

Nancy's father opened the door and inquired, "Is everything alright in here?"

The Doctor turned to him and calmly said, "We're fine, just leave us alone for a while longer."

After some hesitation, he left and shut the door

behind him. Focussing on Emily, the doctor held both of her hands and calmly asked her. "You said that you were in love. Was it mutual?"

Emily smiled. "It was. He showed me how much he loved me in the washroom. He even asked me if he could come over that night. I tidied up the place and had it looking perfect for him." Emily's smile was short lived. "I waited all night for him, but he didn't...", she started to cry. "He didn't show up. That was when you came to see me."

"So, the two of you had sex in the washroom."

"It was more than just sex. It was the physical union of our bodies."

"That's a cramped room. It must've been very uncomfortable."

"You are wrong. He lifted me and sat me on the edge of the sink. We looked into each other's eyes and kissed as our bodies became one. Even when his phone slipped out of his pocket, and I accidentally stepped on it when I slipped off the edge of the sink, he continued to kiss and worship me."

Detective Douglas turned and looked at Sgt Ryan as he told the doctor, "What condition was the phone in?"

The doctor stroked Emily's hair, and asked her, "How was his phone?"

"It was leaning against his foot. When the heel of my shoe hit it, Simon caught me as I lost my balance." Emily smiled and sighed as she gazed into the doctor's eyes. "I smashed his phone and all he cared about was me. What does that tell you about his feelings toward me?"

The doctor smiled and gently ran her hand down the side of Emily's face. "That he obviously adored you."

"But now he is dead." After sobbing for over a minute, she coldly looked at the doctor and said, "But I already told you all this. Why are you asking me this all over again?"

"I just wanted to make sure nothing had changed.

Sometimes, as time passes, people remember things a little differently."

Sgt Ryan looked at Detective Douglas. "So the phone was smashed before the murder. That's why Simon Black's fingers were scratched up. He must've tried to used it to call for help."

The detective grimaced and shook his head. "That means that she was probably the only person that knew it was broken."

"Unless he had mentioned it to his killer."

"Maybe." The detective stared at the sergeant as he thought out loud, "Emily loved him. Simon had just met her. How could a man like that think of her as anything other then a good way to release some energy and pass some time."

The detective's voice resonated in the doctor's ear. She had to look away from Emily and shut her eyes. 'Ask her about Nancy. Find out if she saw Nancy or anyone else flirting with Simon.'

As Emily's tight grip started to turn Dr. Deathridge's fingers pale, the doctor tried to think of a way to restate the detective's question. After biting the side of her bottom lip, she finally said, "Simon was a very handsome man. I bet there were a lot of women flirting with him on Saturday."

Emily loosened her grip as she answered, "They all were. Even Nancy tried her hardest to seduce him. I saw them." Giving out a short chuckle, Emily smiled and said, "I pitied them. Simon isn't stupid. He saw right through them. I am the only one he truly wanted. The moment our eyes first met, we both knew that we were meant to be together."

"So he didn't even look at Nancy?"

"Simon was a thoughtful, considerate man. I caught him politely smiling at her. It was out of kindness, that's all."

"So you were not jealous of Nancy?"

Emily grinned and rocked her head back and forth. "No, not at all. That little tramp was too young for him.

Besides, we both know that her father would have jumped right in and stopped it."

The doctor shut her eyes and paused while Detective Douglas was talking to her. After he was done, she asked Emily, "Was he there?"

"No, not inside the store, but I saw him watching the little tramp through the window. There was no way that he would allow anyone to touch his little girl."

"So he kept a very close watch over her?"

A puzzled look came over Emily's face. "We both know how he hovers over her. That's a funny question to ask. You know everything about everyone here."

Dr. Deathridge rubbed her ear and took a deep breath. In a soft but stern voice, she said, "What I know is my business." After another deep cleansing breath, she added, "I just wanted to know how much you know. Most people here don't really know anything about their neighbours. They live in their own very private worlds, and tend to keep everything to themselves."

The doctor looked at Emily's pale face. Their conversation had sapped even more colour from it, and had began draining it from her lips. "You're exhausted. I had better let you rest. Do you think you can get some sleep?"

Emily shut her eyes and flopped her head on her pillow and said, "I'll try."

Detective Douglas almost screamed into his microphone, "We have a lot more questions we need answered."

The doctor winced as his voice rang in her ear. As casually as she could, she reached up, turned her head and removed the ear piece. While she put it into the rear pocket of her denim jeans, she looked at Emily's pale face.

Doctor Deathridge gently stoked Emily's hair and smiled. "As long as you take the medication that I gave you, you should be fine."

The doctor left Emily's bedroom and grabbed a small cushion from the sofa in the living room. She pressed it against her chest and walked over to Nancy's mother. With the microphone muffled, she briefly went over both Emily's and her daughters medications. After they were done talking, she handed her the cushion and gave her a hug. "If either one of them seem off in any way, don't wait. Call me right away. My phone is always on."

Detective Douglas watched the doctor leave the house and walk to her car. "What happened? I couldn't make out what was being said a while ago."

As she swung open her car door, the doctor abruptly told him, "Client patient confidentiality."

The detective shook his head and barked out, "You know that this is a murder investigation?"

The doctor snapped back, "That has nothing to do with the welfare of my patients. I'm going back to my office. You can meet me there."

The two officers ran up to the doctor as she unlocked the clinic door. Facing the back of her head, the detective told her, "You know that we still haven't identified Simon's killer. There are people in this community that I just can not rule out. I have to know what some of your patients are capable of doing."

As she opened the door to let them in, the doctor's jaw held her teeth tightly together as she spat out, "I told you that I would help in your investigation, but I will not jeopardise my patients' health nor their faith in me." Loosening her jaw slightly, she added, "They expect me to be their confidant. If I start betraying them, I will lose their trust and respect. Without that, I will become nothing more than a pill pusher to them. They will revert back into the messes they were before they got here."

Sgt. Ryan spoke up, "We won't let that happen." While glaring at the detective, he added, "Will we?"

Detective Douglas lowered his head and grasped his hands tightly together. "I don't want to destroy everything you helped create here, but one way or another I will continue to investigate this case. You can either help us find Simon Black's killer, or we will rip this town apart."

The doctor's face turned red as she stood there glaring at him. Before she could speak, Sgt. Ryan said, "Lets go inside were we are less of a public spectacle. Standing out here acting like this isn't doing any of us any good."

Once inside, the doctor turned to the detective. With their noses almost touching, her steely eyes looked straight into his, as she said, "So who do you suspect is the killer? I know everyone in this town. None of my patients had the emotional strength and desire needed to kill that book peddler. They knew that he would be gone as soon as his book signing was over. What possible motive could any one of them have? He was killed when he was getting ready to leave. That fact alone should exonerate them."

The detective placed his left hand on his hip and jabbed the index finger of his right hand against her chin. "As you said, anyone is capable of killing someone under the right circumstances. That even includes you."

Dr. Deathridge slapped his hand away. "You self righteous neanderthal. How could anyone like you understand how fragile these people are. As far as accusing me, I had a room full of patients to verify where I was at the time of the murder."

Seeing the detective bite his lip as he flexed his right hand, Sgt. Ryan tapped him on the shoulder. "Maybe I should step in here."

The doctor turn to him. "Fine with me."

In a calm voice, the sergeant told her, "First of all, we don't need to know everything about every person in this town. A man was killed. There has to be witnesses, and people that know some scraps of information that could help us. We need to find those people and question them." Glancing at the detective, he added, "As far as your patients' files go, all we really need to know is the risk level of certain individuals, so we can strike them off our list of suspects."

As the doctor stepped to the side to face the sergeant, the detective turned to them. "This is still my investigation."

The doctor glanced at him and growled, "How about I give my ear piece and microphone to your sergeant and you go back to your car."

As he was about to speak, the sergeant grabbed his arm and pulled him to the corner of the room. Before his superior could say a word, the sergeant sharply whispered, "What is going on with you? Why are you being so abrasive. We need her help."

Detective Douglas cocked his head to the side and muttered back, "Fine, but get her to tell us everything we need to know."

The doctor piped up, "Within reason. I will not betray my patients' confidence in me."

The detective glared at her. "As long as I can get the evidence I need to convict Simon Black's killer."

After the detective stormed out of the building, the sergeant followed the doctor into her office. As they went inside, the doctor grabbed a hold of the microphone to muffle it, and whispered to the sergeant, "What is up with him? He wasn't this gruff when I first met him. He seems to be getting worse."

The sergeant put his hand over the doctor's to further muffle their voices. "I'm not sure. Maybe it's the fact that he can't steam-roll over the people in this town to get what he wants." With his hand still on her's, he inched back and studied her face. "You have to admit, the people here are not the type that he is used to dealing with."

She glanced down at his hand as it innocently brushed her left breast as he pulled it away. "You maybe right, but I think it is something else."

Realizing what he had done, he yanked his hand behind his back and said, "Sorry."

As the doctor sat down, the sergeant thumbed through his notepad. "Lets begin with Mr. Gamble. What can you tell me about him?"

The doctor smiled and shook her head. "Nancy's father is harmless."

The sergeant cocked his head to the side. "There is a reason why he is on our list of suspects. He is an overprotective parent and was seen lingering outside of the book store at the time of the murder."

The doctor semi smiled at him. "He is always keeping a close eye on Nancy. So he is an overprotective parent. He is harmless."

"That brings up Nancy. Apparently she had changed quite a bit after she found out that Simon Black was coming to town. Could that have heightened his concerns. As you indicated, he was a very protective father."

Dr. Deathridge glanced at her filing cabinet. "Okay, fine, I had a session with him on Saturday morning, and yes it was about Nancy." Tapping the ends of her extending thumbs and fingers together, she added, "He was concerned about her mental well-being. I told him that if he looked in on her from time to time, she would most likely concede and come to terms with how she is acting, and who she really is."

The sergeant nodded his head. "So she sees him in the window and is reminded that everything she does is being scrutinized. She takes a look at herself, realizes that she is acting silly and reverts back to normal."

The doctor twisted her lips to one side and said, "Basically."

"But that doesn't really explain his over protective demeanor?"

The doctor grasped her hands together. "He is a big

man. His stature alone gives him a somewhat menacing ability to control some peoples actions. He doesn't need to resort to using force to get people to listen to him. A few roughly spoken words were usually intimidating enough."

"So is that why you have such a, hum, may I say, robust, male receptionist?"

"Partly, along with being everyone's doctor, at times I am also called in to settle disputes. Having someone big and strong enough to help me defuse some awkward situations can be very useful."

Sergeant Ryan watch her fidget with her pen. "You are not comfortable being the one answering the questions, are you?"

The doctor put the pen down. "Is it that obvious?"

"Yes. You and Detective Douglas are more alike then you think. Neither one of you likes being forced to relinquish control over anything."

She curled her lips inside her mouth and shook her head. "You can't compare the two of us."

Detective Douglas crashed his fist into the passenger side seat. "What are you doing. I never said that you could psychoanalyse me."

The sergeant pulled his ear piece out before continuing, "Detective Douglas can't conduct the investigation in the fashion he wants to, and you can't protect your patients like you feel you should. This murder has put both of you teetering on a greased fence."

The doctor looked at her clasped hands and started to tap her thumbs together. "Maybe you are right, but I would still prefer talking to you over him."

In a soft, almost soothing voice, the sergeant said, "Fine, but try to ease up on him. He has a job to do."

"I know that there is something about the Detective that you are not telling me." She slowly rocked her head back and forth. "But, for now, as long as he respects me, and my patients' need for privacy, I will try to work with him."

The sergeant replaced his ear piece and said, "Are you alright with that?" He smiled at the doctor. The sergeant chuckled. "Detective Douglas said that he could live with that."

"Good."

"The next person we need to learn a little more about is the owner of this town, Roger Blackett." Sergeant Ryan sat back on his chair and studied her response. "We would like to know if he was at the book store on Saturday, and if he was the one who arranged Simon Black's book signing."

Dr. Deathridge covered her mouth with her right hand. As she gazed at the sergeant, she shook her head. "I don't know, but I think it would be very unlikely. He hardly ever leaves his house, and I have never known him to leave town."

"Do you think that there is any chance you can set up an interview with him?"

"He suffers from agoraphobia. Not only is he afraid to go outside, but he is terrified of outsiders and doesn't trust anyone. He does all his communications through a secured three-way landline installed directly to my office and Nancy's house. Her mother is his bookkeeper. She also does a lot of errands for him."

"But land lines can be easily tapped into."

The doctor shook her head. It's all underground with anti bug detectors installed at every end."

"So he does nothing over the air waves?"

The doctor shook her head. "Nothing that he thinks can be intercepted and manipulated in any way by outsiders."

"You are telling me that he has no way of communicating to anyone outside of town."

"That's right." The doctor thought for a moment. "Maybe the post. I think I heard Nancy say something about her mother getting her to post something for him. But that was months ago."

Sgt. Ryan clasped his fingers together and slightly lowered his head. "So he would see us knocking on his door as a gross invasion of privacy." He looked up at the doctor. "So, what kind of interview could you set up for us?"

The doctor tapped her fingernails against the top of her desk. "I will see what I can work out."

The sergeant looked out the window. "It must cost him a lot of money to run this place. Where does he get all of his money?"

Dr. Deathridge also looked out the window. "I am not one hundred percent sure. I was always under the impression that he had inherited it."

Chapter Eight

Sgt Ryan shook the doctor's hand and thanked her for her assistance. It was drizzling outside. He ran to the car and got into the passenger seat. Detective Douglas looked over at him and said, "It's getting late. Maybe we should get a hotel room for the night so we don't have to drive all the way back here in the morning."

"It's not that late."

The detective looked out the driver side window. "The roads could turn into a sheet of ice if it gets any colder. You've seen some of those bends. I just don't want to take any unnecessary chances."

Knowing that the detective's mind was set, the sergeant gently rocked his head and said, "So what is on our agenda?"

"Tomorrow morning, we should go over the book store's records. Surely they must have kept some kind of communication from whoever set up the book signing. Someone had to convey the details of the event to the store and media."

Looking over his shoulder, the sergeant glanced in the direction of the book store. "You are right. His fans must have heard about it from somewhere."

"When we get to the hotel, maybe you can peruse the internet and see what else you can dig up."

The lady at the desk smiled as Detective Douglas entered the lobby. "I see that you have returned. How long do you expect to stay this time."

"I'm not sure." As Sgt. Ryan entered the lobby carrying two hard shelled cases, the detective told her, "And we will be needing two rooms this time."

While staring at the long case in Sgt Ryan's left hand, she pointed at it and asked, "I don't want to sound nosy, but what is in that one?"

Sgt. Ryan politely answered her, "Just some of our

equipment. We are not allowed to leave it unattended in a car overnight."

The lady behind the counter handed the detective two keys, "Take the same room as last time. Your partner can have the one at the end of the hall." The lady bent over and whispered, "It isn't quite as nice as yours."

Sgt. Ryan slid the gun case under his bed. Then he flopped the other case on top of it. Inside the second case was a lap top computer, a compact printer, some blank paper and various small electronic devices. He cleared off the end table next to the bed and turned it into a mini desk.

Shortly after turning on the laptop, he saw several notifications from two of the technicians back at the station. He grabbed his phone and called Detective Douglas. "Come to my room. The tech boys must have been working overtime."

As the detective entered the room, Sgt. Ryan waved him over to his bed. "Sit down, we have a lot of stuff to go through."

The detective pulled the end table away from the wall, to enable him to see the monitor better. As he sat down and leaned sideways to get a better view of the monitor, he said, "What have you got?"

"They ran all the fingerprints, videos, plus the photos you took through the system. We have a ton of data to mull over."

The detective skimmed through the first e-mail. "About 13% of the finger prints were on file. That's a lot higher than normal for this region. The crime rate is generally pretty low around here."

Sgt. Ryan glanced at him, "A lot of the people attending the book signing were probably from down south."

"That might explain part of it."

The sergeant pointed to the screen. "Of the crimes committed, half of the flagged people had only misdemeanours." The sergeant went quiet for a while, then said, "Now that is very strange. Usually the vast majority have only misdemeanours."

"Did they attach any photo ID's to the people they flagged?"

After looking at the bottom of the screen, Sgt. Ryan clicked on the paperclip icon. "Yes, I'm retrieving them now."

The detective reached over and flipped through the files. "Most of the people with just misdemeanours were from out of town. It seems that all the people charged with the more serious crimes live in Blackett Hill. Their photos may be old, but I can still recognise most of them." He scratched his head for a couple seconds before he added, "Some of them have really changed quite a bit."

Sgt Ryan glanced at the photos. "Some of them look like old pictures from a POW camp."

"They were probably doped up. The doctor must have drastically changed their medication."

"Whatever she is doing certainly works. They look younger now than they looked five years ago."

Emily's gaunt face appeared on the monitor. Written beside her image were, 'Assault with a deadly weapon. Uttering death threats. Suicidal.' Beneath it was printed 'Emily Williams'.

Next was Nancy's unflattering photo. Beside her's was, 'Assault and auto theft.' Under it was the name Nancy Green. The officers looked at each other. Detective Douglas broke the silence. "We have a pair of winners here. I just wonder what else we've got."

A half dozen files later, a picture of a much younger Simon Black was on the screen. Next to it was listed, disturbing the peace, trespassing, vandalism and resisting arrest. Under it was the name 'Simon Blakey'.

The sergeant looked at Detective Douglas and said,

"So we now have the dead man's actual birth name. Simon had a pretty rebellious youth but nothing serious."

The detective pointed at the screen. "Look at the dates. They were all before he changed his name and got into writing."

"Maybe writing was part of his rehabilitation therapy. I have heard that writing things down on paper has a way of turning a person's thoughts into something more physical. In order to express an emotion on paper, a person has to draw something from their own personal experiences. This forces them to dredge up their past. According to what I have heard and read, this helps them confront the true reasons why they are the way they are."

"Well it must have helped. Since he changed his name he has stayed out of trouble." Thinking about Simon's murder, he added, "At least with the law."

"But he is still somewhat of a mystery."

Detective Douglas rocked his head back and forth. "So we have his real name. That doesn't change the fact that it was Simon Black, a rich, successful author that was murdered, not the poor, misguided Simon Blakely. That troubled youth died nearly twenty years ago. That seems much too long to have any bearing on his murder."

When Sgt. Ryan isolated the files triggered by the photos the detective snapped, the pair began to squirm even more. Almost everyone in Blackett Hill was using an alias. The list of offences they committed were shocking. The cook that smashed the detective's phone, had been charged with numerous assaults and uttering death threats. The mature waitress had only got out of prison a year ago for attempted murder. The obstinate lady that lived in the house behind the book store had served time for both arson and vandalism.

The detective scratched the back of his head. "I don't know if it is just me, but a lot of these people are starting to look familiar."

Sgt. Ryan looked at him. "Some of them may have been locals. Prison has a way to change a person's appearance."

"You might be right."

Sgt. Ryan looked at the detective. "This town is full of ex-cons. Who knows, you could have even put some of them in jail."

"Maybe." The detective thought of the woman behind the book store and took a deep breath. As he exhaled, he shook his head and said, "Well, I don't care what the doctor says. These records indicate that almost any one of them could be our killer. Maybe Simon recognized one of them. They could've got into a spat that simply spiralled out of hand."

A couple photos later, Dr. Susan Deathridge's face appeared on the monitor. 'Assault causing bodily harm, charges dropped.' The detective scrolled the mouse over to blue highlighted link and double clicked on it. The police file of the case popped on the screen. "She had physically assaulted a prison warden." The next paragraph shed some light on the doctor. "She was a prison psychologist." The detective looked at the sergeant and told him, "So that explains why she's defending these ex-cons."

Sgt. Ryan interlocked his fingers behind his neck and leaned back. "She's treating the town like her own, private, outdoor half-way-house."

The detective slowly read the doctor's file. "Apparently, she stuck the warden on the side of his face with a baton. He had to undergo reconstructive surgery and was in hospital for nearly a month." Glancing over at the sergeant, he said, "I wonder what made him drop the charges? He must've endured a lot of pain and financial loss. I would have had her locked up and sued her for damages."

Sgt Ryan puckered his lips and stared at the screen. "It doesn't really say much about the assault."

Detective Douglas spoke up. "Or why the charges were dropped."

"Something fishy was going on." Sgt. Ryan scrunched his eyebrows. "What if she caught him doing something he shouldn't have been doing. Maybe he was scared it would leak out if it went to court."

"Blackmail? Now, that sounds very plausible."

The next photo they looked at was of Randy Green, Nancy Gamble's father. Beside it was a twelve year old 'driving while under the influence' charge from Alberta.

"Now there is a surprise." Detective Douglas rocked his head back and forth, and said, "I thought he would have had multiple criminal charges against him." He looked at the sergeant and added, "Maybe I got him wrong."

Sgt. Ryan twitched his nose, turned away and coughed. After clearing his throat, he said, "Maybe I'll ask the technicians to make some further inquiries. It sounds weird that he is the only one in town that we came across so far, without a violent past."

"Great idea. Add to your e-mail that I want anything else they can dig up on the doctor, Nancy, Emily and the lady in the house behind the book store. There is something about her that troubles me. She still could be a wild card."

The next batch of files the sergeant opened had hundreds of stills from the videos collected from the truck stop, camp grounds and the gas station in Blackett Hill. As they began to peruse through them, the sergeant turned and looked at Detective Douglas. "The technicians must have run the video through a computer, and selected the images that seem to match the ones from the book store."

"Those fuzzy things. Computers just see measurable and easily identifiable traits. They just see focal points. They don't take into account a person's mannerisms, dress, gait, fashion sense and stature when linking two obscure images together." Glancing at Sgt. Ryan, he added, "That's our job.

That's why we will never be replaced by analytical robots. Robots don't have any gut feelings. They don't see things the way we do."

"But computers are a lot faster."

For the next two hours, the pair flipped through the images and compared them to those from the book store. Licence plates from Michigan, Ohio and New York were more common then those from Manitoba and Quebec. They dismissed the vehicles with families onboard, along with transport trucks, delivery vans, plus business and construction vehicles. They still were left with hundreds of images to compare.

As the detective got up to stretch, the sergeant spoke up, "Here is an easy one. She is even wearing the same outfit that she had on in the book store's video."

Detective Douglas dashed over and gazed at the striking woman in the photo. "I would recognize that figure anywhere. Can we identify her."

Using the car's licence plate, the sergeant downloaded a copy of Cindy MacDonald's New York driver's licence. The photo on it didn't do her justice. Compared to the well manicured woman standing at the counter of the truck stop, the woman in the driver licence photo appeared rather drab and almost pathetic. Her dress, glasses, lifeless haircut, makeup and posture were almost completely different. "If she wasn't driving her own car, I wouldn't have put the two images together."

The detective saw how the young sergeant stared at the screen and chuckled. "Don't get too excited. For all we know, she was just there to meet her favourite author and get his autograph."

"You're probably right. She is most likely back in the states by now."

It was almost two AM when the pair finally decided to call it quits for the night. Knowing that the detective didn't like eating at the restaurant, at seven o'clock in the morning, the housekeeper knocked on his door. "I put some coffee on if you want some."

As he woke up, he thought of what the housekeeper's file said. 'Obstruction of a police investigation, assaulting a police officer and multiple arrests for vagrancy and causing a disturbance.' After looking at the time, he slapped his cheeks a couple times and shook his head. "I'll be down in a couple minutes."

The detective quickly put on his clothes. With his jacket under his arm, he knocked on the sergeant's door. "It's after seven. Get a move on."

From the bottom of the stairs came, "I know, I'm down here waiting for you."

As he reached the lobby, Sgt Ryan handed him a cup of steaming coffee. Detective Douglas placed it on the coffee table, sat at the bench beside it and tied his shoes. "Why didn't you wake me."

"Normally it's the other way around." After taking a sip of coffee, the sergeant grinned and asked him, "So what is on the agenda this morning?"

The detective double checked his itinerary on his phone. "Officer Kelly will be patrolling this area today. I'll give the Hunters' Crossing station a call and see if we can set up a meeting with her. Next, we need to talk to the doctor. There are lots of things about this place that she is not telling us."

"Like this entire town is a glorified half-way house full of ex-cons."

The detective looked at the young sergeant and shook his head. "When I was your age I used to party to the wee hours, and somehow still be up at the crack of dawn. I just can't do that anymore." While rotating his head and yawning, he barely managed to get out, "Now I need at least six hours sleep."

Clamping his jaw tight, the sergeant fought the temptation to crack an 'old man' joke. With a wide grin on his face, he told him, "You know that you left yourself wide open. Telling someone how old they are getting, and not allowing them to make fun of you should be a crime."

"Knock that grin off your face." Detective Douglas straightened his tie. "Lets get some breakfast and make some phone calls."

As the housekeeper poured them some more coffee, they sat opposite to each other at the kitchen table, and pulled out their phones. The detective bit his bottom lip, turned his head and asked the housekeeper, "When does the clinic open?"

"Eight, the lineup should be starting any time now." As she peeked out the window, she added, "Some people bring a cup of coffee with them and turn it into a social event. Nobody seems to visit anyone here. At least at the clinic, everyone is nice and polite. To most of the people here, just standing in a line is a social event. Even if you don't talk to anyone, it's nice being around people that don't treat you like some kind of freak."

Detective Douglas looked at her. He wanted to bring up her past crimes, but held his tongue. Thinking about what she had been convicted of, he wondered why she was being so nice to him. "You really like it here, don't you?"

The housekeeper turned to him and grinned. "What's not to like. The people here are really nice, and I have a safe, warm place to sleep at night." Glancing back at the window, she smiled and added, "The people here leave you alone and nobody harasses you."

Satisfied with the woman's response, the detective took in a deep breath, turned to the sergeant and said, "The doctor is probably at the clinic by now. I'll give her a call. Maybe she can work us in sometime this morning."

When he called the clinic, the receptionist answered

in a cheery voice. "Hello, Dr. Deathridge's office, how can I help you?"

"Hi, this is Detective Douglas. I was wondering about setting up another meeting with the doctor."

The receptionist glanced at his blank monitor. Without even turning it on, he harshly answered, "She is booked solid. If things die down, she might be able to work you in later today. I'll call you back and let you know."

Looking at Sgt. Ryan, the detective said, "It could be a while before we get to see the doctor. I'll see if I can set up a meeting with Officer Kelly."

Sgt. Ryan looked up at him and placed his phone on the table. "No need. I checked her schedule and sent her office a request for a meeting. They had already e-mailed me back. It is set up for nine-thirty at the truck stop."

"Great, that means that we will have time to peek through the book store's records before we need to leave town. Whoever arranged the book signing would've had to notify the store. There has to be some kind of paper trail for us to follow up on."

After a quaint continental breakfast, Sgt. Ryan placed their dishes in the sink. "Thanks, that was very nice of you." With a smile, he added, "It was almost like being at home."

The housekeeper's eyes went kind of puffy. She straightened her back and cried out, "I was just trying to make your stay comfortable." Then stomped into her bedroom and slammed the door shut.

While Sgt. Ryan loaded their equipment back into their car, he turned to Detective Douglas and said, "That was a strange reaction. I was just trying to give her a compliment."

"I think the word home may have triggered a memory. Remember her file, she was homeless for most of her life. She might have a weird outlook on what a traditional home is actually like."

"From her reaction, I take it that it wasn't very pleasant."

They used the sidewalk on the other side of the road from the clinic. On the way to the book store they looked around. Outside of the eight, quiet, fidgeting people standing in front of the clinic, they saw two people quietly opening their shops. Their footsteps almost echoed as they walked down the street. Neither one of them spoke, in fear of being overheard in the still morning air.

Through the book store's window they saw Nancy sweeping the floor in front of the counter. Detective Douglas tried to open the door but it was locked. Startled by the rattling door knob, Nancy dropped the broom she was using. Noticing the two officers standing outside of the door, she wiped her hands on her apron, walked over and unlocked the door. "You gave me a fright. How can I help you."

The detective spoke up, "We would like to have another look around the store if you don't mind."

"Why would I mind?" Nancy's eyebrows fell as she added, "It is not my store."

"That's right. Roger Blackett owns everything in this town."

Nancy pointed to the far right corner of the store. "There is a whole section of reference books in the back, that were brought in just for him. This store is like his own private library. Before the book signing, it had copies of every edition of every Simon Black novel, plus every novelty item associated with them. Over a quarter of this place was like a mini shrine to him."

"So we have been informed." Sgt Ryan looked around the store before saying, "That would make Simon Black a huge part of both you and your boss's lives."

Detective Douglas added, "No wonder Emily was so infatuated with Simon Black. She was practically immersed in his essence every day." Turning to Nancy, he asked her,

"How often does Mr. Blackett come into the store?"

"I'm not sure if he has ever come in here. I don't even know what he looks like." Nancy picked up the broom and started to sweep as she told him, "My mother knows him. She is the one that does all the running around for him."

While the sergeant snooped around the store and disappeared into the back room, the detective asked Nancy, "When was the first time you heard that Simon Black was coming here for a book signing?"

"I think Emily told me about it around two weeks ago."

"Did she say how she found out about it?"

"No, I don't think so. If she did, I can't remember it." Leaning on the broom, she added, "She was so excited about meeting him that she could barely function. The next day, she came to work wearing two completely different shoes."

Sgt. Ryan called out from the back room. "I think I found something."

The detective almost ran into the room and found him kneeling next to the exit door. "What did you find."

The sergeant handed him a sample baggy with a small wad of chewed up paper in it. "Someone used it to fill the hole where the locking bolt goes in. The door will shut, but anyone with a credit card, or any thin object, could work the bolt free and open it."

Looking at the wad, the detective said, "We should be able to get a DNA sample from it. Good work. I don't know how the technicians missed it?"

The sergeant looked at him. "Jamming a door's lock isn't proof of murder."

"I know, but it may give us a suspect."

Chapter Nine

Detective Douglas walked out of the back room holding the plastic bag. Nancy's eyes were drawn to the wad of paper inside it. "I'm sorry. I can explain."

He stopped and looked at her. "Explain what?"

Nancy pointed to the bag. "I must've jammed the lock."

"Why did you do that?"

"Sometimes I forget my keys. Emily told me that if I keep forgetting them, that I may not be able to work here anymore." As tears ran down her face, she blubbered out, "I beg you, please don't tell her."

Not swayed by the young woman's tears, the detective said, "It is not her that you need to worry about. This is a murder investigation. Someone killed Simon Black in this store." Biting his bottom lip the detective rocked his head back and forth. "How many people knew that it was jammed and not really locked at night?"

Nancy shook her head. "How would I know. I guess anyone that used the back door could have seen the paper crammed into the hole."

The detective glanced at the bag and noticed the condensation inside of it. "How often do you pack paper into the hole?"

Nancy used her sleeve to wipe her eyes. "Whenever I'm the one opening the next day, and I remember to."

"Can you remember if you did it on Saturday?"

Shaking her head, she told him, "I can't remember. We were very busy on Saturday. I was absolutely exhausted. I could have. I'm not sure."

Sgt. Ryan overheard the conversation and came out of the back room with more baggies containing wads of paper. "I found these tucked behind a box." He turned and faced Nancy. "How often do you remove the old ones?"

"I try to get them out before Emily gets here." With

her head down, Nancy's sad, wide, glossy eyes looked up at them. "You are not going to tell Emily about them, are you?"

Detective Douglas asked her, "What if someone broke in during the night?"

Nancy wrapped her arms around her chest. "If they don't disarm the alarm, it will go off. Everyone in the entire neighbourhood would hear it."

Sgt Ryan spoke up, "The alarm box is near the front of the store. So, the alarm must have an extended time delay?"

She looked at one and then the other. "Yes, I think it is set for one minute. Sometimes we are carrying stuff, and need to set it down before we are able to disarm it."

As the detective got closer to Nancy, she got a better look at the dark wad of paper in the baggy. "Hold on, that's not one of my wads. I would never put that yucky stuff in my mouth."

The sergeant held up the bags. "Which one are you talking about?"

Nancy pointed to a wad of coloured paper. "There are too many toxic chemicals in that stuff."

Sgt Ryan looked at the dried up wads in the bags he was carrying, then the one the detective had. "They're different. These ones look like they came from the edges of a newspaper. That one looks like it came from a magazine."

Detective Douglas glanced at the sergeant. "Then we'll make this one a top priority."

After handing the bag to the sergeant, Detective Douglas walked over to the counter and asked Nancy, "Where would we find the paperwork pertaining to the book signing? Someone had to have arranged for him to come here. He wouldn't just show up unannounced and uninvited. I would imagine that there would be a lot of work that needs to be done to prepare for such an event."

Looking down at the floor, Nancy answered, "Emily

looked after all that stuff."

The detective scratched his head. "That's fine, but where would she keep the paperwork?"

"Somewhere in one of the filing cabinets in the backroom. They are on the right side next to the washroom."

There were three, four drawer, filing cabinets in the room. Detective Douglas opened the top drawer of the first cabinet. It was stuffed with file folders. The detective had to forcefully wiggle the first one out of it. He turned to the sergeant and told him, "If I start rummaging through these files, I'm going to be late for my meeting with Officer Kelly. How about you stay here and go through them. I'll be back as soon as the meeting is over."

Sgt. Ryan glared at him, "Leave me with all the dirty work while you sit down, drink coffee and eat a donut."

The detective chuckled. "That's one of the perks about being the senior officer."

The truck stop was half full of semi trucks, RVs, pickup trucks and cars. Detective Douglas didn't notice any patrol cars in the parking lot. After parking the car, he went in and picked out a corner booth.

The waitress had already brought him a coffee before Officer Kelly walked in and began looking around. The detective waved her over. "Sit down, you might as well relax and have a coffee while we chat."

Wearing a little more makeup than a female police officer is normally allowed, Officer Kelly glanced around the restaurant. "I was expecting to see Sgt Ryan. Didn't he come with you?"

Seeing the puzzled look on her face, he asked, "Why?"

Officer Kelly released the blast of air from her lungs. "I don't know. I just haven't seen him since he got sick."

The detective grinned. "I needed him to shuffle through a ton of files in the book store in Blackett Hill."

"Oh, I get it, payback for the sick days he took off."

Detective Douglas shrugged his shoulders. "Well, someone has to do it."

As the officer sat down, a waitress came over with a mug and coffee pot. "Can I get you anything?"

Officer Kelly looked at her. "Just coffee for now."

The waitress leaned over and poured her a coffee. "They will be bringing out some fresh muffins in a bit. I know how much you like our blueberry muffins."

Officer Kelly smiled as the waitress topped off the detective's mug. "Thank you for remembering, but not today. This is a business meeting."

Detective Douglas smiled and spoke up, "They sound delicious. Bring us a couple."

As the waitress walked away, the detective looked at the stern looking officer across from him and told her, "My treat."

After releasing a sigh, Officer Kelly informed him, "And I have a bridesmaid's dress that I have to fit into." Tilting her head to the side, she added, "You can take the extra muffin back to Steve, I mean Sgt. Ryan."

Detective Douglas smirked. "Let's just get down to business. On Sunday, did you notice anything strange in the back room of the book store?"

"No, why do you ask?"

"We found out that the lock on the back door had paper jammed into the hole. Anyone could have opened it."

Officer Kelly shook her head. "No, I can't remember anything strange. The door was shut when I got there and most of the shelves looked somewhat neat and orderly."

After taking another sip of coffee, the detective asked, "There were a lot of people at the book signing. Did you or your station receive any complaints?"

"No, I can't remember any. The only problem I had was from one of his American fans. She was weaving in and out of traffic and was honking her horn like she owned the road. I ended up giving her a hefty speeding ticket along with a tongue lashing."

"How did you know she attended the book signing?"

"She had a copy of Polar Diamonds, the book Simon Black just released, lying on the passenger seat."

The waitress placed two muffins on the table. The detective thanked her, and waited for her to leave before continuing. "Can you remember what time that was?"

Officer Kelly instinctively pulled out her newly replaced note pad. She shook her head. "Sometime between three and four. I always have my dash cam on. As soon as I get back to the station, I could lookup the exact time for you."

Detective Douglas bit into a muffin and allowed himself time to think. "So you leave your camera on during your entire shift?"

"Sure, you never know when something can happen."

"So it was on when you drove through Blackett Hill on Saturday?"

"Naturally." She looked at the muffin on the plate in front of her. After gulping a mouthful of coffee, she slid the plate to the far side of the table. "I believe I drove through Blackett Hill a couple times on Saturday."

The detective looked at the second muffin and smiled. "Do you think I could get a copy of Saturday's video."

"Sure, as soon as I get back to the station, I'll make you a copy and leave it at the desk."

"That would be greatly appreciated."

As Officer Kelly stood up, the detective said, "I have one more question for you. Blackett Hill is private property, so why are you patrolling it?"

She looked down at him. "The road going through Blackett Hill is still public. They may own all the property on both sides of it, but as long as they are paying taxes, someone has to patrol it." She started to smile as she added, "Plus, the cheeseburgers at the restaurant are absolutely terrific."

Detective Douglas drove back to Blackett Hill and parked in front of the book store. Looking down the street he noticed that there was no longer a line up in front of the clinic. He gave it a call. The receptionist answered, "Hello, Dr. Deathridge's office, how can I help you?"

"This is Detective Douglas, I was wondering when the doctor will be free. I never got the return phone call that you promised me."

"Oh, sorry about that. I may have forgotten to give her the message."

"Well, can you give it to her now?"

"Sure, right after her current patient leaves."

"Tell her that I'm trying to be nice. " After taking a cleansing breath, he added, "I expect a reply within five minutes. If not, I could get real nasty. I might even start treating the locals like I would any other murder suspects."

The detective ended the call, grabbed the small paper bag off the passenger seat and marched into the book store. By the time he got into the back room, he had managed to regain most of his composure.

Sgt. Ryan was on his knees flipping through files in the bottom drawer of the middle filing cabinet. He glanced at the detective. "I have yet to find a single thing relating to any book signing. I don't think this store has ever had one before Saturday. It must of been their very first one."

The detective handed him the bag. "I take it that you know Officer Kelly outside of duty."

Sgt. Ryan smirked. "Yeah, Maryann is a bridesmaid and I am an usher at a friends wedding in a couple weeks."

"So it's Maryann." Detective Douglas released a soft chuckle. "Just a heads up. I think, Maryann likes you."

Sgt. Ryan ignored his last comment, opened the bag and grinned. "Blueberry, I might have known."

The detective glanced at the over stuffed drawer that the sergeant was looking through. "What a mess."

"It is mostly invoices and records of every sale and return from the past seven years. The residents here use this place like a public library. They buy a book and return it as soon as they are done reading it."

"All that sort of stuff should be filed on a computer."

The sergeant rested on one knee and turned to face the detective. "Have you even seen a computer in this town?"

Before the detective could reply, his phone rang. "Hi, you got Detective Douglas, how can I be of assistance?"

"This is Doctor Deathridge, I heard that you wanted to speak with me."

"Yes, We did a background check on you and some of your patients. It seems that you have not been completely honest with me."

"That is not true. I have told you nothing but the truth. Nobody from this community committed that murder."

"You deceived me, and lied about your patients' real names."

"Their first names had never changed, and I don't believe that I had ever mentioned any of their last names. So, how could I have lied about them."

"What about the Gambles?"

The doctor hesitated before answering. "Well, I may have been a bit misleading with the Greens, but you were the one that referred to them as the Gambles. I just never corrected you."

"So Nancy Gamble's mother is Roger Blackett's book keeper?"

"That is correct."

Detective Douglas took a deep breath. In a commanding voice, he barked out, "This is getting too much. When can we meet? We need to have a serious one on one talk. I need some straight answers. The sooner I get them, the better it will be for everyone in this town."

The doctor paused for a moment. Without raising her

voice, she told him, "Meet me in the back room of the community hall at two o'clock. There is so much stuff in there that it is almost sound proof."

"Why not your office?"

"My files are here. I don't want anyone to think that I gave you access to them."

Detective Douglas took a deep breath. "Fine, we will meet you at the hall at two."

The detective and Sgt Ryan spent the rest of the morning at the book store searching through the files. Other than an invoice for six hundred hard covered, and two hundred soft covered copies of Simon Black's latest book, they found nothing pertaining to the book signing.

While Sgt Ryan stood up and wiped the dust off his knees, the detective told him, "There has to be some kind of paper trail somewhere. Emily must have stashed them somewhere." Glancing at the door leading to the retail floor, he added, "Nancy must know where she hides stuff before she gets a chance to file them."

Nancy heard her name and went into the backroom. "Were you wanting me?"

The detective looked at Nancy's polite, rosy smile and couldn't avoid smiling back. "We were just wondering if you know of anywhere else Emily could have placed the papers pertaining to Simon Black's book signing? Maybe she tucked them somewhere safe, in order to file later."

Nancy looked behind the counter and scratched her head. "I honestly don't know. She was always very methodical about handling paper work. I've never seen any laying around for more then a minute."

Sgt Ryan looked at the detective and said, "However, she had a soft spot for Simon Black. Maybe she put them somewhere a little more private."

"Maybe." As they stepped outside the store, Detective Douglas looked up and down the street and told the sergeant,

"We might as well get something to eat before our meeting with the good doctor."

The sergeant piped up, "I heard the restaurant here makes great cheeseburgers."

Not wanting the sergeant to see his anxiety, Detective Douglas took a deep breath and calmly said, "Sure, I'll drive."

"It's only a couple blocks?"

"That doesn't matter. We're taking the car."

Detective Douglas parked outside the Restaurant's window and peered inside. While sitting behind the steering wheel, he could see five people standing in front of the counter. "How about getting me a cheeseburger, fries and coffee to go."

Sgt. Ryan glanced at the restaurant then back at him, "They have a couple empty booths. We could eat inside."

"Too crowded. I have to make some phone calls and I don't want to be overheard." As the detective passed the sergeant a couple bills, he said, "My treat."

As he waited in line, the sergeant glanced out the window. He saw the detective slam his phone against the dash. "Good thing the dash has lots of padding."

After the sergeant got back in the car with the food and coffees, the detective drove to the campgrounds. He stopped at the entrance and looked around. He saw a picnic table nestled under a large maple tree, turned and told the sergeant, "That will do."

While they were eating, they both looked around at the Spartan conditions. A gust of wind swirled around some of the dead brown, red and yellow leaves that were falling off the trees. Sgt. Ryan finally broke the silence and commented, "I can't see a bunch of nerdy, urban bookworms wanting to stay here."

"Why not? All they need is a dry place to curl up, a warm blanket and a lantern. Most of the bookworms I know have dozens of e-books on their phones and tablets."

Sgt Ryan swatted a mosquito that had landed on his neck. "While, most of the bookworms I know like a fresh smelling, flush toilet and an insect free environment."

Glancing at the time, the detective told him, "We have an hour and a half before our meeting. We might as well spend some of it looking around here. You never know what evidence someone might have accidentally left behind."

As the sergeant used a stick to poke through the trash bins, the detective went into the office. The reception room was empty. The small room contained a rack of local interest and outdoor safety pamphlets, a large map of the campground on the wall, some fold-up maps on the counter and a bell.

The detective rang the bell and heard some shuffling in a back room. A scruffy, white haired man slowly wandered out carrying a steaming mug. After he finished chewing what was in his mouth and washing it down with a sip of tea, he said, "How can I help you?"

After showing him his badge, Detective Douglas said, "We are investigating the murder that happened in Blackett Hill on Saturday."

"I remember you. You got some CDs from my surveillance cameras."

"That's right. They were a great help. They helped us identify a fair number of the people at the book signing on Saturday." The detective glanced out the window and then back at the attendant. "If you don't mind, we would like to poke around the grounds a bit to see if they left anything behind that might help us."

The old man pointed to the window, "Go ahead, take whatever garbage you want. That will mean less for me to get rid of later."

"Great, it should only take a half hour or so." The detective turned to leave and then stopped. "Have you emptied any of the trash bins since they were here?"

The man shook his head and told him, "I probably

won't empty them until I pack everything up for the season."

"Good. Just in case we need another look around, can you call the station and let us know before you do."

"Sure, no problem."

While Sgt. Ryan continued to search through the trash bins, the detective examined the campsites and fire pits. As the detective moved some unburnt chunks of wood around with a long stick, he tried to identify the garbage the campers were trying to burn. Some of the labels on the cans and wrappers were still identifiable.

The detective spotted a couple campsites that were almost hidden behind a grove of bare trees. As he shuffled through the ashes of a small fire, the end of the stick he was using got entangled in a cup shaped piece of fabric netting. Stuck to the outside of it were small burnt clumps of blonde hair. He held the stick as high as he could and yelled out, "Sergeant, what do you make of this?"

Before he even got to the campsite, he recognized what it was. "That looks like the inner lining of a wig."

"A good wig can cost a lot of money. I wonder why anyone would burn one?"

Sgt Ryan walked over to the fire pit to get a better look. "Maybe it got singed by the fire and the owner didn't want to be embarrassed by it."

"I doubt that. A person could take a singed wig into a salon and get it restyled." The detective looked around the small campsite. "I think it was deliberately burnt. Or, maybe someone grabbed it off someone and tossed it in the fire out of spite." He looked around the campsite. "I can't see any fresh tent peg holes in the ground."

"Maybe they decided to sleep in their car."

They went back to the office to see who rented the site. The manager went through his records. "No one was signed in to that particular campsite. It doesn't have any water or electricity going to it. Maybe someone didn't like their neighbours and moved their camp without informing me." Shrugging his shoulders, he added, "It happens all the time."

"Could we get a list of who rented the various campsites for the entire weekend." Turning to the sergeant, the detective said, "Maybe you should stay here and poke around some more."

"More grudge work. I'm getting to see a pattern here."

The detective smiled as he pointed to a nearby trash bin. "Whoever burnt that wig didn't want it to be found. They could have simply tossed it in the bin. The wig may be nothing, but it might have been part of the killer's disguise."

Sgt Ryan sighed and said, "Fine, I'll stay here."

Detective Douglas lost his smile as he said, "We also need to get the techs to concentrate on comparing the video images, not just facial images, from here and the book store. If we can find out who wore that wig, we might have a suspect."

The sergeant looked at him. "Maybe it was a man dressed as a woman."

"A transvestite?"

"I am just saying that maybe we shouldn't rule out anyone."

"You are right. When I call the techs, I'll tell them to go over the video very carefully and focus more of their attention to physical characteristics, like bone structure, height and muscle tone."

As the detective arrived at the community hall, several locals watched him get out of the car and walk inside. Inside, he saw a four women playing cards and a few men tossing a basketball into a hoop attached to the wall. In the far, front corner, the receptionist from the clinic was teaching a self-defence class.

He noticed the doctor standing next to a set of double

doors at the rear of the hall. Everyone stopped what they were doing, and silently watched him walk over to her. "I thought we would be alone."

"Nothing that goes on in this community is totally private. That way everyone knows that they are not being picked on or falsely accused of something they didn't do."

The doctor's words echoed through the hall. As the pair entered the back room, the others resumed what they were doing. One of the women playing cards chuckled. "The doctor will set him straight. If he causes any trouble here, karma will surely catch up to him. He'll regret ever messing with anyone from this town."

The backroom was full of tables, chairs, cleaning supplies, exercise mats, various bags of balls, hockey sticks and a lot of other miscellaneous pieces of furniture and equipment. The detective took a couple chairs off the nearest stack and set them down.

The doctor looked at him and then the chairs. "So you are planning to turn this into a long meeting."

He shook his head and grinned. "We have a lot to hash out." After she sat down, he looked up at her and said. "First, how about you telling me about why you assaulted a prison warden? I like to know what kind of person I am dealing with."

The doctor shook her head and paced back and forth across the floor. "All charges were dropped. In fact, he never even filed a complaint. His doctor was the one that got the police involved."

"According to my information, he needed a lot of reconstructive surgery on both his jaw and cheekbone."

The doctor looked at him and smiled. "Compared to what he did, I felt that he got off lucky."

Detective Douglas's grin widened. "You didn't file any formal complaints about him. We checked. There was nothing in his files that justified the beating you gave him."

"When the people that are doing the crime are the same people that control all the records, what good are they. No one cared or even listened to what I had to say." Doctor Deathridge looked up at the ceiling. "But they sure paid attention when they had to find a replacement for that sorry excuse for a man." The doctor smirked as she added, "I put that meathead out of commission for almost four months."

The detective's solemn face lost some of its colour as he asked, "That's assault. Why didn't he file charges?"

The doctor couldn't help but chuckle. "Do you think that fool didn't want to see me behind bars? He did. The problem is that he had read all of my reports. He knew what I had unearthed. Nobody wanted to see me on a witness stand. If any of my reports went public, it would've disrupted the day to day operations of almost every prison in the country."

The detective cocked his head and looked at her. "So why haven't you gone to the press?"

Doctor Deathridge smiled and snorted. "Fear, they know that I still have all my original documents stashed away. If anything happens to me, they will be released to the media. They are so scared of me that they agreed to not file any charges, plus let me oversee, and make suggestions on all the changes they are now implementing." A wide grin spread across her face as she added, "I won. What else matters."

"What kind of changes are we talking about?"

The doctor sat down on the chair and gazed at him. "A better understanding of how they should be handling extreme introverts, people with mental disorders like PTSD or those who happen to be bi-polar. A lot of them commit suicide long before completing their sentence. In the exercise yard, they were marked as easy targets for gang recruits to attack at random. Most of them can't handle being herded around like livestock. They shouldn't be forced into the general prison population without some kind of provisions in place to protect them."

"So why the warden?"

The doctor looked at him and shook her head. "He laughed at me. I tried to explain to him why the system needed to be changed and he laughed at me. Well karma is a bitch and he became the fall guy." She gave out a chuckle. "He should've listened to me."

Detective Douglas sat back in his chair. "So that's where the members of this strange community came from."

"Mostly, but some were referred to me by judges and fellow psychologists." A grin spread across her face as she leaned forward and told him, "I think that you will find that I have a lot of clout in the legal system."

The detective grinned back and told her, "And how does that help me solve Simon Black's murder?"

"The judges trust my judgement and so should you. My reputation is of the upmost importance to me and this community. If I had even an inkling that one of my patients had committed that murder, I would tell you. I have this entire community to protect."

The detective leaned forward and glared into her eyes. "They look up to you as their protector. If you gave one of them up, what then?"

The doctor's face turned cold. "Murder is murder. If they are presented with all the facts, and there is no doubt about the conclusion, they will be alright."

After a brief staring match, the detective finally lowered his head. "So I just have to trust your judgement?"

Dr. Deathridge grinned. "That's right."

"What about Emily, am I able to question her yet? I still haven't found out who orchestrated the book signing. Other than some book invoices, there was nothing in the store pertaining to it."

"I'll try to find that information out for you, but no promises. That poor girl has been through enough trauma."

"We will need the actual documents. Any paperwork that she could give us would be greatly appreciated." Detective Douglas looked into the doctor's steely eyes, and added, "We need to find out the real reason why Simon Black came here, and why he was murdered, and who set up the book signing."

As the doctor stood up, she looked down at him and said, "I'll see what I can do, but I can't promise anything."

Detective Douglas looked around as everyone watched him leave. Their wide grins and soft chuckles infuriated him. It was only after he left the building that he realised that the entire meeting was a setup. He stopped, turned back and looked at the door. "The doctor used the meeting as a publicity ploy. She wanted them to see me slither out like a scolded school boy. I hope they all had a good laugh because this case is not over with yet."

Chapter Ten

On the way back to the campground, Detective Douglas thought about his conversation with the doctor. As the faces of the smiling people watching him leave the building ran through his mind, a shiver ran up his spine. "There should be a tall, barbed wire fence around that entire town."

As he pulled up to the camp's office, he saw Sgt. Ryan and the owner inside, standing next to the counter. When he went inside, he found them slumped over a marked up map of the different campsites. "Have you found anything."

Sgt. Ryan turned and faced him. "We figure that at least five, extra, hike-in campsites were being utilized. Some of the cars were packed full. Whoever used that site could have been sitting in a back seat for all we know. The problem is that some people arrived on Thursday. Some even made a semi weekend out of it and never left until Sunday morning."

"We need a list of all the people that stayed here." The detective glanced at the map. "The people using the extra sites were probably part of a large group that rented a nearby campsite. That way they could still be together, while having more tent space to sleep in during the night."

"But I never saw any fresh peg holes."

"Maybe they just weighted in down with all their stuff."

The owner raised his hand. "There's a problem with that list. I only wrote down the name of the person who was paying for the site, along with their vehicle's plate number and how many were in the party."

The sergeant looked at the detective. "Maybe we should concentrate on the larger parties."

"Maybe." Detective Douglas rocked his head back and forth as he told Sgt. Ryan, "I think we should leave this job up to the technicians. They should be able to digitally enhance some of the various videos and give us still photos of the people sitting in the back seat. Hopefully, they can find someone wearing a wig."

The sergeant smiled. "Or different hair colour, cut or style."

The detective felt his phone vibrate. He took it out and read a brief text. After taking a few deep breaths he turned to the sergeant and said, "Officer Kelly will be at the station in about an hour to drop off her dash cam video from the weekend. She said that she would leave them at the desk. How about you go to the station and drop off what's left of the wig, plus those videos, to the tech department."

As he thought about seeing Maryann, a child like grin grew on the sergeant's face. "Sure, But I will be needing the car." It suddenly dawned on him, "What will you be doing while I'm gone?"

The detective walked over to the window and stared at the road. He thought about the doctor's almost one sided conversation, and the grinning faces of the town folk as he left building. With a blank look on his face he finally answered him, "Making my presence known. Sometimes just the knowledge that someone is out there snooping around, and asking questions, can make a person slip up."

Detective Douglas looked at the old man behind the counter and then out of the window again. "Even an innocent nod of my head might lead the guilty person to think I'm on to them. I just want to rock the boat a wee bit. I want to see if it changes anyone's daily routine."

The sergeant rubbed his forehead. "So you will be just walking around town and making everyone feel as uncomfortable as you possibly can."

"That is about the size of it." The detective saw the old man listening in to their conversation. "I don't trust ex-cons." Shaking his head, he added, "Despite what the good doctor wants, she can't completely shackle me. I am investigating a murder."

The old man took a couple steps back and slowly rocked his head back and forth. "If you cause any trouble in that town, karma will get you in spades. No one causes trouble in that town. If you do, you will live to regret it."

On the way back to Blackett Hill, the detective thought about what the man said. "What does karma have to do with governing the people in town? That's just plain stupid."

Without taking his eyes off the road, the sergeant responded, "In a way, it could act like a moral code of conduct. You act out of line, you get what you deserve. If anything bad happens to anyone, it is because they somehow did something wrong. Since it is a shrouded community, outside of the doctor, who actually knows if that person actually did anything wrong or not. The people here will assume it was the person's karma that had punished them. In a way, the doctor has somehow turned karma into the town's invisible police force."

The Detective smiled and nodded his head. "In a weird way, that makes sense."

Sgt. Ryan dropped the detective off in front of the book store. Before Detective Douglas shut the door, he told the sergeant, "Take your time. I'll just be wandering around stirring things up and seeing if anyone bites. I'll be fine."

The sergeant warned him, "Simon Black came here and stirred things up. He's dead. Watch your back. These people like their quiet, little town just the way it is. They don't like outsiders. Even if no one here killed Simon, that doesn't mean they won't try to kill you."

The detective shrugged off the sergeant's warning. As he walked down the main street, he peered into every window and tried to make eye contact with every person he saw. *'I'll show her what I can do. She can't shackle me. I don't care if everyone in this cockamamie community despises me. I have a job to do and I'll do it.'*

When the residents saw him, they would hide, look away or cower. Feeling somewhat empowered, he started to swagger. This yielded a very negative effect. The window blinds of the next store were being shut as he approached. He was being shunned.

He tested the door. It wasn't locked, so he entered. Before the door could close behind him, everyone inside had vanished. He could hear them shuffling around behind the counters and aisles stocked with various hardware supplies. As he walked from one aisle to another, he noticed both front and back doors open and close. *'These are not people. They are scurrying around like rodents.'*

The door of the grocery store was locked. When he put his ear next to the window, he could hear people whispering to each other inside. Looking around, he saw no one. The street was empty. Everyone was avoiding him. "Well be that way."

As he got to the hotel, he found that its front door was also locked. He looked up at the sky and saw dark rain clouds off in the distance. Clenching his fist, he looked at the cars parked in front of the restaurant. "They can't shun me. There are too many outsiders in there."

In the alley next to the restaurant, one of the cooks was tossing a bag of garbage into a bin. He saw the detective. Without shutting the lid, he raced back inside.

Detective Douglas hastened his pace and was inside before the cook had time to make his way through the kitchen. The grin on his face widened as he walked up to the counter. The cook glared at him as he stood in the kitchen behind the waist high, swinging doors.

The mature salt and pepper haired waitress saw him and sharply said, "What do you want?"

"A coffee." After looking at the desserts displayed in the glass counter, he added, "And a piece of strawberry-rhubarb pie."

He watched the waitress tremble as she took a cup from the bottom of a rack next to the coffee machine. She trembled even more as she poured the coffee into it, and placed the slice of pie on the plate. After placing slightly more than it cost on the counter, he sat at the booth next to the door of the men's washroom. He pulled out his phone and placed it on the table. As he sipped his coffee, he looked around the room.

None of the outsiders paid any attention to him. However, the locals tried to avoid looking in his direction. *'So this is what it means to be shunned.'*

The detective picked up his phone and went through his emails. He cringed after reading a few of them. As he sat back, his head hit the wall behind him. Out of pure frustration, he smacked the back of his head against the wall several times and closed his eyes. When he reopened his eyes, he saw the young waitress staring at him from behind the counter. As she quickly looked away, he forced himself to smile, and picked up his fork.

The pie tasted much better than he expected. It tasted too good. He grabbed the salt shaker and sprinkled some of it over the pie. He took a small bite and could barely swallow it. *'That will make it last a lot longer.'*

Half of the pie was still left a half hour later. He stared at his empty coffee cup as he watched the rain pelt the window. Seeing the young waitress serving coffees to the people in the next booth, he loudly asked, "What no refills?"

The young waitress stopped what she was doing, froze for a brief moment, then walked away. Detective Douglas shook his head. "I guess not."

The sound of the rain drowned out most of the chatter from the other customers. He looked around the room and then at the washroom door. After pocketing his phone, he grabbed his cup and stood up.

As he turned towards the washroom, water splashed

onto his sock. He looked down and saw a small puddle that had formed next to the doorway. He stepped over it as he went into the washroom. While placing his coffee cup on the small counter he noticed that the window was slightly ajar. At both ends of the window seal, tiny streams of rainwater ran down the wall and onto the floor.

When he was finished using the urinal, he washed his hands and filled his cup with water. After drinking half of it, he filled it back up. "Note to self, next time not as much salt."

Holding his cup in his left hand, Detective Douglas slid the bar used to lock the washroom door with his right. He turned the door knob and started to pull the door towards him. Suddenly something sharp struck his back. His hair stood on end as a sudden surge of high voltage electricity ran through his entire body,

As he desperately tried to open the door to escape, an even stronger jolt engulfed him. He used his right hand to push against the doorframe in an attempt to turn around to see his attacker. His legs wouldn't budge. As his torso shifted, his left hand swung to the right. The cup struck the edge of the sink. Wet shards were strewn over the small counter. Unable to let go of the broken handle, droplets of blood dripped from his tight fist.

Using all the strength he could muster, he turned his head as far as he could. All he ended up seeing was his own frazzled image in the mirror above the sink.

As he tried to hold onto the edge of the sink, he could feel the voltage getting stronger. After a few seconds, his pulsating body collapsed to the floor. As his right hand repetitively smacked the toilet again and again, his left leg kicked the door shut. With his eyes bulging out, he finally lost consciousness.

The young waitress saw an elderly man knocking on the washroom door. His knocks got progressively louder, and rose above the rain pelting the windows and roof. Even the people at the far end of the restaurant began to stare at him. The waitress went over to him and asked, "What seems to be the problem?"

The man turned to her. Without unclenching his teeth, he said, "I need to go. Some fool has been in there for almost half an hour. He won't even answer me."

The waitress ran and got the young muscular cook. He tried the door knob. "It's locked." As he leaned against the door, he felt the top of the door wiggle. "It can't be locked. Something must be wedged against the bottom of it."

The impatient, grey haired man gripped his hands together. "Well unwedge it. I got to go."

After bracing his left foot against the floor mounted table where the detective had been sitting, the cook got down on one knee and put his shoulder against the door. The waitress helped him push. The door opened a crack. Suddenly there was less resistance and it opened half way. As the cook held the door open, the waitress peered inside. "It's that rude cop. He is passed out on the floor. His legs are jammed against the door."

The cook told her, "If I hold the door open, do you think you can squeeze inside?"

"I should be able to."

The waitress wiggled and carefully worked her way inside. Once inside, she shut the door to make more room to work. Grabbing one leg at a time, she flopped the detective's legs against the counter and opened the door.

While the cook dragged Detective Douglas out, the impatient man stepped over his limp body and went inside. "Finally!"

The waitress glanced at the rain pounding against the window. "You can't drag him outside. Not in this weather."

The cook puffed out his cheeks. His lips flapped against each other as he released a loud burst of air, followed by, "So what do you think we should do with him."

The waitress got behind Detective Douglas's head and grabbed his shoulders. "Lets just put him back in his seat and pretend he just fell asleep."

The next thing Detective Douglas remembered was Sgt. Ryan slapping his face and saying. "What happened to you?"

Detective Douglas tried to focus on the sergeant's fuzzy face. "Someone used a stun gun on me."

Doctor Deathridge slipped through the small crowd in front of the booth and asked, "Did you see who it was?"

"No my back was turned."

The sergeant ripped off the piece of paper that someone had taped to the detective's chest. As he looked around the restaurant, he yelled out, "Who taped this on him?"

The seasoned waitress stepped forward. "I did. I don't want any customers to think that we allow drunks to waltz in here and pass out."

Detective Douglas slowly reach out, grabbed the note and read it out loud. "Karma's a bitch."

The doctor smiled slightly as she shone her flashlight in Detective Douglas's eyes and checked his vitals. "He'll be fine."

She noticed his blood stained hand. When she opened his fist to look at his palm, she saw several plastic bandages taped across it. She carefully removed them and pulled out a couple, small, curved, ceramic shards from his palm. Most of the cuts were superficial. Only a couple were still bleeding. "Who gave him a ceramic cup?

The seasoned waitress stepped forward and told her, "Being an outsider, I thought he could handle one."

"But, who was going to wash it when he was done? You know the rules." The doctor shook her head. "I thought those cups were all thrown out?"

The cook spoke up. "We only have a few left. Some of our regular customers ask for them."

"Well get rid of them."

The doctor watched the cook grab a plastic tote and placed the bottom rack of cups in it. As he left, she began to disinfected the wound. After she finished wrapping the detective's hand, she smiled and told him, "They should stop bleeding within an hour. I would still recommend that you leave the bandage on overnight."

With a small degree of force, she twisted the detective sideways and pulled the back of his jacket and shirt over his head. "You really got burnt, didn't you?"

The detective barked back, "Someone tried to fry me!"

As she bandaged up his back, she told him, "That's going to be sore for a few days."

Sgt. Ryan helped the detective into the hotel lobby. As he sat him down on the bench, he asked him, "What did you do this time?"

Bent over with his hands covering his pale face, Detective Douglas slowly answered him, "I tried to shake things up." While slowly shaking his head, he added, "First they shunned me. Then they tried to fry me."

Sgt. Ryan looked at the two, small charred holes in the back of the detective's jacket. "It wasn't karma that shocked you. Someone had to have pulled the trigger. You are lucky that they stopped there. The doctor warned you. These people are not your run of the mill urban thugs. Didn't you read their files. You can't go around threatening them. They could take a step backwards and go utterly berserk."

The detective turned his head and looked at Sgt. Ryan. "Like whoever killed Simon Black." After a couple of deep breaths, he continued, "There is a good chance that whoever shocked me, is probably our killer. If I'm right, the killer lives in Blackett Hill."

The sergeant stared at him. "Maybe, but you are not

dead. This could have been just a warning."

Sgt. Ryan helped the detective to his room and sat him on the bed. The detective put his arm behind his back. His fingertips could barely reach the area where the electrodes struck him. "Right where a person can't reach. Maybe it was someone with some training."

"Outside of some police and special forces units, the type of stun gun that was used is next to impossible to get in Canada. From the files I've seen, I don't think anyone here could even pass the screening process to qualify to use one. Maybe it was just a lucky shot."

"What about the PTSD patients? There has to be some ex-soldiers or cops in town with some training with them. Maybe we just haven't got any files on them yet."

"That's possible, but you do know that most PTSD victims are not soldiers or cops."

The detective looked up at the sergeant and said, "Sometimes I wonder who is running this investigation, you or me."

Sgt. Ryan grinned and released a small chuckle. "You are. I am just here to make sure you don't screw it up." He saw the detective's fists beginning to tighten up. "Fine, I'm here to assist you, and not undermine you."

The detective gazed into the sergeant's eyes as he said, "I know that you have been chatting with my wife. She inadvertently sent me a text message that was actually intended for you."

The sergeant shrugged his shoulders. "She is worried about you."

"Why should she be? Just because she isn't here to hover over me like a mother hen! That's no reason for her to be worried about me. She should just keep her nose in the kitchen where it belongs."

Sergeant Ryan placed the palms of both of his hands in front of him. "Ease up on her. She knows that you are mad at her, and when you are frustrated and angry, you have a tendency to make rash decisions."

The sergeant put his hand on the detective's shoulder. "She knows that she upset you, but you weren't there. She felt that she was being forced to make all the decisions on her own. If you had been there, it wouldn't have happened."

Detective Douglas shook his head. "But the woman is colour blind."

"She told me that she had asked the painter to pick the colours for her. Maybe he didn't know about her condition."

"But I hate pink, purple, or any of those girlish colours." The detective covered his face with his hands. "Now it's going to cost me over double to get the house painted. Why did she have to paint every room at one time?"

"She told me that the painters gave her a great deal, and they were only free that day. She didn't want to wait until it was too cold to open the windows, to air the place out. Check your messages. She tried to get a hold of you."

"Yeah, but at the time my phone was busted."

"And how many times did you flip through your messages without responding before it broke? It takes quite a while to paint every room in a house."

Detective Douglas shrug his shoulders. "Whatever."

The sergeant shook his head and added, "Well lets hope that she can at least get the bedroom repainted before you get back."

"But terra cotta, how could she ever think that I could possibly sleep in a pink bedroom?" Detective Douglas looked at his partner. "And why does she think I need babysitting. I am a senior police detective in charge of murder investigations. I can look after myself."

The sergeant leaned back and glanced at the two charred marks on the detective's back. "Like I said, when you are angry, she worries about you."

After the detective had some time to recover, he went to the sergeant's room. While lying on the bed, he watched the sergeant go over the footage taken from Officer Kelly's dash cam. Glancing at the computer screen he noticed the relatively low volume of traffic on both the highway and the road leading to Blackett Hill. "I wonder what would come up, if we ran all the plate numbers on her videos?"

Sergeant Ryan chuckled. "A waste of man hours."

"There can't be more then a thousand plates." The detective sat up. "The techs could compare them to the other lists in no time. It could eliminate a bunch of suspects and help us figure out who was where."

The sergeant smiled. "So now you think that it could actually be someone other than one of a townies?"

"Give me some credit." The detective glared at him. "I know how to investigate a murder."

As the video of Officer Kelly pulling over the car that she had told him about came on the screen, Detective Douglas sat up and wiggled closer to the sergeant to get a better look. "I remember her from the book store footage. Look at her haircut. She is the one that lost it and had a mini fit."

"But she was racing to get away from there. I don't think she was intending to turn around and race all the way back to kill him."

Detective Douglas put his arms behind his head and lay back on the bed. "Probably not, unless she wanted to get a ticket to use as an alibi."

Sgt. Ryan continued to peruse through the footage. Shortly after swapping memory sticks, he found the footage from when Officer Kelly drove through Blackett Hill. "We should run all these plates through the computer."

"This video was taken almost four hours before the murder." Detective Douglas turned to the sergeant and told him, "But, at least we know that they were at the book signing. It might be worth a shot."

Officer Kelly had slowed down as she passed the book store. Sgt. Ryan reduced the speed of the video to one eighth.

Sgt Ryan noticed two men arguing in the alleyway next to the store, and paused the video. Detective Douglas looked at the time stamp, '15:35'. "That's not the time the lady behind the store told me."

"Maybe she got confused."

Even after Officer Kelly turned around and was driving out of town, the two men were still arguing. As the sergeant saw the scruffy looking man strike the slightly taller, well dressed man's shoulder, he paused the video. "We might have something here."

He played the two three second scenes over and over in slow motion, trying to identify the well dressed man. As he was being struck by the shorter man, he slightly twisted his body. Half of his face flashed in and quickly back out of view. The man's blue striped tie briefly stood still before falling back into place. Despite the blurred image Detective Douglas had an inkling of who it was. "Look at his suit and tie. That's Robert Swayze, Simon Black's agent."

"But he isn't wearing any glasses."

The detective smirked. "Have you ever heard of contacts? He probably only wears glasses when he goes out in public."

The sergeant took a closer look at the blurred, still image on the screen. "You could be right." Looking down at the time stamp'15:39', he added, "That must have happened just before he left for his meeting."

"Yeah, but why was he in a heated argument in a small town in the middle of nowhere? Besides Simon Black, who would he even know in Blackett Hill? Something is not right. For him to have an argument with someone in Blackett Hill is strange." Detective Douglas folded his hands behind his head and reiterated, "In fact, this entire murder is very strange."

Chapter Eleven

Detective Douglas rapped on Robert Swayze's hotel door. "Wait a minute", radiated from the room. As Robert peered through the peephole, he said, "Oh, it's you again."

Robert undid the security chain, opened the door and stepped back into the room to allow Detective Douglas to step inside. Sgt. Ryan followed him in and shut the door. As the sergeant smelt the air, he picked up the same fragrance as before. "Did you have a woman visit you?"

Robert smiled, and said, "No, just the cleaning lady."

Sgt. Ryan cocked his head to the side and looked at him. "She wears a very distinctive perfume. Most hotels don't allow their cleaning crew to wear any fragrances at all."

"Well apparently either this one does." Robert's smile turned into a grin, as he slowly added, "Or maybe the girl's a bit of a rebel."

Detective Douglas stepped between them. "The reason that we came here tonight is to ask you about an incident that happened last Saturday."

Robert's face turned serious. "I thought I answered all your questions?"

"Well apparently a few more questions came up."

"Like what?"

The detective smacked his lips. "Well, first of all, who were you arguing with in the alleyway next to the book store around three-thirty Saturday afternoon?"

Robert's mouth cracked open. It took him a few seconds to respond. "When I went out to get some fresh air, some local followed me outside. We got into a brief heated conversation about Simon Black's book signing. That's all." Robert shook his head. "Except for the two ladies that ran the book store, it seemed like no one in that stupid little village wanted anything to do with Simon's book signing."

"Do you know who he was?"

Robert flung his right hand in the air. "How would I

know? I never met him before."

"All right." Detective Douglas wasn't impressed by Robert's theatrics. In a firm but steady voice, he asked him, "So, what were you arguing about?"

Robert glanced at the wall and then back at the detective. "Simon Black of course. Somehow, he knew that I was Simon Black's agent, and even called me by my full name."

The sergeant butted in. "Are you sure that he didn't overhear you mention it to someone?"

Detective Douglas glared at the sergeant, then looked at Robert. "Or maybe he got it from the internet. Maybe he sent you a manuscript and you turned it down."

Robert thought for a moment. "Writing a book requires focus and a lot of hard tedious work. You saw the people that live in that town. Do you think anyone there is even capable of doing the research that would be required to write a book?" He pointed at the detective. "Would you pick up a book written by one of them? I don't think so."

"They may be a bit odd, but they are not stupid." Detective Douglas adjusted his shoulder blades to help relieve the lingering pain in his back. "To tell you the truth, I'm not really sure what they are capable of."

Robert looked at the detective. "The man in that alley wasn't tech savvy in the least. You should have seen the way he looked at me when the alarm on my phone went off. He was utterly terrified of it." Placing his hand over his heart, he added, "I honestly don't know why he objected so adamantly to Simon being in town."

Detective Douglas looked at Robert and studied his open arms and semi-confused manner. Believing he was telling the truth, he asked, "So how did your little spat end."

"By him yelling, 'this is not over', and storming off."

Detective Douglas cocked his head to the side and asked him, "What do you think he meant by, 'this is not over?'"

Robert raised his arms and shook them in the air. "He thought I arranged the book signing in order to turn the town into some kind of tourist attraction. You should have heard him. The man was a complete lunatic."

The detective glanced at the sergeant, and then looked back at Robert. "Do you think he was capable of cornering Simon, and in a moment of rage, killed him?"

Robert shook his head and released a barely audible snort. "The guy was crazy. After he left, I even had a good chuckle. The man was frightened of his own shadow. He was obviously quite harmless."

"Never-the-less, we need to check him out. You never know what some people are capable of."

Robert glanced at the sergeant and then back at the detective. "So who was he?"

Detective Douglas put his notepad back into his pocket, looked up at him and smiled, "We are not one hundred percent sure. It seems that nobody in Blackett Hill is who they appear to be."

It was getting late. As they walked down the hallway Sgt Ryan looked at the detective. "So, do you really think you know who the other guy is, or was that just a line?"

"I have a hunch."

Detective Douglas thought about going home. The mere thought of sleeping in a pink, 'terra-cotta' room made him shudder. "Sergeant, I think that I'm just going to get a room here tonight."

Sgt. Ryan quickly glanced back at him as they walked down the stairs. "Your place can't be that bad? Think about your wife. Think about how bad she must feel."

The detective released a deep sigh and slowly shook his head. "She knows how much I hate pink. The painter is a man. He must've questioned her choice of colours. I think she did it on purpose."

"Why would she do that?"

"For turning the spare bedroom room into a den." Detective Douglas glanced at the sergeant, and added, "Every man needs a man cave. She wanted to keep it as a spare bedroom, incase one of the kids come for a visit." He snorted as he shook his head, "Now it's a bare, pink room. She told the painters to cram my stuff in garbage bags and pile them in the middle of the floor."

"So you get a new coat of paint on the walls before you put your stuff back up." Seeing the detective shake his head, the sergeant said, "Come on, once the lights are turned off, you can't tell what colour the walls are."

Detective Douglas shook his head some more. "Yeah, but I'll still know that I am sleeping in a pink room."

Sgt. Ryan had to stop himself from laughing. "You are awfully insecure for a tough guy."

The detective wouldn't answer him. After a moment of silence, he changed the subject. "We have to positively identify that strange, awkward looking man."

The sergeant quickly replied, "Robert said that he followed him out of the bookstore. Even if the video is a little fuzzy, we still should be able to match it. If we are lucky, we may even get something that we could use to identify him."

"If he is a local, he probably has a record. Wouldn't it be really nice if we are able to match his image to someone in the system. "

After Detective Douglas booked a room, he walked back to the station. He spent the next couple hours going through the footage taken from the book store and Officer Kelly's dash cam.

As he ran through the book store footage at eight times normal speed, he caught a glimpse of the unshaven, sloppily dressed man that was harassing Nancy. He stopped the video and studied the image. "He appears to be the right height, and seems to be wearing the same clothes."

The fuzzy photo was too obscure to run through the computer's database. After studying a half dozen stills, he felt confident that it was the same man.

He printed over a dozen still and cropped images. Satisfied that they were the best he was going to get, he took them back to the hotel with him. As he lay on his bed, he compared the fuzzy images to the ones from Officer Kelly's dash cam. "It has to be the same man."

The next morning, the detective stood by the car and waited for the sergeant to arrive. As he pulled into the parking lot, the detective waved him over. "We have to go back to Blackett Hill. I have isolated some images of the mystery man, but they are too fuzzy for the computer to identify."

"Why can't we just give them to the techs and see what magic they can do with them?"

Detective Douglas shook his head. "Robert Swayze said he was probably a local. If he is, fuzzy or not, the doctor should be able to identify him with a mere glance."

The detective opened the front passenger door and tossed Sgt. Ryan the car keys. As the sergeant got into the driver's seat, he told him, "That could save us a lot of time."

As Detective Douglas got in and buckled his seat belt, he added, "Plus we will already be in Blackett Hill to hopefully question him."

As they approached the campground, the sergeant slowed down. They couldn't see any vehicles parked inside it as they drove past it. A large, shiny lock hung from the end of the long, orange steel tube that acted as a swinging gate. The detective turned to the sergeant and said, "Funny, even the owner isn't there this morning."

The sergeant shrugged his left shoulder and replied, "As he said, it is his off season."

As they drove into Blackett Hill, they noticed that there was no line up in front of the clinic. The sergeant parked the car in front of it. Detective Douglas got out, walked over to the window and peered into the reception room. "I think we are in luck. There are only a few people inside."

Before the clinic's door closed behind them, the receptionist harshly said, "So you are back. What do you want this time?"

Detective Douglas grinned. "The usual. We need to talk to the doctor, again."

The tall, broad shouldered man stepped out from behind the desk. As he gazed down at them, he extended his arm and pointed in a circular motion at the people seated on the bench. "They were here first. You will just have to wait your turn. That should be around twenty to thirty minutes."

The detective looked up at him. "Put us down after these people and we will be back in thirty minutes."

"That is not how it works. If you are not in line and someone else comes in, I have to put them in ahead of you."

Detective Douglas glared at him. "Not if you want to keep this town on the map. I got a job to do, and I'll turn this place into a ghost town if I have to, in order to get it done."

Both officers could see the receptionist's muscles tense up. After he took a few deep breaths, he relaxed his clenched fists, and calmly said, "Very well. I'll let you in, in half an hour."

Sgt. Ryan checked the time as they left the clinic and strolled over to the book store. Nancy stood behind the counter sticking sale signs on some discounted books. She looked up as the two officers approached her. With a forced smile on her face, she said, "How can I help you today?"

Detective Douglas stared at her. "Nothing much. I just have some questions to ask you about the man that was pestering you during the book signing on Saturday."

Nancy straightened her shoulders. "Oh, him. I thought I had already told you everything I know about him."

"I've gone over what you had said, but I still want to know a wee bit more. For instance, in the images we retrieved from the store's cameras, I noticed that he wasn't holding on to one of Simon Black's books. Did he even stand in line to meet him?"

Nancy stood still and thought for a moment. "That's strange. I think you are right. I can't remember seeing him standing in line. He was just skulking around the store acting weird."

As the sergeant looked around the store, Detective Douglas asked her, "To your recollection, did he even try to speak to Mr. Black?"

Wringing her hands together, Nancy muttered, "I don't know. I was trying to ignore him. I guess I was hoping that he would just go away and leave me alone."

"So when you did see him, what was he doing?"

Nancy rocked her head back and forth. "It seemed like he was hiding. Maybe he was like me and felt a bit uncomfortable with all the outsiders in the store." She looked at the detective and bit her bottom lip. "Maybe I was a bit harsh with him."

Detective Douglas tried to analyse Nancy's body language. All he could see was an uncomfortable, jittery girl, that wouldn't look at his face. "I know that you don't like me asking you all these questions, but I have no choice in the matter."

From half way across the room, Sgt Ryan asked her, "You just said that he might have been afraid of all the outsiders in the store. Was he from around here?"

Nancy felt a little more at ease as she answered him. "Like I had said before, I never saw him before Saturday."

Sgt. Ryan walked toward her as he said, "This is a relatively closed community. Is it possible that he could still live in Blackett Hill?"

Nancy looked at the slightly confused sergeant and

then at the stern detective. "It is unlikely but it's not impossible. Most of the folks in town keep to themselves. Some hardly, if ever, leave their homes. There might be a bunch of people here that I haven't met."

Thirty-two minutes had passed by the time they got back to the clinic. The detective saw that more people had arrived. The receptionist, pointed at the detective's face. "You were late. I didn't know when you would be back, so I let a patient in ahead of you." Shaking his head, he defiantly added, "It's all your fault."

Sgt. Ryan checked the time and placed his hand on the detective's shoulder. "He's right. Let's just chill for a couple minutes. These appointments are generally pretty quick."

The red faced detective brushed the sergeant's hand away. While staring at the receptionist, he blurted out, "Very well, but it better be fast."

Sergeant Ryan picked a pamphlet off the coffee table and walked to the wall which the detective was leaning against. "This is the first clinic I've ever been to that didn't have stacks of old magazines."

The detective nodded his head. "Yeah, everything about this clinic is strange."

In less then a minute, the doctor's door opened and a woman walked out. Spotting the two officers, she looked down at the floor and quickly scooted passed them. The receptionist looked at the detective and cocked his head toward the doctor's door.

The detective stood up and said, "Our turn."

The sergeant strolled behind him. Looking at the receptionist, he mouthed out, "Sorry."

Once inside the doctor's office, the sergeant shut the door and stood next to it. Detective Douglas sat down on the chair in front of the doctor's desk. The Doctor strummed her fingers on her desktop as she stared at him. "So what do you want this time?"

Detective Douglas took a couple cropped images from his jacket and placed them on her desk. "Do you know this man?"

Doctor Deathridge, picked them up and looked at the fuzzy images. "He looks like Roger Blackett."

The detective grabbed the arms of his chair and almost stood up. "The owner of this place."

The doctor cocked her head and studied the cropped and blown up images some more. "These pictures are not the greatest, but it could be him. Where were they taken."

The detective sat back down and told her, "The book store. They were taken during Simon Black's book signing."

"That can't be. He never leaves his large, private, wooded property."

After a brief pause, Detective Douglas looked up at the ceiling. "And why is that?"

"I have already told you. He's terrified of outsiders and their intrusive technology."

"That's right. He has agoraphobia." He thought of a moment before adding, "But there is a phone in almost every building in town? Why would he install them?"

"In case of emergencies. You will find that they are all set to pre-programmed calls only, so outsiders can't harass any of the people here."

"But I can call yours."

"Both mine and Mrs. Green's private lines are fully functional. We need to communicate with the outside world."

The detective leaned forward and asked her, "So what would get someone like Roger Blackett to leave his safe, comfortable house, and go to the book store?"

With a puzzled look on her face, the nervous doctor replied, "Maybe he was trying to work at easing his fears. I've been trying to get him to leave his house more often. If the man in the picture is actually him, it will be the first time he has ventured off his property in almost a year."

Sgt. Ryan spoke up. "So, what happened a year ago?"

The doctor looked away from the detective, and focussed on the sergeant. "His eyes were hurting him. I coaxed him into coming to the clinic so I could give him a proper eye examination. It ended up that he just needed stronger reading glasses."

Detective Douglas loudly sighed, tilted his head and said, "None of this explains why a man with extreme agoraphobia would come to town, and pick an argument with a so-called outsider."

The doctor rubbed the back of her head. "If that was Roger Blackett, and if he did pick a fight with anyone, anyone at all, it would have to be over something very, very serious." Shaking her head, she added, "Because that doesn't sound like anything he would do."

In a sharp tone, the detective interrupted the doctor's train of thought. "What about murder? Could you be wrong about that too?"

The doctor leaned back and grinned. "You must be kidding me. That is really stretching it."

"Well something had to have rattled him enough to get him to leave his house." The detective placed his hands on the doctor's desk. "First, he left his little sanctuary. Second, he was seen skulking around a crowded book store, seemingly interested in Simon Black, but not his new book. Third, he picked an argument with Simon Black's literary agent."

Doctor Deathridge shook her head and chuckled. "You are barking up the wrong tree. It wasn't him. It couldn't have been him. First of all, Simon was twice Roger's size. Second, Roger was terrified of the outside world. Even if that was him, with all those outsiders, he would have slithered out of there the first opportunity he got. If he didn't, his condition would have paralysed him. And last of all, he's a coward. Even if he had a few words and pushed Simon's agent, any lengthy argument would have driven him speechless. In the entire time that I have known him, he has never stood up for himself, not even once."

Detective Douglas relaxed slightly. "Well maybe something happened that gave him a real, good reason to."

The doctor looked at him. "Like what? He has lots of money. He has a comfortable home that he feels safe in. He doesn't really need anyone or anything to make him happy. What possible reason could he have?"

"Maybe he saw Simon Black's arrival as some kind of invasion. He could place Blackett Hill on the map, for real. That would upend everything he worked for."

The doctor stood up and leaned against her desk. "But you are forgetting that it is private property. He could simply block off both entrances to the community."

Detective Douglas smugly informed her, "But the road is public property. That's why its plowed in the winter and the police patrol it."

Dr. Deathridge smiled and sat down. "The county has offered us the road numerous times. They told Roger Blackett that he could have it for one dollar, plus lawyers' fees and any other expenses associated with the transfer. Like you indirectly stated, the road is a burden on the county."

The detective smiled back at her. "But the argument outside of the book store still puts him near the top of our list of suspects. We need to question him."

"He will never agree to be questioned."

Detective Douglas's raised his eyebrows and chuckled. "He may have no choice about it."

"He has a lot of top notch lawyers at his disposal." Doctor Deathridge leaned forward, grinned and glanced over at her file cabinet. "With his documented emotional and medical condition, they'll rip you apart if you even try to go anywhere near him."

Staring at the sergeant, she added, "Velvet gloves,

that is what you need to wear in this town. Without them, you will both be prison bound, and I'll make sure of it."

Sergeant Ryan felt uneasy as the doctor turned and glared at him. He took it as a warning. She knew how closely Detective Douglas and he interacted. His mouth turned suddenly dry as he tried to swallow the lump in his throat.

Chapter Twelve

As they walked to their car, Sgt. Ryan said, "I wonder where Roger Blackett really gets all his money from?"

Detective Douglas barely glanced at him. "He was an only child. When his parents died, he must've got everything. He was probably spoiled rotten from the day he was born. No wonder he became an agoraphobic. Why leave home when you have everything you want at your fingertips."

The sergeant smiled, and said, "I don't know about that. If I had all kinds of money, I would explore the world, and experience everything I could."

The detective looked at the sergeant. "Did you see him? I don't think he's the physical sort. I see him more as a collector, or book worm."

"Appearances can be deceiving. You never know what a person really looks like under loose fitting clothes." The sergeant chuckled. "In fact, even tight fitting clothes. I've seen some seemingly fit, gorgeous women turn into doughy slobs after they peel off their tight fitting, spandex undergarments."

The detective smiled. "I can agree with that. You should see my wife before and after a party."

Sgt. Ryan glared at him, and said, "Lets not bring her into this conversation." As the sergeant pulled out the keys to their car, he added, "Never-the-less we should look into both his and his parents' past. I would like to find out how much money they actually left him." Looking at the detective, he added, "Plus, the rich almost always have skeletons in their closets. Maybe one of them resurfaced."

As the detective walked around to the front passenger side door, he commented, "I'm just wondering who gets the royalties from all of Simon Black's books now? That could add up to a tidy sum. Maybe even enough to kill for."

"Maybe we will get a better insight into the money trail at Simon Black's funeral. Computers can only tell us what we ask them to. We need to know who to investigate, what we need to know about them, plus, where to search for other information relevant to the case. Remember, the techs can't do our jobs for us. They need us to tell them what we want them to look for."

Detective Douglas snickered, "Did you get that out of a textbook?" After looking at his watch, he added, "The funeral is almost four hours away. We have time to do a little more digging before we need to leave."

After Sgt. Ryan unlocked the driver's door, he got in and said, "I'll continue to dig into Simon Black's past. I have already got a few connections at his publishing house."

As Detective Douglas got in and strapped on his seatbelt, he replied, "That's fine, I wanted to look into Roger Blackett's past anyways. I think it'll be very interesting to see how he can afford to maintain an entire town, plus support all of its special-needs occupants."

The drive back to the police station in English Lookout was intense. So far, all of the records that they had on Simon Black and Roger Blackett had been fairly vague and mundane. Knowing that they needed to dig a lot deeper, the pair bantered back and forth various obscure ways that they might be able to access more detailed records about them. Unfortunately most of them were illegal.

As the pair walked into the station they were not much further ahead. Sgt. Ryan glanced at Detective Douglas. "I'll squeeze my connections at Simon Black's publishing house. Hopefully something pops up. If not, lets hope that we can get a lead on his beneficiaries at the funeral."

Detective Douglas stopped next to his desk and turned to the Sergeant. "And I'll dig into property titles. That should give me some insight into how Roger Blackett paid for them. He may have inherited his parents' estate, but that paved, public road indicates to me that he had to have bought some additional properties in order to build Blackett Hill."

Looking at the clock on the wall, he added, "Lets see what we can dig up in a couple hours. I would like to get to the funeral a little early."

Detective Douglas found out that only a small part of Roger Blackett's present estate was inherited. Even at the relatively cheap price for land in that region, it took Roger Blackett almost a decade to obtain the rest, piece by piece.

The detective spent a lot of time skimming through all the sales. In a lot of the transactions, Roger Blackett paid well over the market value for the properties. In three cases he paid almost double. All of them were paid in cash with 'as-is' under terms. After seeing the same term repeated over and over, the detective muttered, "He definitely didn't want anyone to back away from any of the sales."

Due to different time zones, Sgt Ryan caught almost everyone at the publishing house during their staggered breaks or lunches. Robert Swayze's secretary finally picked up the phone. While trying to swallow a mouthful of a ham and cheese sandwich, she said, "Hello." A couple seconds passed before she managed to get out, "Robert Swayze's office."

"Hi, this is Sgt. Ryan. I am with the Royal Canadian Mounted Police. I spoke to you a while ago about Simon Black."

The secretary finished swallowing the piece of sandwich and washed it down with a swig of water. "Yeah, I remember talking to you."

"I am investigating the possibility that money could be the motive behind Simon Black's murder. I was wondering if you could tell me anything about his financial agreement with your firm. I am mainly interested in who will be getting the royalties from his book sales, now that he is dead?"

The secretary moved her lunch to the side of her desk and readjusted her keyboard. After bringing up Simon Black's file, she told the sergeant, "You might need to get a warrant in order for me to release any of this to you. Simon's agreement wasn't exactly straight forward. In fact, it was a bit complicated."

"In what way?"

"Most writers receive all of their royalties. That means that they can simply leave it to anyone they want in their will. In Simon's case, the royalties were split. For some reason a man named Roger Blackett gets forty percent of Simon Black's earnings." The secretary suddenly realised what she had just revealed. "I didn't tell you anything! It just slipped out. If you tell anyone that you got that information from me, I'll deny it. I worked extremely hard to get where I am. I need this job."

"Don't worry. I'll go through all the proper channels and pretend you didn't say a thing. We don't want anything that might go to court, tainted in any way."

After releasing a sigh of relief, the secretary said, "Thanks."

The sergeant grinned and took a deep breath. "You are very welcome. Don't worry, your little slip-up will be our secret. It may have even helped solve Simon Black's murder."

Sgt. Ryan walked over and leaned on Detective Douglas's desk. With a wide grin on his face, he asked him, "So, what have you found out?"

The detective looked up at him and said, "Wipe that childish grin off your face. Just tell me what you found out."

The sergeant softened his smile and said, "I think you may be right. Roger Blackett might be our killer."

"What made you come to that conclusion?"

"He gets forty percent of all Simon Black's royalties. With Simon dead, he most likely gets it all. That's a lot of motive."

The detective looked at the land transaction on his computer screen. "Well that certainly explains what I've found. Roger had paid cash for almost everything. Outside of the land purchases, the man has no credit history at all, not even a credit card."

"At least you got his bank account number."

"Not yet, he paid by certified cheque. At least they were all issued by the same branch of the Royal Bank of Canada. That gives us a starting point."

Sgt. Ryan rubbed the back of his head. "He can't pay for everything by certified cheque. What about bills, like electricity and furnace fuel? In order to run that so-called town of his, he must deal with hundreds of bills each month."

Detective Douglas looked at the sergeant. "No one can do anything now-a-days without leaving some kind of money trail behind them. I'll find it."

"Maybe he set up a company to deal with the town's finances. I think that the power company might be our best lead. Those guys really like getting their money."

As planned, the two officers pulled up to the local funeral home a half an hour early. The large parking lot in front of it was overcrowded. Sgt. Ryan mumbled, "I thought this was going to be a small private funeral." Glancing at the detective, he said, "This place is too small for a huge, celebrity funeral. Why would someone like him want to be buried here anyways?"

"I don't know. He lives in Toronto." As the sergeant began to parallel park into a tight spot two blocks away from the funeral home, Detective Douglas added, "I don't know who made the funeral arrangements, but we need to check that out."

By the time they got back to the funeral home, the lineup in front of it was curved onto the sidewalk. Detective Douglas stopped and looked at the lineup. "Who are all these people, and where did they come from?"

"They are probably his fans."

"I know that. But, how did they know when and where his funeral was going to be held?"

The sergeant shook his head and smiled. "We are in the age of enlightenment. One word on the internet can spread to millions of online zombies within seconds."

"But who put that information out there? I checked the funeral home's, Simon Black's and his publisher's web sites and found nothing about Simon's funeral."

"Maybe someone at the funeral home was a fan, and leaked it."

"That could mean their job. I don't buy it. Jobs are too scarce here."

Everyone in line stared at them as they strolled past them and walked right up to the door. After they presented their badges and identified themselves, the doorman let them squeeze in. Detective Douglas peeked into the chapel. All the seats were taken and the sides and back were crowded with bystanders. Spotting a sign saying 'Office' and an arrow, he told Sgt. Ryan, "Stay here and keep your eyes open. I'm going to see if I can find the owner."

The office door was open. Detective Douglas peeked inside. He saw the owner slumped over his desk, talking on the phone. Not wanting to startle him, he knocked on the open door and said, "Can I come in."

The funeral director glared at him, "What do you want?"

Detective Douglas straightened his posture and flashed his badge. "I just wanted to talk to you about Simon Black's funeral arrangements."

"That was quick." The owner put down his phone and added, "I was just talking to the desk sergeant at the station. I wasn't expecting such a huge crowd of people. This was supposed to be a quiet, solemn affair. I was only expecting a handful of close friends and a few business acquaintances."

"So why were you calling the police?"

"Crowd control. I have another funeral in two hours and only one chapel."

"Do you have anywhere else that you could move the other service to?"

"Maybe one of the churches." He placed his hands on the sides of his head, and added, "But what about her family and friends? Some of them have travelled a long way to get here. How can I conduct two funerals, at two different places, at the same time?"

The detective shrugged his shoulders. "Simple, just delay the service part of this one. The procession wanting to pay their respects to Simon Black could eat up the entire afternoon. The other funeral should be over by then."

The frantic man glared at him. "But who is going to oversee this one? I still can't be in two places at the same time."

Detective Douglas forced himself to smile. "I could make some calls and arrange to have some plain clothed officers oversee things here. That way you can take care of the other funeral. I am sure that once the dead woman's family sees the crowd, they would appreciate the change in venue."

"Well any extra cost to them will be going on Simon Black's tab. They shouldn't have to pay a cent for this sort of inconvenience." The funeral director sat straight up in his chair. "In fact, they should get a discount. Simon Black caused this mess, and he should pay for it. Or at least his beneficiaries should."

The detective glanced out the window. "They may even get a bill from the station."

The funeral director changed the sign next to the door. Hastily constructed signs indicating the change in venue, were posted at both the entrance and exit to the funeral home's parking lot.

A plain clothed police officer was stationed outside of the funeral home. As cars stopped to inquire about the second funeral, she explained the situation to them and handed out copies of a map to the church. With the police help, moving the second funeral's location was not as difficult as the funeral director had originally imagined.

As the line of fans began to circle around the block, sporadic outbreaks of rage occurred as people tried to butt in line. Two more uniformed police officers had to be brought in to keep the peace.

Inside, Detective Douglas stood on one side of the viewing room where the mahogany casket was on display, and Sgt. Ryan on the other. The red and black velvet lined, mahogany casket was surrounded by all kinds and types of flower arrangements. The largest wreaths were set on a raised, two tiered platform behind the casket. The rest were arranged on multi tiered displays situated at both ends of the casket. In front of the colourful displays were countless vases and the smaller flower arrangements. There were flowers and roses of every colour from white to black.

Many of the arrangements had broken red hearts pierced by a black arrow in the middle. Some of the painted arrows were real. Others were merely fake, bolt shaped pens, like those sold in the book stores novelty section. The arrangement that caught the detective's eye, was what appeared to be a broken human heart, skewered by a crossbow bolt, and set on a bed of a dozen white roses facing one direction, and a dozen black ones facing the other.

The detective glanced at the high definition, video cameras fixed to all four corners of the ceiling in the viewing room. There was a fifth camera above the main entrance angled downward at the coffin. He shook his head. '*The only faces that camera could capture would be from people leaving. Unfortunately, most people look down when they leave a funeral.*'

Detective Douglas walked up to the coffin to get a better look at the striking flower arrangement. 'You were my one and only love, your #1 fan, Marion', was typed on the tag.

Near the front of the coffin, almost hidden amongst a wall of flower arrangements, the detective noticed a large, wide, camera lens with an unobstructed view. That camera was aimed towards the front of the coffin. Under his breath, Detective Douglas mumbled, "We might actually end up getting some photos good enough to run through the computer."

Sitting in the front, centre pew that was normally designated for immediate family, were Robert Swayze, an attractive woman that the detective recognized from the book store's video, two older men, Nancy Gamble and her mother. Behind them were numerous people that he recognized from the videos they had reviewed.

Sgt. Ryan looked around at the people that managed to get a seat, and thought, *'I hope those people signed the visitors book. With the cameras in this place, it would make it much easier to identify them.'* Sgt. Ryan discreetly pulled out his notepad and jotted down a quick reminder for himself.

Sgt. Ryan stared at the twitchy woman in her thirties, who was sitting right behind Robert Swayze. Something about her looked familiar. Her black shawl, dark sunglasses and long, curly, black hair partially concealed her seemingly, very, attractive face. Her hands were entangled in the black leather jacket on her lap, possibly to keep them still and stop her from fidgeting. Unable to place her, the sergeant glanced over the rest of the crowd. Something about the woman's mannerisms constantly drew his attention back to her.

The woman caught him staring at her and looked down at her jacket. The third time she caught him, she glanced at him, studied him for a few seconds then looked away. After an hour and a half, like many of the others, she got up, placed her jacket on her seat in order to save it, and walked toward the washroom.

The sergeant followed her. Getting a glimpse of him off the side of an almost mirror polished, brass statue of an angel, she turned around. "What do you want? You have been staring at me ever since you got here."

The plain clothed sergeant stopped and raised his open right hand towards her. "It's all right. I'm one of the police officers investigating Simon Black's murder. I can show you my badge if you want."

With one hand on the washroom door's doorknob, she impatiently asked, "So, why are you following me?"

"I'm not." Sgt. Ryan pointed to the men's washroom just on the other side of the women's, and added, "I just had to use the washroom." With a half smile, he continued, "I had too much coffee beforehand. We weren't expecting such a large turnout."

The woman straightened her posture and blurted out, "But he was a magnificent, world famous author. I was hoping he would get a much, much better sendoff than this."

As the ends of her shawl draped down her sides, the sergeant got a better look at her. The loose, black dress she wore couldn't hide the couple extra kilos she carried to help smooth out her strong muscular curves. While she had been sitting down, her shawl had covered the gap in the front of her low cut, mid-thigh dress along with the top of her thighs. He smiled as he imagined her wearing it on a romantic date, or out dancing with her girlfriends. Despite all the makeup she wore, close up, he could see the attractive, but slightly weathered face beneath it.

He couldn't stop smiling as he asked her, "Why would you expect a huge turnout? To my knowledge, the funeral wasn't posted anywhere. How did you find out when and where it was being held?"

Marion chuckled. "You don't even know who I am, and you are supposed to be investigating his murder?" She put her hand on top of her head and vigorously shook it. "I'm the president of his largest fan club. After he was reported killed, I was on the phone with every funeral home in both

Toronto and around here. Posing as a fussy, grieving widow, I eventually figured out it was here, and posted it on my website."

The sergeant rubbed the back of his neck. "How did you figure it out?"

She grinned and looked around at the angelic paintings on the wall. "I went online and simply looked for gaps in various funeral homes' posted schedules. Funeral homes don't normally have any gaps." Looking at the attentive sergeant, she added, "You would be amazed at what a funeral director will reveal, when a fussy widow wants to make sure her dead husband's funeral isn't situated next to someone he didn't get along with.

The sergeant grinned and shook his head. "So you are the person that is responsible for all of this."

"All of what? I was just letting his fans know what was happening. They deserved that much respect." Marion pointed to the people patiently standing in the line waiting to view Simon Black's coffin, and say their good-byes. "He had become a huge part of their lives. Every time he released another book, they not only lusted for it, they devoured it with great appreciation. Now, they will never get to enjoy another new novel written by him. They needed closure."

The sergeant cocked his head to the side and said, "I guess I've never appreciated any author in that way. I like to read, but a lot of the authors I read are long dead."

"Imagine you just finished reading all the books one of them wrote, and then they suddenly died. If you had a chance, wouldn't you want the opportunity to show how much their novels meant to you? That is what I gave to Simon Black's fans."

The sergeant released a soft snort. "I guess I sort of see your point."

With the palms of her hands stuck out in front of her, she tilted her head and asked him, "So, now can I please go to the washroom, or do you have any more questions for me?"

Sgt. Ryan's eyes glistened as he smiled at her. "Sure, but I still may look at you from time to time after you get back to your seat."

Marion's eyebrows began to rise as she smiled back at said, "Well, alright, as long as I know the reason why you are staring at me."

A uniformed police officer accompanied the funeral director outside. Using a bullhorn, he informed Simon's fans that the visitation would be briefly halted in order for the funeral director to conduct the funeral service. To help prevent any trouble, he also informed them that visitations would immediately resume after the service.

Once he got back inside the chapel, the funeral director roped off the front portion of it. After the mourners next to the coffin said their final good-byes to Simon's corpse and left, he also roped off the hallway.

After his opening speech, he asked Robert Swayze to step up to the microphone to say a few words. Robert stood up and walked up to the elaborately carved podium situated at the foot of the coffin. Both Marion and Sgt. Ryan stood behind the thick, red, felt covered rope that blocked off the hallway.

As Robert looked around the crowded room he began to speak. "Simon Black was not only a great author, he was a magnificent and compassionate human being as well. Simon respected his fans in a way very few authors were capable of. He had more book signings, and made more public appearances than any author I know. He also gave more than his share to the mental health charities that were closest to his heart, and was a man to be admired. I only wish that I was more like him. Along with all his terrific and loyal fans, I will greatly miss him."

Robert looked at Simon's body lying in the coffin. A thin, skin coloured scarf was tucked around his neck to conceal his fatal wound. "I know that he had much more to give us. He was the best author any agent could have the privilege to work with. I will dearly miss him."

The funeral director stepped over to the microphone. "Now a brief word from Simon's trusted Lawyer and long time confidant, Steven Henderson."

As one of the old men sitting in the front pew got up and stood behind the microphone, all of Robert's attention was on him. Simon's senior lawyer, was a man of few words. Robert had initially given Simon, Steven Henderson's business card. The stone faced man rarely expressed neither like nor dislike towards any of his clients. However, Simon Black was a rare exception.

After his opening introduction, he began reading his cue cards. "Contrary to public opinion, writing was not Simon Black's true love. Despite Simon's numerous great works of thrilling literature, and countless female partners, he once told me that his adopted brother Roger Blackett was the only person or thing that really mattered to him."

He raise his right arm in the air as he continued his speech. "Although it wasn't physical or sexual in nature, his love for him was as deep as humanly possible." As he lowered his arm, he looked around the room. "Neither of these two broken men had any close, family members left. Together, they created their own family, and it was built on trust and loyalty. For that I admire both of them. Despite what anyone says to the contrary, I know that Simon Black was a good and decent man. He will be greatly missed by his countless devoted fans, and even more by those, like me, that got to know the private and sincere man behind the novels."

Looking down at the coffin, he added, "It is strange for a man in my profession to get the opportunity to work for a truly decent man. I am glad I had that opportunity, and I will truly miss him."

Overwhelmed with grief, Marion grabbed and

squeezed Sgt. Ryan's hand. He watched her turn and sink her tear covered face between his arm and chest. Not knowing what to do, he just stood there and didn't say a word.

After the brief service was over, the funeral director unhooked the thick red rope to allow the visitations to continue. As the director walked over to the hallway to unlatch the rope in front of them, Marion eased away from the sergeant. She opened her eyes and saw the sergeant's jacket. With a twisted smile on her face, she looked up at him and said, "I'm sorry, I smudged lipstick and mascara all over your coat."

Sgt. Ryan smiled and softly replied, "That's alright, that stuff isn't that hard to get off."

"I hope your girlfriend doesn't get the wrong idea."

Sgt. Ryan smiled. "Don't have one."

"Wife?"

"Nope."

Marion smiled, opened her small purse and pulled out a card. "Here, send me the bill."

Sgt. Ryan looked at the card. "So, you are a nurse."

"Yeah, that's why I read. Working long hours helping sick and injured people, plus having to deal with a bunch of rude hypochondriacs vying for your attention, a person needs a good book to escape into." Marion smiled and cocked her head to the side. "When I read one of Simon Black's books, I wasn't at the hospital anymore, I was in Paris, London, Australia, or maybe even the Yukon. He turned my breaks into mini vacations. He was such a magnificent author. I'm really going to miss him."

As he looked closely at her face, something seemed obscure. It wasn't until she turned and walked away that he realized that her hairline had changed. '*She is wearing a wig. It must have been pushed out of place when she pressed her head against me.*'

Chapter Thirteen

With only twelve mourners left in line, Detective Douglas left the chapel and went to the funeral director's office. He knocked on the door. The owner answered, "Give me a minute."

After about three minutes, Nancy's mother walked out of the office. Detective Douglas stepped in front of her. "This is a surprise. I never expected to see you here."

Mrs. Green glanced up at him. "We had to go over all of the extra funeral expenses. With the funeral taking much longer than was expected, plus having to move that poor woman's funeral service across town, what I previously paid him wasn't nearly enough."

"I'm a bit confused." The detective tilted his head. "So you are the person that is paying for all of Simon Black's funeral expenses?"

Mrs. Green nodded her head. "Indirectly, Yes."

"So who is actually paying for it?"

"Roger Blackett." Mrs. Green looked at him with a puzzled look on her face. "I look after all of Blackett Hill's and Roger Blackett's personal expenses. I thought everyone knew that."

"I thought that you were just his book keeper and errand girl." Detective Douglas stared at her and said, "So you are telling me, Mr. Blackett doesn't look after any of the day-to-day expenses at all? He must really trust you."

"And why shouldn't he?"

"I thought he had serious trust issues. That was why he didn't trust the internet, or any other form of non-physical communication."

"Yes, he has some very serious trust issues. That is why he hired me. I handle all of his and the community's bills, transactions, notifications and any needed outside correspondence. His bank manager issues me with a certified cheque to cover everything, at the start of each month."

Detective Douglas shook his head. "I just pictured him as a control freak. I thought he would be scrutinizing every bill he got to make sure he wasn't being ripped off."

Getting a little cross, Mrs. Green blurted back, "Roger doesn't like dealing with people, let alone mindless companies. When we go over the books each month, he does question the cost of various items. However, he has complete faith in my judgement."

"Looking after the finances of a community the size of Blackett Hill must be a lot of hard work. Mr. Blackett has transferred a lot of responsibility onto your shoulders."

"Nothing that my husband and I can't handle." She straightened up her back, and informed him, "Roger is an extremely, smart man. He knows what's going on in the world around him. When you were at the book store, didn't you notice all the reference books. Most of them were brought in for him. He is not some isolated, backwards hermit, and he doesn't shirk any of his responsibilities."

Detective Douglas cocked his head to the side, and asked her, "But Nancy said that she had never met him. How does he get the books?"

Mrs. Green grinned and rocked her head back and forth. "I take them with me when I visit him, and return the ones he is finished with when I get back."

"So I was wrong about a few things." The detective rubbed the back of his neck with his right hand. In a calm voice, he asked Mrs. Green, "Since Roger Blackett suffers from agoraphobia, how does he communicate with his bank manager? How does his manager know how much to give you each month?"

Getting a little annoyed, the frustrated woman blurted out, "Only Roger and his manager have keys to the brief case that I courier back and forth between them. I have no idea what is in it. The bank manager takes the case to his office. After about half an hour, he brings it back along with a certified check. Then I split the money into the various accounts that I work from."

"So you don't actually know anything about his true net worth? How do you do his income taxes?"

She scrunched up her face, glared at him and said, "I'm in a bit of a hurry. Nancy is in a rough state and I have to get her home."

Not wanting her to leave, the detective side stepped in front of her. "So you talk to Roger more than anyone else. What can you tell me about his relationship with Simon Black?"

"Like I said, I'm in a hurry." Mrs. Green reached into her jacket's inner, breast pocket and pulled out a business card. "Here, call me. We can set up a time later. Right now, I have to go."

The detective peered out a window and watched Mrs. Green run across the parking lot, and climb into the driver's seat of her car. As they drove off, the light coming from the row of short, pole lights in front of the funeral home shone through the car's side windows. Inside of it, the detective saw the silhouettes of Mrs. Green and Nancy in the front, plus Mr. Green and a thin nervous man huddled in the back.

The funeral home owner stepped out of his office and asked him, "Were you wanting to see me?"

"Yes." The detective slowly turned around to face him. "Lets go into your office."

As Detective Douglas shut the door behind him, he said, "Mrs. Green has already answered a few of the questions I was going to ask you."

"So I take it you have more?"

"Just a few."

After the detective sat down and pulled his chair closer to the owner's desk, he said, "Simon Black was a huge celebrity. Why was such a small funeral being arranged for him?"

The owner meshed his fingers together, while he answered, "That was what the client wanted. Roger Blackett's lawyer requested that I was to make arrangements for a small, private ceremony, as per Simon Black's will. No one expected such a huge turnout. Poor Mrs. Green was caught in the middle. She didn't know what was happening."

"You could have turned them away."

"This place is my livelihood. If they rioted, I could lose everything." The owner stood up and began to pace the floor. "After some wrangling, Mr. Henderson, Mrs. Green and I worked out a compromise."

"Which was?"

"Renting and setting up a video camera so Roger Blackett could at least watch and hear what was going on. He really wanted to be here." The owner stopped pacing and looked at the detective. "Apparently, as soon as he saw the crowd, he covered himself up in a blanket and hid in the back of Mrs. Green's car during the entire thing. Mr. Green had to stay with him, to make sure he was all right."

The detective bit his bottom lip and thought for a few seconds. "So I take it that the video camera you rented took high quality images of everyone, plus everything they said at the front of the room." Looking up at the owner, he said, "I need a copy of the video from that camera."

"I can't. Mrs. Green took it with her."

"How, she was in here with you?"

"Her daughter Nancy removed it."

"How did you know she took it?"

The owner pointed to the image in the corner of his computer screen. "I watched her do it."

Detective Douglas scratched his head. "Well at least you can give me a copy of the video from your cameras."

The owner looked at him, smiled and semi waved his left hand. "No problem, just give me five minutes."

"Well I might as well wait here for it." After

swivelling his chair back and forth for a couple minutes, the detective asked him, "So, what's going to happen to Simon Black's body?"

"He is being cremated. Apparently, Roger Blackett wants his ashes." The owner grinned and rocked his head. "What he does with them is his business, not mine."

As the two officers left the funeral home, Sgt. Ryan turned to Detective Douglas and said, "I don't know how relevant it is, but I think I found out who's wig we found."

The detective glanced at him. "Whose?"

"A lady named Marion LaPointe. I was talking to her when I went to the washroom."

Detective Douglas glared at him. "In the men's washroom?"

The sergeant's eyebrows lowered as he glared back at him. "No, we chatted outside of the women's washroom."

The detective smiled and snorted. The sergeant looked around at the dark, nearly empty parking lot. "Miss Lapointe was also the one that discovered Simon Black's funeral arrangements, and posted them online. She has a website devoted to him."

On their way back to the station, Detective Douglas turned and asked the sergeant, "I'm starving, how about picking up something at the coffee shop."

Sgt Ryan pulled up to the drive-thru intercom and placed his order. "A number three combo with a large regular coffee." He glanced at Detective Douglas. He had all five digits on his right hand extended. "And a number five combo with a large, black coffee for my partner."

"What donuts do you want with them?"

"Apple fritters."

They pulled out of the drive-thru and went back to the station. Despite how late it was getting, they took their meals back to their desks and logged onto their computers.

Sgt. Ryan made further inquires into obtaining Simon

Black's financial records from his publisher, along with Roger Blackett's banking information. He knew that the process to obtain financial records could take hours, days and sometimes even weeks to get. While he waited for feedback, he took a bite of his tuna sandwich and did a little research into Marion LaPointe's background.

Despite Officer Kelly's video of Marion wanting to get away from Blackett Hill as fast as she could, the sergeant still had some lingering doubts. Was it her mannerisms that made the sergeant leery of her, or was it her wig, or maybe her smile. He wasn't sure. Glancing at the makeup on his jacket, he smiled. Maybe it was just her.

At the same time, Detective Douglas was trying to find a connection between Simon Black and Roger Blackett. Roger Blackett's past was practically a blank slate. He never had a driver's licence, passport or even a credit card. The only government documents he could find were Roger's birth certificate and social security number, both of which had been issued before his parent's died, and they never expire. Even his Ontario Health Card had lapsed. Beyond that, Detective Douglas found his name linked to over a dozen local land purchases.

When Roger's parents died, he had inherited their house and the surrounding wooded property, but very little else. He had no visible income or means to support himself. However, within four years, he had managed to purchase the property next to his. Detective Douglas looked at the date. "Now that can't be a coincidence."

He punched 'Simon Black's books', into the computer. After finding a list of publication dates, he muttered, "It's flimsy, but at least it is a connection." Shortly after Simon's first best selling novel was published, Roger was rolling in money. *"He must have been getting royalties from Simon's books right from the get go. That means that they had met sometime before Simon's first book was even written. How does a housebound man who is afraid of the internet and even phones, meet someone as outgoing as Simon Black?"*

Looking into both Simon Black's and Simon Blakey's pasts was tedious. Most of the web sites he looked at were dedicated solely to his renowned, best selling novels. Only a few even mentioned his actual birth name. Only two mentioned his previous, failed, short story career that was marred by bad reviews.

It was nearly 10 PM before Detective Douglas clicked on Marion LaPointe's website. The banner across the home page was a bleeding, broken heart pierced by a black arrow. "So that's where that motif came from."

He clicked on the page titled 'The Beginning'. It was as if Marion researched every aspect of Simon's life, from childhood until that very day. He rocked his head back and forth as a new page suddenly appeared.

The page was dedicated to Simon's funeral. When he got to the middle of the page he had to stop and take a deep breath. Marion had posted a candid picture showing the left tiered flower rack. In the picture, Sgt Ryan was standing at one end of the rack, and the head of Simon's coffin appearing to the right of it. Below it read, 'Plain clothed police officers were mixed amongst the mourners. Obviously, they don't have a solid suspect in Simon Black's murder case. Lets hope that any information that they did gather can help them apprehend Simon's killer, and we can have closure on this senseless murder. If you heard or saw anything that you think could help them solve the case, please notify the police.'

At the bottom of the page was a snap shot of Sgt. Ryan's card. *'He is not the one looking after this investigation, I am.'*

After skimming through Marion's website, Detective Douglas spent another five minutes flipping through some of the linked websites. Then he leaned back in his chair and thought for a while. Glancing over at Sgt. Ryan, he asked him, "Did you see Marion LaPointe's website?"

"Yeah, I'm going through it for the third time right now." Without looking away from his monitor, he added, "She has researched his entire life. There has to be a clue in here somewhere."

"So you saw your picture?"

Sgt Ryan looked at him and chuckled. "Three quarters of the picture was flowers. I only hope that I didn't ruin her phone when she took it."

"Well, I am just glad that she is such a dedicated nerd." Turning towards his monitor, the detective added, "Thanks to her, I think I know how Roger and Simon are connected."

Sgt. Ryan got up and walked over to Detective Douglas's desk, he said, "What do you mean? I went through her entire website at least three times and found nothing." Then he leaned over and looked at the split screens on the Detective's monitor.

The detective rolled his chair back a bit to give the sergeant a better view. "Compare the dates that Simon's books hit the best sellers lists, to the dates that Roger had the money to purchase properties. That can't be a coincidence." The detective looked at the sergeant and added, "Roger had gone from rags to riches, at the same time that Simon went from a struggling hack to a best selling author."

Sgt. Ryan squatted next to Detective Douglas's desk and scrutinized the dates on the two screens. "We already knew that Roger got a percentage of Simon's royalties. We just don't know why."

Detective Douglas leaned forward and selected 'The Beginning' page, of Marion LaPointe's website. "According to Miss LaPointe's research, he came up with his first novel while he was teaching."

He clicked on school's name and its website appeared on the screen. "He taught at a correspondence school."

The sergeant looked at the detective. "But they are done through emails and file attachments? I can't imagine Roger having anything to do with a computer. How could he even sign up for a internet class?"

The detective click back onto Marion's website. As he looked up at the sergeant, he said, "Did you read the complete paragraph covering his teaching career?"

"I thought so! What did I miss?"

"He also tutored people with special needs." He glanced at the sergeant and grinned. "That means a more customized teaching style. They could have corresponded through the mail. Maybe Roger became his muse. You never know how some relationships start."

Sgt. Ryan looked at the time, '11:05'. "It's way too late to get a hold of anyone from the school."

Detective Douglas clicked off his monitor. "Yeah, maybe it is time to call it quits."

As the sergeant walked towards the door he looked back. Detective Douglas was slouched over with his head buried in his hands. "Come on, terra cotta is not that bad. Go home and see your wife. She probably misses you."

The detective peeked through his fingers. "You have been chatting with her, haven't you?"

"Only a couple times today. She's sorry, and the painters are willing to come back to paint it any colour you want. She even has some swatches she wants you to look at."

The detective scratched his head and looked up at the ceiling. "I guess I should go home. If I leave it to her who knows what colour she'll pick next. It might even be worse."

The next morning, Sgt. Ryan saw Detective Douglas walk into the station with one hand pressed against his lower back. "You are running late. Had a hard night?"

"Yeah, I knew that I shouldn't have gone home last night. She had swatches all right. Every colour was worse than the next."

Detective Douglas stared at the sergeant as he continued his rant. "She kept harping on and on about how everything was my fault for not being there to pick them out in the first place. I got so mad that I ended up sleeping on the couch."

Sgt Ryan grinned a bit, as he told the detective, "Well, she isn't a mind reader, and she is colour-blind."

While stretching his back the detective grumbled, "That old excuse. We've been married for almost thirty years. She should know what I like and don't like by now."

Sgt. Ryan shook his head, smiled and quietly muttered, "She should get a medal."

As the detective finally reached Sgt. Ryan's desk, he asked him, "Did you get a hold of the school?"

"About twenty minutes ago. You were right. Roger Blackett was one of Simon Blakey's students."

Detective Douglas leaned on the desk and asked. "What about the time line?"

"You were also right about that too. It ended after a year and a half. That was when Simon published his first best seller. The school had no records of any correspondence, of any kind, with Roger Blackett after that."

The detective grinned. "So Roger could've helped Simon write his first novel. That could be why he gets such a large percentage of Simon's royalties. Maybe Roger can prove it and was blackmailing Simon."

Sgt. Ryan leaned back and swivelled his chair towards the detective. "Roger doesn't have any published work of any kind to his credit, not even a newspaper clipping. Even if he somehow helped Simon write his books, it was still up to Simon to market and sell them. After all, it is his face on the book jacket."

Ignoring his sore back, Detective Douglas began vigorously pacing the floor. "But now Simon's books can sell themselves. With him gone, Roger could keep all the royalties for himself. That's a lot of money."

Sgt. Ryan cocked his head and looked at the detective. "What if Roger was just Simon's muse and he outgrew him. Maybe he found another muse. Maybe he came here to tell Roger that he wanted out of their agreement." Looking up at the ceiling, he reluctantly told the detective, "If that happened, Roger could lose everything. Without a constant flow of money coming in, Blackett Hill wouldn't be able to survive."

"True."

"If anyone in Blackett Hill found out about it, it could devastate them. If that happened, and word got around, we could have a lot more suspects to consider."

"But they would also have to be aware of the financial agreement between Simon and Roger. That's a lot of information to overhear. As far as we know, Roger is the only person in Blackett Hill that knew about the arrangement."

"I suppose you are right."

Detective Douglas glanced at Sgt. Ryan and smugly told him, "Judging from the videos I've seen, I doubt that any of the locals caught wind of it. Plus, I don't think that Simon Black is the type to blab personal, financial information to strangers." Detective Douglas stopped pacing, turned and smiled at Sgt Ryan. "I think we found our man."

Sgt. Ryan lowered his head. "What about what was said at the funeral?"

The detective grinned. "Words, just words. People get a little sappy at funerals. They feel that they have to find something up-lifting and heart wrenching about the deceased, to help comfort the sad sacs in the audience."

Sgt. Ryan sat back on his chair and placed his left hand behind his head. "What if his lawyer was wrong? What if Roger was more than just Simon's muse? We never considered the possibility that Simon was bi-sexual. What if they struck up an affair?"

Detective Douglas started to pace the floor some more. "Roger Blackett hardly has anything to do with the outside world, whereas Simon relishes it." After releasing an audible smirk, he stood still. "But it is strange that a good looking guy like Simon is still single. According to what I read about him, he could have had anyone he wanted male or female."

"That's right." The sergeant closed his eyes. After a couple seconds he casually added, "What if Roger saw Simon flirting with Emily and got jealous. If they were having an affair, considering how isolated Roger's life is, that would devastate him. That could easily blossom into a plausible motive."

Detective Douglas stared at him. "That's one possibility. Considering that the killer most likely used an improvised weapon, the murder was done on the spur of the moment. A jealous fit of rage seems to fit."

The detective slowed his pacing as he thought of the spat in the alleyway next to the book store. "What if Roger thought that Robert Swayze was trying to interfere with his relationship with Simon. Even if it wasn't sexual in nature, it wouldn't matter. Roger would still feel threatened. Why else would he leave his private sanctuary and venture into town. Remember all the questions he asked Nancy. They were mostly about why Simon was even in Blackett Hill. Maybe he was worried that Simon came there to end their relationship. That could have been what the fight was all about."

"Maybe we should question Robert Swayze some more before he leaves the country."

The sergeant looked around the room as he said, "Here is another thought, Simon liked the ladies. There must be a lot of jealous husbands out there."

"That doesn't fit." The detective stopped pacing and leaned on the sergeant's desk. "In order to stab him to death in a small washroom, Simon had to have known his killer. The murder was both spur of the moment and personal. However, if a wig was involved that means at least some degree of premeditation." While slightly shaking his head, he bit his lower lip. "You are right about one thing, Robert Swayze's spat in the alleyway is probably the key to unlocking this case."

Sgt. Ryan called the hotel where Robert was staying. The receptionist politely informed him that she saw Robert step out. Hearing this, he strongly requested that she call the station the moment he returns and ask for Sgt. Ryan.

Overhearing the entire conversation, Detective Douglas said, "He could be gone for most of the day. Maybe we should use that time to look into Simon's, Roger's and Robert Swayze's pasts."

The sergeant spoke up, "Plus Roger and Simon's financial history. We can't rule out money as a motive."

Detective Douglas stood up, put his hands on his hips and arched his back. "Love and money, the silly things that people are willing to kill for. Even if Roger didn't have a sexual arrangement with Simon, with his warped, paranoid mind, who knows what excuses he might've conjured up."

Sgt. Ryan rubbed his chin as he interrupted him. "Simon travelled around the world promoting his books. There wouldn't be much time for them to see each other. We need to keep in mind, Roger refuses to use any kind of long distance phone service or electronic devise."

"But, if Roger was simply Simon's muse, they could have developed some kind of weird, non-sexual, long distance bond. Between a writer's vivid imagination and a man that lives in his own little world, they could be a perfect match. Maybe they invented their own unique take on reality."

Sgt Ryan tapped the tip of his pen against his desk while he took some time to think. "Enough 'what ifs'." In a solemn voice, he turned and asked Detective Douglas, "So, do you actually think that Roger could have murdered Simon?" The detective sat on his chair. After taking a long, deep breath, he finally answered him. "Roger's weird, isolated, little world is his life. If he felt that his delusional reality was about to end, I believe he could commit murder. To him, that would be equivalent to someone pressing a loaded gun against his forehead. "

Sgt. Ryan nodded his head and said, "I can see that."

Detective Douglas scratched the back of his head while he added, "Someone or something threatened him. Why else would Roger be willing to face all his anxieties in order to go to the book store." He glanced at Sgt. Ryan. "Remember all the questions he asked Nancy, and the spat with Robert? He desperately wanted to know why Simon was in Blackett Hill, yet he didn't attempt to talk to him, at least not with anyone around. Everything seems to fit, but I'm just not sure which scenario is the right one."

"Simon knows Roger. He would've had no problem inviting him into a tiny washroom for a private chat." Sgt Ryan looked over at the detective. "We have no concrete evidence. We can't just give the prosecutor our conjecture and expect him to get a conviction. We need physical proof."

Both men shook their heads to clear their minds, and refocus their energy. Sgt. Ryan got on the phone and hounded the office workers at Simon's publishing house. Meanwhile, Detective Douglas surfed the internet for hints into Simon's sexual history.

The detective found out that like Roger, Simon was basically a loner. When he was ten, his parents were killed in a car crash. That destroyed his faith in others. He felt that he couldn't rely on anyone and had to look after himself.

As a foster child, despite being surround by other kids, Simon felt totally alone. His awkward demeanor made him a target for bullies. To escape their torment, during lunches he sunk all of his energy into his high school's newspaper. During his graduating year, he had a late growth spurt. Almost overnight, the girls began to see past his awkward, nerdy demeanor. The sudden influx of affection, spurred him into writing a series of uplifting, short stories, which he inserted into the school's newspaper. When a regional magazine thought that they were worthy of republication, Simon thought he had found his true calling.

While waiting for some replies to his emails, Sgt Ryan thought about how Simon's short story career never really flourished. He picked up his phone and called Marion. After some polite opening banter, he asked her, "How did Simon Black's short stories compare to his novels?"

"They were quite different. His short stories were full of youthful emotion, but they had very little substance. In comparison, his novels were deep, with more substance and their characters were much more profound and believable."

"But you are sure that they were definitely written by the same person?"

The phone went silent for a few seconds. "What are you getting at?"

"I was doing some research into Simon Black's past. He had turned into a complete different person after he released his first novel. Every aspect of his life changed. He became a bolder, confident, and much more image focussed man. He went from a tall, bean pole to a towering hunk."

Marion chuckled. "He wrote a global, best selling novel. That kind of recognition can change a person." Thinking of Simon's appearance, she smiled and added, "And lets face it, having a great body helps him sell books."

In a serious voice, Sgt. Ryan told Marion, "But as you said yourself, even his writing style had changed. We have found out that whatever happened, happened while he was tutoring Roger Blackett." The line went silent. After hearing no reply, the sergeant said, "Are you still there?"

"Yes, I'm still here. I just never thought of that

before." Sgt Ryan could hear Marion's deep breaths, as she paused before continuing, "I never knew anything about Roger before the funeral service. As soon as I got back to my room, I looked him up. In a weird way, what you said makes sense. By tutoring Roger, Simon was forced to see the world through someone else's viewpoint. He became obsessed with helping people with emotional problems. He became the spokesman for numerous organizations. Maybe through helping Roger, both his life and writing became more grounded. Maybe that's why his writing changed and evolved the way it did."

"I guess that is possible." Sgt. Ryan looked at his note pad before continuing. "If Roger became Simon's muse, how much contact would he need to keep everything going?"

"None, heard of some authors that use historical figures as muses. Just knowing that they existed is sometimes good enough."

After bantering a few more niceties back and forth, the sergeant put down his phone. On his computer, he reviewed his incoming emails. While he was replying to them, he smiled as his thoughts drifted back to his easy-going conversation with Marion.

On the other side of the room, Detective Douglas dug further into Simon's past. He found out that Simon's personal life hadn't really changed much. His ex-girlfriends' rants, left him believing that Simon was still confused and very suspicious of anyone trying to get close to him. According to all the records he could find, Simon's longest relationship had only lasted a few months. However all of his relationships were with women.

As Sgt. Ryan tapped on his shoulder, the detective jerked his head away from the screen. "What is it?"

"The receptionist from the hotel called. Robert Swayze just got back."

"Great, lets go and have a talk with him."

"First, I should tell you that according to the records I was just emailed, we were right. Roger Blackett now collects all of the royalties from all of Simon Black's books. That's a lot of money for being someone's muse."

Detective Douglas scratched the back of his head. "I know that he is agoraphobic, but with all this extra money, he could be a flight risk. At least now, we have some evidence to back us up." He bit his bottom lip and sighed before adding, "I think we better bring him in for questioning."

The sergeant slowly rocked his head back and forth. "I don't think we have enough to hold him, and remember what the doctor told us."

Twisting his head to the side, the detective lowered his right eyebrow and said, "Yesterday morning he wasn't even a believable suspect. Right now, everything seems to be pointing straight at him. At this rate, we should have all the physical proof we'll need to convict him by tomorrow night."

"And what about his lawyers?"

The detective shook his head and grinned. "Lawyers, lawyers, lawyers, everyone has lawyers. All they are is expensive mouth pieces. Unless we give them something to chew on, all they can do is file a bunch of unsubstantiated complaints." The detective grabbed the sergeant's shoulders, looked him straight in the eyes, and added, "The trick is to not give them anything to chew on."

Chapter Fourteen

Two police cruisers followed Sgt. Ryan and Detective Douglas up to the pair of rusty, locked, steel gates that blocked the entrance to Roger Blackett's private property. Bolted to the gates were signs that read, 'Owner is not responsible for any vehicle damage occurred on property', 'Enter at own personal risk', 'Owner it not responsible for any personal injuries occurred while on property including accidental death', plus three evenly spaced, 'No trespassing' notices. In small print at the bottom of each sign, was the name and contact number of a Toronto based, lawyer firm.

After reading the signs, Detective Douglas chuckled. "Well, I guess they don't apply to us."

Without hesitation an officer went to the trunk of his car, took out a pair of bolt cutters and snapped the chain that secured them. After the officer opened the gate Sgt. Ryan crept his car towards it. He looked at the overgrown ditch on both sides of the gate. "If anyone wanted in, all they would have to do is walk around them."

Detective Douglas looked at the thorn bushes that concealed most of the muddy swamp on both sides of the laneway. "If they do, they better be wearing thick, chest waders, cause they would be covered in muck."

The long, gravel driveway that wound through the wooded property was pitted with potholes. Overhanging limbs from the unkept trees next to the driveway, rubbed against the top and sides of their car. A large pothole caused Sgt. Ryan to smack the top of his head on the car's roof. He turned to Detective Douglas, and told him. "This is not what I expected. With all his money, I would have thought he would have at least a paved driveway."

Detective Douglas smirked. "We know he is quite eccentric. The guy definitely wants to be left alone. In fact, he probably sees this overgrown driveway as a way to deter unwelcome visitors."

The sergeant pulled the car up to Roger Blackett's old, slightly rundown, family home. He got out of the car and stood next to it as he looked around. "This place is a dump."

Curled up strips of old, dark green paint were peeling off the wood, planked siding that covered the outside of the small, one story house. Rolls of neatly stacked firewood lined its exterior walls, leaving only a small gap for the doorway. Several rugged, multi-paned windows peeked over the top of the piled wood. The south side of its roof was covered in solar panels. Most of them were for generating electricity, but some were designed to heat water. The tall mast of a wind turbine was fastened to the far peak of the house. There were no signs of any telephone, cable or electrical lines leading up to the house. It was completely off the grid.

While he was walking to the door, Detective Douglas saw the bottom corner of a curtain fold open and fall shut. After knocking on the door and getting no reply, he yelled out, "Roger Blackett, I know you are home. We have a warrant to take you in for questioning, plus a court order to search your house. If you don't let us in, we may be forced to break the door open."

The screen door released a loud squeal as Detective Douglas opened it. He tried the main door. It wouldn't budge. "It's locked." He turned to the officer standing behind him and said, "Get the ram." Staring at the closed door, he yelled out, "This is your last chance. Open the door or we will be forced to break it down."

Two uniformed officers retrieved a small battering ram from the trunk of their cruiser. The detective held the screen door open as they got into position to bash the door.

The detective yelled out, "Last chance." Hearing no reply told the officers, "Do it."

As the ram struck the door with a loud 'BANG', Roger walked out of the woods carrying a bolt action, .22 calibre rifle in his hands. Two dead rabbits dangled from his belt.

Shocked at what he was seeing, he yelled out, "What do you think you are doing?"

Seeing the rifle, the two officers standing behind the ones holding the battering ram turned, drew their pistols and yelled out, "Put down your weapon!"

Roger froze as the officers cautiously approached him. As one of them traded his pistol for a tazer, he repeated their demand. "Put the gun down or I will be forced to put you down."

Roger never moved a muscle as Sgt. Ryan walked past the two officers. As he grabbed Roger's rifle with both hands, he softly told him, "Let it go, just let it go."

While staring into Roger's blank eyes, the sergeant jerked the rifle free and handed it to one of the officers. "We have a warrant to take you into custody for questioning about the murder of Simon Black."

Sgt. Ryan turned to the closest officer and told her, "Take him to your cruiser. Try to explain to him the reasons why we are taking him into custody, and clearly tell him his rights." He took a deep breath before adding, "Please, make sure that you get it all on camera. In his state he may not remember anything, and it could come back on us."

The officer standing next to her pointed to the dead rabbits, and asked, "What should we do with them? We can't take them with us. They'll bleed all over the back of the car."

As Detective Douglas walked up to the police cruiser, he glanced at the rabbits and said, "Chuck them into the woods. The wildlife will get rid of them for us."

As the male officer pulled out his handcuffs, the detective told him, "Be gentle with the cuffs. I was told that this guy has some top notch attorneys." Seeing the hunting knife dangling from his belt, he added, "But I would confiscate that knife and clean out his pockets. You don't know what kind of gear he carries into the woods with him. He is not quite right in the head. No one knows how he is going to react to all of this."

The female officer snapped back, "Yes sir."

As she tried to push Roger's hands together, his arms wouldn't move. "This guy is much stronger then he appears. Ben, I'll need some help getting the cuffs on him."

As the male officer squeezed his arms together, she cuffed him. In a trance-like state, Roger slowly shuffled his feet as the two officers escorted him to the cruiser.

Detective Douglas glanced at worried sergeant. "He'll be fine. I already told the jailer to have a padded cell ready for him." Glancing at the house, he added, "Now, lets see if we can find anything inside that might wrap this case up."

After the police cruiser left, Detective Douglas looked at the other two officers. "Check the shed, smoke house, wood piles and around the outside of the house. Look for anything that is out of place, recently buried or appear to be deliberately hidden."

As he entered the doorway, Sgt. Ryan looked at the door latch and then the scratched door frame. Wooden splinters and metal pieces of its latch were scattered on the floor. "The door wasn't even locked. There is no locking mechanism. It was just stuck."

Detective Douglas looked down at the remnants and shrugged his shoulders. "Well, now it's unstuck." Looking at the window near the door, he saw that the corners of the curtain were shredded. "He might have a cat."

The decor of the two bedroom house was Spartan in nature. They were two doors on the wall to his left, and another door plus a doorway on the wall across from him. Detective Douglas stayed in the livingroom as Sgt. Ryan looked through the rest of the house.

The door closest to the front door, led to what the sergeant assumed was once Roger's parent's bedroom. Roger had converted it into a library. The walls were lined with firmly attached homemade wooden shelves. Even the space under the window had shelves stuffed full of books. The closet was full of tools and extra parts for the wind turbine, water pump and solar panels.

In the middle of the room, there was a wooden rocking chair and box-like coffee table with a half dozen books neatly placed on it. The sergeant perused through the books. There were neatly organized books from almost every genre in the room, from old, children's books to modern slasher ones. "Roger must have kept every book he ever read. The guy's a book hoarder."

The next door led to Roger's bedroom. It was much smaller, and had only the bare necessities. It contained a single bed, a lamp, a couple family pictures on the wall, a night table full of socks and underwear, a large, locked, metal gun cabinet and a fall coat hanging on a coat hook on the back of the door.

Hanging in the closet, he found two old pairs of coveralls, some old clothes, a winter coat and a couple sweaters. On the floor, was an empty laundry basket, a pair of warm winter boots and a pair of moccasins. On the shelf above the clothes rack were a few extra blankets and a pillow.

In the small bathroom there was a cabinet with a washing bowl on it, a compost toilet, a small sit-in tub, a small mirror and a towel rack. A large first-aid kit hung on the wall behind the toilet. Attached to the wall above the cabinet were two, water reservoirs. Beyond the soap, toothpaste razor, towels and a glass, the place was uncluttered.

As the sergeant entered the doorway to the kitchen, he noticed that the sink was on the same wall as the bathroom's. A counter with a large window above it, ran down most of the north wall. The shelves on the walls of the kitchen were well stocked with canned and vacuum sealed food. There were also two, insulated, stainless steel mugs, three plates, four bowls and a handful of cutlery. In a drawer below the counter, Sgt. Ryan found a few tins of cat food. On the floor next to a wooden cat dish, he noticed an assortment of scattered, small bones.

An antique kitchen stove rested at the east end of the kitchen. Joined sections of black stove pipe led into the stone chimney that stuck through a section of the south wall. He noticed some tiny holes in the flue. Sgt. Ryan hovered his hand above the stove. After feeling the heat coming from it, he opened the fire door and looked at the dying embers.

Attached to the rafters along the middle of the kitchen, were two clothes lines. Two pairs of socks and some underwear were folded over one of them.

Before Sgt Ryan left the kitchen he noticed the arced scratches on the floor in front of the back door. He yelled out, "He didn't use the front door. He used the back. That's also how his cat got out. The door has a small flap in it."

Detective Douglas yelled back. "So that's why the front, screen door squeaked so badly."

The livingroom took up a third of the house. In the far corner of the room was a crude, massive fireplace. The stone chimney had built-in vents to help circulate the heat. It ran straight up the wall, and through the peak of the house. The detective noticed a faint wisp of smoke seeping out of the fireplace insert's slightly opened door.

Looking up, he saw a pair of cross-country skis and a pair of snowshoes on top of the rafters. Several long sections of steel tube, probably for a wind turbine's mast, and a bunch of wide planks suitable for shelves, were neatly stacked above the doorway leading into the kitchen. A large, motionless, ceiling fan was mounted in the middle of the ceiling.

Stuffed bookshelves filled the rest of the east wall all the way up to the rafters. Next to the shelves, a five rung step stool leaned against the south wall.

The detective quickly glanced through the book titles. From bottom to top there were two complete sets of encyclopedias, a vast assortment of reference and do-it-yourself books from every walk of life including both civilian and military, a whole shelf on off-the-grid living, a shelf that primarily dealt with psychiatry, and on the very top shelves there were books on various religions, beliefs and philosophies.

On an old desk under the window facing the driveway was an old personal word processor. Beside the glorified electric typewriter were stacks of papers, notepads, an external disk drive, plus a strange electrical box that had four USB ports on the front of it. In one of the ports was a external thumb drive. Detective Douglas released a faint chuckle. "I guess he wasn't totally afraid of technology."

The only real luxuries in the entire house were a reclining chair, a very comfortable looking desk chair, and a cherry wood, book cabinet with two, narrow glass doors.

Inside the cabinet was a complete set of Simon Black's novels, including the newly published Polar Diamonds. When the detective looked through the front of them, his eyebrows began to rise. None of them were signed.

As Sgt. Ryan entered the livingroom, Detective Douglas glanced at him. "Find anything interesting?"

"Nothing, the man lived like a hermit. How can anyone with his kind of money, live like this? He has three changes of identical clothes and all of them are worn down to threads."

"The ones he had on were in decent shape. He must wear the same clothes until they fall apart. He probably only wears the ones you found when he does a wash."

The sergeant noticed a small trail of smoke leaking out of the fireplace insert. "It's been too warm for two fires. The kitchen stove is still throwing off plenty of heat. I wonder what he was burning."

As the sergeant spoke, Detective Douglas looked at a couple small, glowing, red embers through the glass doors of the fireplace insert. "You could be right."

Using a small narrow fireplace shovel and poker, Detective Douglas began removing all the charred paper, debris and most of the ashes. He carefully spread them out on the stone tiles in front of the fireplace insert. The fresh air reignited the edges of a couple small pieces of paper. Detective Douglas used the poker to separate them from the rest of the debris.

Sgt. Ryan kneeled beside him and looked at the burnt piece of typed paper and charred wood. Detective Douglas glanced at him. "I don't want to disturb these remnants to much. Lets take some photos, pack them up, document everything and send them to the lab."

Waving one of the officers over, he told him, "Get some boxes from the trunk of the car. Line them with some blankets from the bedroom. After the remnants are cold, carefully place them in the boxes. I don't want any of the remains to be squashed. Some of those brittle remains may contain fragments of the murder weapon, or evidence of motive, so be careful."

As the pair got back to English Lookout, Detective Douglas looked at the time. "Roger wouldn't even be processed yet. Maybe we should go to the hotel and question Robert Swayze some more."

The receptionist smiled as Detective Douglas walked into the hotel. "Your favourite guest is still in his room."

He smiled back at her. "Thank you. Something important came up, and we had to deal with it first."

The sergeant caught his smile. As they walked to the elevator, he whispered to him, "I hope that she isn't the reason you have been avoiding going home."

The detective was still smiling as he told him, "No, but at my age, it is nice to know that women still find you attractive."

Detective Douglas knocked on the door, waited a few

seconds and knocked again. Finally Robert came to the door and peered through the peephole. "You again."

As Robert opened the door his robe slipped open, revealing the right edge of his bare stomach, hip and front of his leg. Turning away, he retied his robe and sat down on his bed. "Can't a man have any peace in this town."

Detective Douglas walked over and stood in front of him. "I'm sorry, but I have to ask you some more questions."

Robert waved his right arm in the air. "Fire away."

"First of all, I think I should inform you that we have Roger Blackett in custody. He lives in Blackett Hill and we believe that he has more than enough motive to commit the murder."

Robert stood up and almost butted heads with the detective. "What do you mean? What motive could he possibly have? Did you even check into that crazy lady at the book signing?"

"She has an alibi." The detective glanced at the gap at the front of Robert's robe and looked away. "We know that Roger Blackett now gets all the royalties from Simon Black's books. That's a lot of money. Plus we believe that the bond between them is much more then that of a writer and his muse. That could be an addition motive to kill him."

The colour started to leave Robert's face as he plopped back down on the bed. "Are you crazy? You have no idea what you have done. I hope you put a suicide watch on him." The fingers on his right hand started to nervously tap his leg. "With his condition, he can't survive in prison."

The detective turned to face him. "You seem to know a lot about him. Didn't you tell us that you never met him before the book signing?"

"I didn't, but my relationship with Simon was transparent. He told me everything. And yes, Roger was much more than just his muse. He was his corner stone. Without Roger, Simon couldn't even produce a short novelette that was worthy of publication." Robert looked up at the detective. "If anything happens to Roger I will let the entire world know that it was entirely your fault."

Detective Douglas shut his eyes and took a deep breath. Upon opening them, he said, "So Roger meant a lot to Simon, but what did Simon mean to Roger?"

Robert waved his hands in front of him. "Yes, Simon made sure that Roger was well paid for his services." He shook his head as he added, "Roger cherished his awkward and very extraordinary relationship with Simon. He would never hurt him. He was his one and only link to the outside world. He basically lived through Simon."

"What about Dr. Deathridge?"

Robert almost shouted out, "She was his doctor." He lowered his voice slightly. "Roger needed someone like Simon to bounce his thoughts and images of the outside world off. He can't get feedback from a book. Dr. Deathridge is a closed minded mother hen. She lives in her own little world. Simon of the other hand, was someone that Roger could semi experience a vast array of cultures, arts, activities and cuisines through. There is no way he would kill him."

Detective Douglas stepped back and gave Robert some time to cool down. He noticed Sgt. Ryan leaning against the washroom door as if he trying to listen to something inside. Sgt. Ryan saw him. With a subtle smile on his face, he rubbed the side of his nose with his forefinger.

Detective Douglas gave him a quick half smile back, before returning his attention to Robert. With his hands grasped together, he asked him, "So, what about all the money he'll be getting? Money like that could buy a man a lot of friends."

Robert shook his head. "He didn't need any more money. As a matter of fact, I can even produce documents showing that Roger wanted to scale back his share of the royalties. At the beginning, he was getting half. Then

Simon's book sales went through the roof. At the time of Simon's death, he was about to lower percentage of the royalties to a quarter."

The detective's eyebrows dropped as he said, "Why!"

Roger grinned as he said, "I don't know. If you want, when I get back to my office, I can send you a copy of the letter he sent me." After slapping his thighs, his voice started to mutter. "Now, he will be lucky if he can keep his private, little town going."

Detective Douglas stepped towards him and tilted his head. "But he will be getting all of Simon's royalties."

Robert soberly looked at him. "Sure, but without new books coming to market, that will quickly dry up."

"What do you mean? Explain it to me."

"Without new books coming to market, an author can't generate new sales. His books get shoved into bargain bins at a loss, to make room for new, more profitable ones." Robert looked up at the ceiling. "People like buying new books. If all they want is something to read to pass some time, most book lovers have friends to swap with. They also have libraries and second hand book stores to search through. They don't want to pay for an old book."

With a puzzled, scrunched up face, Detective Douglas looked down at Robert and said, "So you really don't think Roger could have killed Simon?"

"And risk everything? No way. He's too smart to be that stupid. He knows how the publishing industry works." Vigorously shaking his head, he added, "Besides, he is way to too sensitive."

Detective Douglas rocked his head back and forth. "When we picked him up, he had two dead rabbits dangling from his belt. He can't be that sensitive."

"But they were just meat for his table." Robert took a deep breath and lowered his head. "I bet Roger even said a prayer to them. From what Simon told me about him, he was a bit religious." He quickly looked back up at Detective Douglas and blurted out." Killing a rabbit and killing the man that he loved, are totally different."

Detective Douglas's eyebrows raised as he asked him, "When you say loved, what do you mean?"

Robert waved his hands in front of him. "Simon was not gay, and to my knowledge neither was Roger, if that is what you mean." He lowered his hands as he said, "He loved him, not as a lover, but as a true friend, a confidant and like a close brother. Even if they had some kind of dispute, Roger's deep rooted feelings toward Simon would prevent him from resorting to any kind of violence."

"You really believe that?"

Robert looked up at him and soberly said, "Yes, yes I do."

Detective Douglas took a deep breath and exhaled it through his nose. "Well I guess that is it for now. Still, I would like to be informed if you plan to leave town."

Robert straightened his robe. "No problem. I wasn't planning on leaving until after Simon's body is cremated, and his ashes scattered."

As they were walking down the stairs to the lobby, Sgt. Ryan glanced at the detective. "You knew that he had a woman in there, didn't you."

The detective grinned. "Why did you think it took him so long to answer the door?"

Sgt. Ryan snickered. "Well by the looks of it, Robert's straight."

"But I am still not sure about Roger. Two unattached men being that close, still sounds fishy to me."

Sgt. Ryan stopped in front of the staircase doorway, and told the detective, "You know, Marion is staying here."

"Do you know which room?"

The sergeant pulled out is notepad and checked his notes. "She is in room 417."

After she heard a knock on the door, Marion looked through the peep hole, saw Sgt. Ryan and smiled. As she unlocked the door and opened it, she said, "I thought you might want to talk to me some more."

As Detective Douglas pushed the sergeant aside, he said, "I'm Detective Douglas. I'm in charge of the investigation of Simon Black's death. I was wondering if we could come in and ask you a few questions?"

Marion's smile disappeared. "Sure." As she stepped aside, she added, "Come on in."

The detective blocked Marion's view of the sergeant while he told her, "You have got an interesting website."

"Thank you, I've worked hard to get it the way it is."

"I'm interested in your research. Do you keep any files on it?"

Marion's face turned cold. "Sure, I need them to double check any new facts that come up. I wouldn't want people to think I am some kind of hack. Everything on my site has been thoroughly researched and verified."

In a bit of a huff, she pulled out her laptop, flopped it on the dresser and turned it on. "If you want, I can download you any file you want."

The detective snickered, "Sure."

As Marion and Detective Douglas stood in front of the dresser, Sgt. Ryan poked around the room. With his phone out, he candidly took pictures of everything he could, including several of Marion.

Marion handed the detective a memory stick, and told him, "I want Simon's killer in jail. Too bad there is no death penalty in Canada." Trying to calm down, she took a deep breath. "If you think I can do anything, anything at all to help you catch him, just ask."

Detective Douglas smiled. "Thank you, but I think this should be enough." As he shoved the stick into his pocket, he added, "I wish there were more people out there like you. That would make my job a lot easier."

It wasn't until the detective turned around to leave, that Marion noticed Sgt. Ryan staring at her. Her face started to warm up, as she said, "I forgot you were here."

The sergeant smiled. "That's all right. We can chat later."

As the sergeant walked down the hallway, Marion stood in the doorway. Sgt. Ryan glanced back, said, "Hopefully I will see you before you leave."

"We will see."

As they walked into the police station, Dr. Deathridge almost leaped off the bench she was sitting on. She ran towards Detective Douglas yelling, "Are you a complete moron? How could you bring Roger in for questioning?"

With her low cut sweater pressed against him, she glared into his eyes and demanded, "Where is he? I need to make sure he is alright."

Detective Douglas placed his left arm across his chest to shield her breasts from view as he looked down at her. "Calm down. I know what you told me about him, but we had to consider him as a high flight risk. We had to bring him in."

"You had plenty of other options. You never so much as asked for my help. I could have sat him down and helped you, but you blew it. If he does anything to himself because of this, I will hold you personally responsible."

"What is he, a fragile Russian egg or something? In my experience people are people. Yes, some are a little more emotional than others, but they still have the same needs and wants as the next one."

The doctor was furious. As she clenched her fist and started to swing at the detective's face, Sgt. Ryan grabbed her arm. As he struggled to control her arm, he said, "Telling an officer off is just public disobedience, but striking an officer is assault. Do you really want me to get my handcuffs out and lock you up?"

The doctor stepped back and wrestled her arm away from the sergeant. "No, but you know what I am capable of. If anything happens to Roger, it will be more than just karma that will get you. It will be the demons of hell itself, and I have a whole bunch of them in my pocket. When his lawyers get here, you'll be in deep, serious trouble."

As the doctor stormed back to the bench and sat down, Detective Douglas told her, "He'll be alright. I made sure that everyone here knew they had to treat him with ultra soft, silk lined gloves."

"Well I am still not leaving until I am sure he is safe."

As he walked passed her, the detective shook his head and said, "Suit yourself."

In a snarling voice, she told him, "His lawyers are going to have a field day with you."

The door leading into the room full of chart boards and cluttered desks had barely enough time to shut behind them, before Sgt. Ryan turned to Detective Douglas. "You know that Roger may not be our killer. What happens if he's not?"

"Right now, all arrows point to him." The detective looked at the sergeant and told him, "If he is innocent, he'll be released with no harm done."

The sergeant shook his head. "He is not like the rest of us. He could get PTSD. Something this traumatic could linger on for a long, long time."

Detective Douglas placed his hand on the sergeant's shoulder. "Look, we did everything by the book. The guys that wrote it were no dummies. They knew what they were doing."

Sgt. Ryan looked at the detective's hand. "So when do you want to question him?"

After releasing a subtle smirk, the detective told him, "I think we should let the doctor and him simmer a bit longer.

Once they realize that we are the ones in control, they will become a lot more cooperative."

"What about his lawyers?"

"They won't be here until tomorrow at the earliest. By that time, we should be able to prove to them that we are doing everything by the book, and treating their client with all the care he requires."

As the sergeant sat down at his desk, he checked his messages. Among them was one from Marion. He clicked on it. 'Just letting you know that I will be staying in the area until Simon's ashes are spread. If you need to ask me anything, just send me a message.' The smiley faces at the beginning and end of the message made him smile.

Going to Marion's website, Sgt. Ryan tried to see past all the stuff about Simon Black and get a feel for the site's creator. It was written as if Simon was almost god-like. "This lady worshipped him."

After rereading every page with a new viewpoint, he went to the footage from the book store. He saw Marion storm out of the store. The passage Simon wrote in her book had made her furious. He paused at the image of her turning around and glancing back at Simon as she left the store. With it on the screen, he walked over to Detective Douglas. "I think we may have another viable candidate for Simon Black's murder. Marion was a little more than just obsessed with Simon, she actually loved him. Maybe she deliberately sped, and wanted to get a ticket in order to give herself an alibi."

Detective Douglas sat back in his chair and looked at him. "I think you just want Roger to be innocent. Trust me, we have the right man."

Sgt. Ryan placed his hands on the detective's desk. "Well I am not sure of that. What if Marion is the killer?"

After releasing a sigh, the detective lowered his head. "Fine, take a few hours and try to convince me otherwise." Looking up at him, he added, "Meanwhile, I'm going to see what provisions have been made for our prime suspect. I don't want to give his lawyers or Dr. Deathridge any ammunition to work with."

Before the detective returned, Sgt. Ryan had amassed a half dozen images. "I have photos of Marion entering and leaving the campsite."

The sergeant spread the photos over the top of the detectives desk. Pointing to the one on the right, he said, "When she arrived, she was wearing a wig."

"Why wasn't her car licence registered at the office?"

"She entered as a guest, visiting some friends. If you look at the next photo taken only a few hours later, you will see her driving out without a wig."

"Why didn't the techs get her licence plate number?"

The sergeant shuffled around a few photos and pointed at her licence plate. "It had one of those tinted plastic covers used to try to fool toll road cameras. Even if it wasn't dirty, the sun was reflecting off it. The techs would've had a very difficult time trying to make it out. When she left, the car behind her was right on her bumper."

"Still, she has an alibi."

The sergeant grinned, "No she doesn't. Check out the next photos. I rechecked Officer Kelly's footage and saw a car matching Marion's heading back towards town as she was issuing another ticket."

The detective looked at the next two photos. One showed Marion's car as Officer Kelly was giving her a ticket. The second was an identical car passing Officer Kelly as she was issuing another ticket. "This doesn't prove anything. I can't make out the licence plate. It could be two different cars."

"Two cars of the same make, model, colour and both with tinted licence plate covers. With the volume of cars on the road, that has to be very strange."

Detective Douglas glanced at the last two photos.

"When were these taken?"

"While you were questioning Marion at the hotel, I was discretely walking around her room taking snapshots. Compare the pictures I took of her in her hotel room to the others we have. Her makeup made her look completely different." The last photo was of the contents of her makeup case. As the detective studied it, the sergeant said, "Luckily, all I had to do is tap the top of it with my shoe to open it enough to peek inside."

The detective studied the photo. "For a nurse, she has quite the array of makeup."

Sgt. Ryan smiled. "So, do you think I have enough to warrant further investigation?"

"Unfortunately, I do." Looking up at the ceiling he mumbled, "Now we have two suspects."

Sgt. Ryan grinned as he replied, "But only one killer."

After rubbing the back of his neck, Detective Douglas clicked on the linked feed from the camera in Roger's private, padded cell. "For now, lets check up on suspect number one." Roger was curled up in the corner of his padded cell with his head between his knees.

The detective stood up, marched down the hall and glared at the corporal on guard duty. "Has this detainee been given drugs or something?"

"No, nothing at all. I've even had someone go in and check if he was still breathing."

The detective turned around and looked at Sgt. Ryan. "The way Roger is now, we are not going to be able to get anything from him."

"Nope." Looking back at the exit, the sergeant added, "I just hope that he snaps out of it before his lawyers get here."

Chapter Fifteen

Sgt. Ryan walked out to the waiting room and sat beside Dr. Deathridge. She looked at him with clenched teeth and snorted. "Well, is that neanderthal going to let me see Roger Blackett or not?"

The sergeant kept his voice low. "Before you see him, Detective Douglas wants to talk to you."

She sprung off the bench and glared down at him. "Well lets go and see him."

The sergeant stood up and led her down a hallway. He then nodded his head in the direction of a security door. "Follow me."

After her handbag was searched by the officer that had been sitting at the desk, she walked through a metal detector and joined Sgt. Ryan inside. The sergeant barely glanced at her before he led her down another hallway. "Detective Douglas is in room four. This matter is rather delicate. He thought that it would be best if no one was listening in on what was said."

"And without lawyers being present."

The sergeant glanced at her. "Sometimes, they can make things a little more complicated then they need to be."

As the uneasy doctor slowly entered the room, she stared at the large mirror that almost covered an entire wall. "Is anyone behind that?"

Sitting on a chair behind a heavy, wooden table, Detective Douglas told her, "I made sure that nobody was in there, and I also made sure that everything was switched off. Nothing we say in here will be recorded in any way."

"Isn't that against police protocol?"

"I wanted to keep this conversation strictly between the three of us."

The doctor leaned against the mirror and looked at him. "No cameras either?"

The detective shook his head. "No cameras either."

The doctor wondered, '*What if someone entered the observation room after the detective told her that nobody was there.*' Not wanting anyone to read her lips, she turned her back to the mirror. She opened her purse and pulled out a gel pen and a pad of thin paper. "First, I want a large glass of water."

The detective glanced at Sgt. Ryan and said, "Go and get her a bottle of water."

"NO, I said I wanted it in a large glass, not a bottle."

Sgt. Ryan stared at her and said, "Fine, I'll find a glass to put it in."

Nothing was said until the sergeant came back. She looked at the bottle and the smooth sided, plastic glass. "Are you going to pour it out for me or not?"

Detective Douglas glared at her. "Jeez, he is not your servant."

Sgt. Ryan glanced at him, then back at the doctor. After biting his bottom lip, he opened the bottle and filled the glass to almost the rim. "Is that what you wanted?"

The doctor grinned at him and calmly said, "Yes it is, thank you."

As Sgt. Ryan stood next to the door, Detective Douglas stared at the quirky, defiant doctor. "As you anticipated, Roger is not cooperating with us. However, he is still our prime suspect. If you want to clear him, you will have to help us."

The doctor glanced at both officers and started to write on her pad. After she was finished, she showed the detective what she had wrote. 'Just in case this place is bugged, I am not going to say another word. If you want my help, you will first need to release Roger into my custody.' She flipped to the next page. 'I will assure you that he will not leave his house and you can even post an officer outside as long as he remains out of Roger's sight."

Detective Douglas's right hand reached for the pad.

The doctor quickly yanked it away and shook her head.

Throwing his arm in the air, he yelled out, "What is this? I told you that nothing in this room is turned on. Nobody is watching us."

She flipped the page, and began to jot down another message, using a bit larger letters. When she was done, she showed him the four paged message. 'You have not given me any reason to trust you. My whole style of therapy depends on trust. If I can't trust you, how can Roger. I know him. Until he feels that you will actually listen to him, he won't mumble a word. He doesn't trust cops. He believes they are all nothing but overpaid, corrupt bullies and extortionists.'

After reading what she wrote, Detective Douglas glanced at Sgt. Ryan, then back at her. "So what are you proposing?"

The doctor lifted her knee, rested her foot against the wall, and used her thigh to write on. After she was done, she held the pad in front of the detective's face. He leaned forward and quickly reached for the pad of paper. He was too slow. She managed to pull it away.

After shaking her head in disgust, she slowly moved it back in front of him. The detective stood up and yelled, "This is getting silly. In fact, it's plain stupid!"

The doctor turned and started to walk towards the door. Detective Douglas lowered his voice. "Fine, we'll play it your way, but I will remember this."

The doctor stopped and started to chuckle as she showed the sergeant what she had written. 'First, I want the sergeant to interview him, without you, and in my presence. Second, you will need to give me a few days to settle him down. He needs time to recover from the psychological trauma you put him through. Third, HE NEEDS TO GO HOME! He will slowly die in a cell. If that happens, I'll see to it that you are charged with his murder.'

On the last page, she had written, 'His lawyers have

already hired a helicopter. If he is not released, they will be here in a matter of hours.'

Sgt. Ryan grinned. "Can I tell him."

The detective spoke up, "What's it say?"

"She is willing to help us but not while he is being detained. Due to the trauma we put him through, it'll be days before we can interview him." A large grin emerged on the sergeant's face as he added, "Now don't be mad, but she also insists that I am the one that conducts the interviews."

The detective stood up and yelled, "A few days! We are conducting a murder investigation."

The sergeant shook his head. "Apparently, his lawyers have already hired a helicopter. If he isn't immediately released under the doctor's care, they will be here in a matter of hours. You saw Roger, and you know the doctor's clout. Do you want this police station mocked by every newspaper and media outlet out there?"

The doctor turned towards the detective and broke her silence. "It's that or nothing."

Standing next to the table, she bent over and dunked the pad of paper into the water. As she stirred the water with one finger, the detective noticed that she didn't even leave a smudged fingerprint on the glass. The detective watched the thin paper slowly disintegrated. As he looked up and their eye's met, she told him, "This is not my first off-the-record police interview."

As the water in the glass turned blue from the gel ink, the detective told her. "Even if I allow him to leave under your supervision, he has to remain under police surveillance. As I told you, he is our prime suspect in Simon Black's murder, and he is still considered a flight risk."

Dr. Deathridge removed her finger from the water, smiled and said, "That's fine, as long as they are not within sight of Roger's house. I don't want him to see them."

Sgt. Ryan used the doctor's taillights to help him get

through the dark, twisted driveway. As he got out of the car, the only sound he heard was a faint squeak coming from the wind turbine as it turned directions. "It's like being in a horror movie."

He helped the doctor get Roger out of her car. With his arm semi curled around Roger's chest, he almost dragged him into the house. After the doctor turned on a few lights, he picked Roger up, carried him into his bedroom and laid him on the bed.

As Sgt. Ryan stood up and caught his breath, he looked around the room. "He doesn't need much to keep him happy, does he? This place is pretty sparse."

Dr. Deathridge stood in the doorway with a large strapped bag over her shoulder. "The more things a person has, the less he can focus on what is really important."

Sgt. Ryan watched the doctor remove Roger's shoes and belt before she tucked him into his bed. "I don't know if it matters, but I have had some doubts about Roger's guilt."

The doctor glared at him, "So why put him through all this?"

The sergeant rocked his head back and forth. "Detective Douglas is still convinced that he murdered Simon Black. Maybe we can convince him otherwise."

The doctor took a deep breath. "That would be nice. It amazes me how the police force could allow such a narrow minded neanderthal like that, keep the position he has."

The next morning, Detective Douglas examined the financial agreements that Simon's publishing house had faxed to the station. At the start, Roger had received fifty percent of the royalties. After the last land purchase, it was reduced to forty percent. A typed letter from the secretary stated that she heard of the further reduction, but had no paperwork pertaining to it. It could take a few days to trace it down.

Sgt. Ryan sat at his desk and called Officer Kelly. "I heard that you had a few days off."

"Yeah." The officer looked at the large box on her coffee table containing her bridesmaid dress, as she added, "So what do you want Marq?"

"I was wondering if you could keep an eye on a suspect for us?"

"So you want me to work for you off the books?" Maryann looked at the bags of wedding decorations that lined two walls of her living room. I have a bridesmaid dress to alter and a bunch of errands to do before the wedding."

The sergeant brushed his fingers through his hair. "I'll owe you a couple dances at the wedding." Hearing dead air, he rubbed his chin and added, "I could even help you with some of your errands."

"So why can't you do it?"

"Because it's a woman."

Maryann thought a bit before she tilted her head and chuckled. "I bet she's pretty."

Sgt. Ryan bit his lip and muttered, "Somewhat, and a couple years older. The problem is that I think she has a crush on me."

Maryann release a loud sigh. "I thought so. Women can't get enough of you, can they?"

"It's not my fault. Blame my parents. It's their genes that made me look the way I do."

"Well, they did a magnificent job." After rubbing her tongue back and forth over her front top teeth a few times, she broke her brief silence. "So Marq, where is this stake out going to take place?"

"In the hotel down the street from the station. The clerk informed me that the room next to her's is vacant."

"What about the room across from her?"

"It's occupied. The room next to her's is much better. You can attach a microphone to the wall and hear everything. That way you can make whatever alterations you need to your dress, and still record what's going on." Hearing no response, he rubbed the back of his neck. "While you are getting your alterations done, I could do some of your errands for you."

After a long hesitation, Officer Kelly grinned and said, "Okay Marq, I can think of a couple errands you could do for me. However, you will still owe me a couple of slow dances."

After releasing a sigh of relief, Sgt. Ryan told her, "Great, I'll make sure that you don't regret it."

Marion was walking down the stairs as Officer Kelly carried her bridesmaid dress into the hotel. With her long hair draped over her shoulders, no sunglasses or makeup on, Marion didn't recognize her.

As they passed one another at the bottom of the stairs, Marion looked at the dress and forced herself to smile. "That's gorgeous. I was a bridesmaid once, and that dress was beyond ugly."

The grey smudges under Marion's swollen, glossy eyes told the officer that she had been crying. "This is going to be my third time." Trying not to reveal who she was, she put on a wide smile. "You should have seen my second dress. It was a puffy, pink monstrosity with huge purple and red flowers all over it. They made us look like a bunch of enormous garden gnomes."

Marion couldn't help but chuckle. After glancing at the door, she told her, "Thanks, I needed that. Maybe we will run into each other again before you leave."

"The wedding is over a week away, so maybe." Officer Kelly stretched her arm out slightly and rubbed the back of her hand against hers. "You look like you could use a friendly ear. I'm Maryann. I'm staying in room 419. If you need anything, just knock on my door."

"I'll think about it."

Looking down at the dress, Maryann added, "But give me a minute to get to it, because I'll probably be in the middle of doing some last minute alterations to this dress. You know what that is like."

Marion stood still, turned and looked into the officer's eyes. After forcing herself to smile, she said, "I never introduced myself. I'm Marion." As she started to look away she said, "I may just take you up on your offer."

"Good, I may need the odd break. I hate sewing."

The errands that Maryann asked Sgt. Ryan to do were mostly bull work. Borrowing a truck, loading all the chairs and tables needed for the wedding reception, and storing them in a corner of the hall, took him most of the day.

After he was done, he sat in the truck and called her. After she said hello, he told her, "I thought halls had their own tables and chairs?"

"They do, but the bride didn't like the ones they have. It's my job to make sure she is happy on her special day."

"I think you got the better part of this deal. Did you realize how many loads it took, and how many sets of stairs I had to lug all that stuff up? How many guests are they expecting?"

"Hey, you are the one that asked me for a favour. You knew that they both came from large families." Maryann grinned as she added, "I just saw it as an easy way to get out of some of the grunt work."

"Thanks, thanks a lot."

Maryann started to laugh as someone knocked on the door. "Hold on, someone is at the door."

Looking through the peephole, she saw Marion. "It's Marion, I have to go."

After tossing a sweater over the surveillance equipment, she opened the door. Marion stepped inside and wrapped her arms around her neck and began to cry. "I really need someone to talk to. I don't know if I can get through this all by myself."

In an effort to comfort her, Maryann began to gently stroke her hair. "What's wrong?"

Marion sank her wet face into Maryann's shoulder. "I just lost the love of my life, and I just don't know what to do anymore."

Maryann hugged her back. "It takes time to recover from a lose."

As Marion's tears soaked through Maryann's top, she mumbled, "My life no longer has any meaning. I can't even look at myself in a mirror anymore." Placing her hand on the side of Maryann's face, she asked her, "Can I stay with you for a while? I really need to be with someone right now."

Maryann softly patted the back of Marion's head and told her, "Sure, sure you can."

After looking at the time, Detective Douglas sighed. "I can't go back to that ugly, pink house."

Leaving his car in the lot, he walked to the hotel. The receptionist twirled a finger in her hair and smiled as she handed him his key. "I put you just down the hall from your favourite person of interest. For some reason, the fourth floor seems to be where all the action is."

The detective smiled back. While the smiling receptionist bit her bottom lip, he nodded his head. "Thanks for being so thoughtful. I'll probably see you tomorrow."

The receptionist, released a tiny chuckle. "Can't wait."

Detective Douglas walked up the stairs to the fourth floor. As he opened the door, he saw Cindy MacDonald leave Robert's room wearing a tight black, low cut dress. While standing in the doorway, he couldn't help but hear her giggle as she told Robert, "I'll be back as soon as I can, don't you dare go anywhere."

Detective Douglas managed to close the door before she saw him. Through the door's small glass window, he watched her walk past the elevator towards the stairway. He quickly climbed up another flight of stairs. As he watched Cindy walking down the stairs to the lobby, he mumbled, "So what is a gorgeous woman like that doing with a pompous bookworm like Robert."

When he thought it was clear, he went down to the lobby and asked the receptionist, "Are either of the rooms next to Robert Swayze's room available?"

The receptionist smiled and slowly gyrated her shoulders. "No, but room 411 is. It's right across the hall from his." After licking her upper lip, she asked him, "So are things starting to get interesting up there?"

Detective Douglas smiled back at her and rolled his eyes. "They are getting interesting, that's for sure."

After making a trip back to the station, the detective carried a small case back to his hotel room. He placed the case on the bed and opened it. Inside of it was a camera, suction cups, strips of putty adhesive and a bunch of cables. It took him about twenty minutes to fasten the camera over the wide-view peephole in the door. Through the camera's large viewing screen, he could see everything it was recording.

The following morning, Dr. Deathridge's patients were being shuttled to Roger's house. The doctor had already dragged Roger's desk and chair into his bedroom so he could use his modified word processor.

Instead of replacing the worn out hinges on the screen door, the doctor used a large chuck of firewood to hold it open. Thankfully, the police department had already repaired the damage they did to the front door, and even replaced the hinges.

With the bedroom door shut, the doctor unfolded a card table and some collapsible chairs. As Mr. Green dropped off her first patient of the day, she was still rearranging her make-shift desk.

At first, Roger's nonstop typing made it hard for her to fully concentrate on her patients' problems. After a while, the clicking and banging became merely background noise.

As Detective Douglas entered, the doctor stood up and yelled, "Can't you see that I am with a patient?"

The detective grinned. "Didn't you hear me knock."

"No!"

"Well I did." Detective Douglas looked around the livingroom. He didn't recognize the thirty something, year old man that was sitting in the chair across from her. "Right now, all I care about is Simon Black's murder investigation." Hearing the typing, the detective pointed his thumb towards Roger's bedroom door. "So, when will he be ready to be interviewed?"

"Give him a couple more days."

The detective went over to Roger's bedroom door and cracked it open. Peering inside, he saw him pounding the keys of his word processor. "He looks fine to me."

After telling her patient to wait outside, Dr. Deathridge walked over to the detective and told him, "He is in his own fantasy world. He can't even hear us."

The detective went into the bedroom and started to talk to Roger. "Hello." He raised his voice and continued, "Hello there, is anyone home?"

The speed of Roger's typing slightly increased as the detective asked, "So, what are you typing?"

As Detective Douglas waved his hand in front of Roger's eyes, Roger tilted his head and kept on typing. The detective reached in front of him, grabbed the paper in the word processor and yanked it out. Roger turned, swung his arm and punched the side of the detective's face. The unexpected blow made the detective step back. Roger leaped out of his chair and grabbed the Detective's collar. The pair tumbled to the floor.

Dr. Deathridge ran and grabbed a hold of Roger. With her arms wrapped around his upper arms and chest, she pulled him away from the flailing detective. Detective Douglas landed a few solid punches to Roger's face and chest as the defenceless man kicked, screamed and spat onto Detective Douglas's face.

The detective yelled out, "That's assault. I'll have him behind bars for that."

The doctor glared at him. "You assaulted him first. You invaded his personal space. Right now he doesn't even have the capability of understanding right from wrong, however you do, or at least you should. For a man in your position, you sure don't know much about the law."

The doctor used her entire body to flip her struggling benefactor onto the bed. While pinning her irrate patient face down on the mattress, the doctor pulled a needle from her smock, uncapped it with her thumb, and gave him an injection to calm him down.

Detective Douglas stood back and watched her as he wiped off his face with his sleeve and rubbed his cheek. "He is not nearly as fragile as you make him out to be." After wiping a few drops of blood from his lip, he looked at his sleeve and added, "He is just faking it."

Dr. Deathridge glared at him. "And how many years did you study medicine?" As the doctor spread some blankets over her comatose patient, she added, "You are just an ape with a badge. You can't see anything beyond your hairy knuckles."

While the doctor finished tucking Roger in, the detective scanned the page he had removed from the word processor. "This is gibberish." After skimming through a few of the pages stacked next to the word processor, he looked at the busy doctor. "Does he actually think that this bunch of garbage is suppose to be some sort of readable story? My five year old nephew could make up something better than this."

The doctor glared back at him and sharply said, "Just put them back the way you found them."

"All right, all right." Detective Douglas slowly placed the papers back on the pile. "I wouldn't want to ruin his make-believe masterpiece. Everyone thinks they could be a writer. Being friends with one must make him fantasise it even more than all the other wannabes out there."

Stroking the side of Roger's face, the doctor told the detective, "Just leave. I don't know why you even came here in the first place. I told you that he wouldn't be ready to be interviewed."

Detective Douglas placed his hands on his hips, and blurted out, "As I have told you over and over again, I have a murder to solve."

The doctor glared at him. "And I'll be talking to Roger's lawyers. By the time this is all over, you will be lucky if you don't end up behind bars."

"Lawyers." Detective Douglas stumped out of the bedroom and shut the door behind him. As he stood in the livingroom and looked around, he noticed that the ash bucket next to the fireplace was full of papers. He walked over and bent down to look at them. The typed papers were marked up in red ink. Along with the corrections, they had lots of circles, 'X's' and lines stroking out sections of text.

The detective glanced around the room. Beneath the short legged, book cabinet, a black and white cat stared at him. As their eyes met, the cat dashed into the kitchen.

The detective looked at the closed bedroom door. He quickly grabbed a handful of papers and tucked them under his jacket as he stood up.

In a voice, loud enough for the doctor to hear, Detective Douglas said, "Well I'm not going to get anything from him today. I might as well leave. I'll tell the sergeant tomorrow. Try to have him ready to be interviewed, so we can get on with our investigation."

"Are you crazy!" The doctor yelled back, "Tomorrow of all days. That's when they will be spreading Simon's ashes. Maybe the following day, but definitely not tomorrow."

Back at the station, the detective placed the papers he took on Sgt. Ryan's desk. "What do you make of these?'

The sergeant quickly perused them, before answering, "It's part of a rough outline of a story. It's hard to tell what the story is really about because these pages are obviously from somewhere in the middle of it. Maybe once the editing is done, Peter, the main character, might be a little more believable."

Detective Douglas chuckled, "On the papers I read, the main character's name was Barry."

"Maybe it was a different story?"

"Maybe. Those pages came from his ash bucket. The ones I glanced through back at his place, were fresh off his glorified typewriter."

Detective Douglas bit his bottom lip and started to pace back and forth between their desks. "Do you think it could be possible that Roger might have helped Simon write his books? Maybe he was the idea man. Maybe Simon took Roger's crude outlines and reworded them to create his masterpieces."

"Maybe." Sgt. Ryan slowly placed the papers on his desk. "Robert did say that Roger was more then just Simon's muse. Maybe Simon learned to understand Roger's ramblings when he was his tutor. I've heard that it takes longer to plan out a novel than to actually write it. Maybe he just saw an opportunity and took it. After all, almost every word of the end product would be his. Roger would simply be his generously paid assistant."

The detective looked at the sergeant. "If that's the case, all Simon would need is Roger's rough outlines. He could've got Mrs. Green to mail Simon the memory chips. She doesn't have to know what's on them. They don't even have to see or even talk to each other. Simon could be in Europe and still be able to write."

Sgt. Ryan thought for a moment. "So, Roger lets

Simon polish his stories, and looks after getting them published. He's not in it for the fame. It wouldn't matter to him whose name they were published under."

"Fifty percent of the work. Fifty percent of the money." The detective shook his head. "However, if Roger is now trying to polish his own writing, he might believe that he no longer needs Simon. He could still keep his privacy by using a pseudonym. We are still where we were. Roger is still the prime suspect."

"This is all conjecture." Sgt Ryan pointed his finger in the air. "What about Roger wanting to lower his percentage of the royalties?"

The detective gazed at him. "Who said the reduced royalties were his idea? All we got is Robert's word for it."

Chapter Sixteen

The following morning, Sgt. Ryan slowly tried to make sense of the marked up pages that Detective Douglas took from the ash bin. The volume of red ink on them, indicated to him that Roger wasn't very happy with them. The sergeant looked at the clock, nine-fifteen. He put on his jacket and grabbed the papers. Glancing over at Detective Douglas, he said, "We have to get going or we'll be late for the ceremony."

The detective noticed the time in the corner of his computer monitor. "You are right." Seeing the papers in Sgt. Ryan's hand, he asked, "What are you going to do with those?"

"Marion will be there. I thought that I would show them to her. Maybe she can tell us if they are just the wild rambling's of a want-to-be writer, or maybe something else."

"Just make sure that no one sees you. I don't want either the doctor or Roger to know that I took them. Despite being in an ash bucket, they weren't technically garbage, and free for the taking."

The sergeant smiled and shook his head. "Do you take me for an idiot."

The officer stationed at the end of Roger's driveway waved, and opened the gate for the officers. As they approached the house, they saw a truck along with five other vehicles parked in front of a row of trees. As Sgt. Ryan backed the car in place next to them, he spotted Marion. Her arm was curled around Maryann's waist, with her hand rested on her hip.

The detective caught the sergeant's stare. Seeing the two women, he asked, "What is Officer Kelly doing with Marion LaPointe?"

Sgt. Ryan's attention was focussed on the two women. "I asked her to keep an eye on her. I guess they hit it off."

With one hand on the door handle, Detective Douglas

said, "I just hope that she hasn't jeopardised our case in any way."

The slack jawed sergeant took a moment to answer. "She's a professional. I'm sure everything is fine."

On the freshly cut, weed infested lawn in front of the house, a large orange, yellow and red balloon was slowly being inflated. Falling leaves from the nearby trees littered the entire area. Mrs. Green stood next to the four person basket. By the way she pointed and moved her hands and arms, the detective surmised that she was giving the balloon's pilot some last minute instructions. Nancy stood behind her.

A long, piercing squeak drew everyone's attention to the front door of the cabin. The rusty, worn out hinges of the exterior screen door released more high notes as it opened the rest of the way. Everyone watched as Dr. Deathridge slowly exited the house, with her right arm wrapped around the pale, and visibly upset Roger.

In contrast to the other well dressed mourners, Roger wore his everyday clothes. His arms were tightly wrapped around the eight sided, trophy shaped, cherry wood urn that contained Simon's ashes. With it pressed tightly against his chest, only the upper third of the crest shaped, inscribed brass plate was visible.

Detective Douglas looked around at the small gathering. Along with Marion and Officer Kelly, were Roger, the doctor, Robert Swayze and Cindy, Nancy and her parents, Simon's lawyers, Emily and the crew manning the balloon. Being as discreet as possible, he began snapping photos and short videos of everyone there.

The sergeant walked over to Mrs. Green and asked her, "What's up with the balloon?"

In a subdued voice, she replied, "In his will, Simon requested that his ashes were to be scattered over Roger's property. In order to do that, we needed a permit. Simon wanted us to use a helicopter, but a tethered balloon was the only way his lawyers could appease the bureaucrats. I guess they were afraid that some of the ashes would drift over Roger's property line, and somehow devalue his neighbours property."

Everyone watched the balloon slowly rise into the calm air above the tethered basket. The pilot extended his hand and grabbed Roger's left hand. After the doctor helped Roger get inside the basket, she stepped away from it. While continuing to hug the urn with his right arm, Roger grabbed the edge of the basket with his left hand.

He nervously watched the three balloon handlers loosen the tethers. The balloon floated above the anchored trailer that hauled a huge, heavy winch. As it slowly released more and more cable the balloon went further and further in the air.

As the balloon continued its ascent, Nancy and her mother walked around the small crowd handing out umbrellas. Mrs. Green put on a fake smile while she handed one to Detective Douglas, and said, "Just in case some of the ashes float this way. We don't want any of them leaving the property."

Nancy saw Emily leaning against the corner of the house. Her tears had made some of her makeup run down her cheeks. Nancy walked over to her and tried to hold her hand. Emily pulled her's away and tucked both of her hands under her armpits.

To the people on the ground, it seemed like the balloon barely rose above the multi-coloured, half barren trees. In fact, it was well over twice that high. Roger could see far past the six hundred plus acres of wooded property that his parents had left him. He looked westward towards Blackett Hill. Between the tall pine trees that rose above the canopy, he could barely make out the black rooves of the two story buildings, that lined the main street.

The basket jerked and began to swivel as it came to a

halt. The pilot looked at Roger and told him, "We reached our limit. This is as high as we can go."

The people below watched as Roger removed the biodegradable bag from the urn. As he poured the ashes out, a gentle breeze lifted them into the air. What seemed to take minutes, actually took only seconds before the cloud of ash slowly dispersed into the dense forest below.

When Roger released the bag, the wind inflated it into a mini balloon. Dust particles continued to fall out of it as it slowly drifted out of sight of the people on the ground. Roger watched it get tangled on a dead branch of a maple tree.

Several minutes passed before Roger finally turned to the pilot and told him, "It's done."

The pilot called the man the standing next to the winch. "It's time, bring us down."

The winch operator turned it on, and lowered the balloon. As soon as the ropes dangling from the balloon got within reach, Mr. Green helped the other men secure them to the ground. Dr. Deathridge ran towards the basket. With the ground still a metre and a half below him, Roger opened the door, sat down and slid out. As Roger's feet hit the ground, Mr. Green grabbed his waist and kept him upright.

The doctor wrapped Roger's arm around her neck. Mr. Green slowly let go of Roger and stepped back. Staying one step behind them, his hands hovered close to Roger's waist as the pair slowly made their way to the house.

Detective Douglas almost ran as he tried to cut them off. Seeing him approaching them, the doctor stopped.

Feeling uneasy, Roger's face lost what little colour it had. His body folded as he collapsed onto the ground. Mr. Green attempted to grab him, but failed. Roger's limp body slid through his arms.

The Doctor glared at the detective. "What do you think you are doing? This is not the proper time nor place for your bossy, ape like attitude. Just stand back and leave us alone."

The detective stood there and watched Mr. Green bend down, wrap Roger's left arm around his neck and carry him to the house. The toe of Roger's left boot dragged across the ground. The doctor ran ahead and held the door open. Mrs. Green followed them into the house. The rest of the crowd, including the balloon handlers, stood around speechless.

After the shock wore off, the two lawyers walked past the detective, looked at him and shook their heads. When they knocked on the door, Mrs. Green opened it. During a brief exchange of words, the older lawyer handed her a large brown envelope. Their voices were too low for the detective to make out. After shaking Mrs. Green's hand, the pair turned around and walked directly to their car. Detective Douglas could only surmise that the envelope contained their final bill.

Looking around, Detective Douglas saw a couple members of the balloon crew soliciting the crowd for balloon rides before they deflated it. Sgt. Ryan was standing at the edge of the driveway, talking to Marion and Officer Kelly. Emily was sitting on the ground staring at the grove of trees where most of Simon's ashes had landed. Nancy was standing on her toes looking up at the balloon's pilot, as he opened it's door. Behind her, while holding a ladder, two members of the balloon's crew were grinning as they admired the beautiful, sleek young woman's figure.

The detective set the camera on his phone to video and started to covertly record everyone there. Robert and Cindy's migration over to the porch caught his interest. He watched them adjust a few pieces of firewood, and slowly turn a section of the wood pile along the front of the house, into a rough, crude bench. He knew that as soon as they sat down, the two city dwellers would soil, if not ruin their expensive, fancy clothes.

Detective Douglas smiled as Robert tried to remove the sticky, pine pitch from his hands with a couple of tissues. He watched Robert shake his head as he took off his jacket and spread it over the lowered section. As the pair sat down, held hands and stared at each other, the detective thought, *"Why not wait in their car? They must be planning on staying a while."*

Detective Douglas leaned against a maple tree and watched how everyone interacted. Periodically, he would glance at the awkward couple on the porch. With their arms folded on their laps, they both looked as if they were expecting something exciting to happen. Occasionally, Cindy nervously adjusted her wide brimmed hat, along with various parts of her short, black, skin tight dress. Partly hidden behind the tree trunk, the detective pretended to read through the notes in his notepad, while spying on the seemingly, eager couple.

Fifteen minutes had passed before Mrs. Green exited the house and handed Robert a large, thick envelope. He immediately sat back down and pulled out the large wad of papers. After he finished reading the first page, Cindy smiled and giggled as he passed it to her. The detective rocked his head gently back and forth, as he muttered, "If that is Roger's scribbling, they are probably having a really, good laugh. Even if Robert takes pity on him and publishes that pile of crap, there is no way Roger would be able to save his town with that rubbish."

Detective Douglas watched the balloon being lowered and its crew eagerly help Nancy dismount. He didn't notice Marion and the sergeant walk over to Officer Kelly's car. After a brief search for them, he spotted the back of their heads as they leaned against the far side of the it. Through its windows he noticed the odd piece of paper being passed back and forth. The detective shook his head and mumbled, "This whole thing is a huge farce."

As Marion started to read the pages Sgt. Ryan had handed to her, she gasped. "Where did you get these?"

The sergeant bit his lip before answering her. "I can't tell you." He tilted his head and gazed into her eyes, as he added, "By your reaction, I take it that you know what they are?"

She looked at him as if he had three heads. "Of course I do, don't you?"

Sgt. Ryan smiled at her. "I think I do, but I wanted to be absolutely sure. Tell me, what do you think it is?"

"It's part of a very rough, first draft of an unpublished Simon Black novel."

The sergeant was briefly speechless. "With all the spelling, grammar and typos, how can you tell that Simon Black is the one that wrote it?"

"His voice and style are clearly there." Marion stared at the sergeant. "I was a bit surprised by the amount of typos and mistakes in it. It was as if he wasn't using any spelling or grammar settings on his computer." With a bit of a giggle, she grinned and added, "I guess that's why they call it a rough outline. I bet his second draft was a whole lot cleaner. He marked almost every mistake that I noticed."

"But you are positive that Simon Black wrote this?"

While crossing her heart with her forefinger, she replied, "Absolutely."

Sgt. Ryan pulled out his wallet and handed her a couple twenty dollar bills. "Here, how about you and your new friend go up in the balloon before they deflate it."

Marion smiled at him and released a tiny chuckle. "Sure, that would be nice. I was curious to see how far Simon's ashes had spread."

As she started to walk towards Maryann, she stopped and turned her head. With a grin on her face, she told him, "You are aware that I had all ready paid them for a ride?"

Tilting his head to the side, the sergeant smiled and

said, "I had a notion. At least this way you might think of me while you are up there."

After locking the papers in the car, the sergeant walked over to Detective Douglas. "Something is not adding up. Marion swears that those papers are a first draft of a new Simon Black novel. She was absolutely positive that it was Simon that wrote them. If Roger actually wrote all the novels, that means Simon was just a front man."

Detective Douglas glanced at Sgt. Ryan. "That gives Roger Blackett an even bigger motive to kill Simon. With him no longer able to command the spotlight, he can waltz in and take over."

The sergeant grinned. "Only if he could muster the strength and courage to leave his property."

Detective Douglas glanced at Robert. "I bet he knew the truth from the very beginning. Look at him and that piece of eye candy. He doesn't seem to be missing Simon very much."

Sgt. Ryan looked at them. "Are they reading some of the stuff that Roger was working on, or something he had already finished editing?"

"Probably the latter." The detective snorted and lowered his head. "I bet Robert started to concoct a plan to fleece that simpleton the moment he found out that Simon was killed." He started to chuckle. "That's why he was defending Roger so adamantly. He won't be very happy when I put Roger behind bars."

Sgt. Ryan looked at the couple then back at Detective Douglas. "You do know that Robert can actually profit from Simon's Death, don't you? He might have a legitimate motive."

The detective shook his head. "Even if Roger wrote those books, he's an agoraphobe. He can't go out on book tours. Robert could actually lose money." After staring at the couple sitting on the wood pile, he added, "They know something we don't."

Sgt. Ryan rocked his head back and forth a couple times. "To me, Roger killing Simon doesn't really make any sense at all."

Detective Douglas turned and looked at the sergeant. "Even prisoners can write and publish books. Maybe Roger and Robert worked out a way to keep Blackett Hill going."

"But in a penal institution, he can only keep a small percentage of his earnings. Blackett Hill would be bankrupt in no time at all."

"You have to remember, killers don't always think things completely through. They don't normally plan on getting caught."

Chapter Seventeen

Sgt. Ryan saw Emily sitting on the grass staring at some trees. He walked over and sat down beside her. "How are you doing?"

Emily slowly turned, looked at him, and mumbled, "He's dead."

Sgt Ryan noticed her dilated pupils. "I know he's dead. But what I would like to know is how are you coping with it."

With a slight slur in her speech, Emily told him, "Fine, I guess. The sky is still blue, the sun came up this morning and the pine trees are still green. Everyone tells me that it will just take time to get over Simon's death." Looking at the ground, she added, "I can't see how it ever will."

The sergeant watched a tear drop run down her cheek and fall onto her black sweater. "It will, just give it time."

Ignoring what he said, Emily looked back at the trees. "When I die, I want my ashes to be scattered with his. That way we could spend eternity together."

Sgt. Ryan glanced at the trees, and told her, "In a few days, his ashes will become part of the ecosystem and live on forever. You, on the other hand, will still have a life to live."

"A part of me knows that, the rest doesn't care."

Sgt. Ryan reached out and held her hand. "Can I ask you something?"

Emily looked at his hand, she meekly said, "Sure, but I can't guarantee I will answer you."

The sergeant jerked his head towards the porch. "Look at the couple sitting on the porch. Do you remember seeing them in the store on the day of the book signing?"

Emily looked at them and tilted her head. "Yes, they were both there."

"On that dreadful day, when was the last time you saw them?"

In a bit of a stupor, Emily greatly slurred her words

as she said, "That flirt had the same hat on, plus a wig. I'm sure that she was still there when I left." Emily gazed at Sgt. Ryan. "The man had a blue suit on, but he didn't stick out like she did."

Emily took another look at the couple. Her eyebrows drooped as she told the sergeant, "Funny thing is that they both were dressed in almost the same shade of blue."

As Emily's attention went back to the grove of trees, The sergeant asked her, "Do you know who setup the book signing in the first place? Who originally contacted you?"

Emily turned her head and stared at him. "I'm not sure. The first letter had Simon Black's publisher's letterhead on it, but there was no name or signature on the bottom. I was just so happy to finally get a chance to meet him."

"Where is this letter now?"

"The last time I saw it, it was in the top desk drawer in my room. I took it home as a keepsake."

"There had to be more than that one piece of correspondence. Where is the rest?"

Looking at her lap, she answered, "They are all in my drawer. They had nothing to do with any kind of financial transactions, so I thought I would just keep them for myself."

"Were any of them signed?"

A smile spread across Emily's face. "Only one. It was hand written and signed by Simon Black himself. I couldn't believe it when I saw his signature on the bottom of it."

Sgt. Ryan swallowed and tried hard not to change his tone as he asked her, "Was it on the same stationary?"

"No, it was from some hotel in Montreal." Emily sighed as she turned and looked at the sergeant. "He wanted to personally thank me for agreeing to let him promote his new book in my store. I never thought that anyone like him would write such a personal letter to me."

The Sergeant took a deep breath. After a brief pause he asked her, "Could you tell by the writing style whether

Simon wrote the other letters or not?"

"The tone of the other letters were completely different. They were very formal. There wasn't anything elegant or personal about them. They were almost like a form letter, or something from a lawyer's office."

The sergeant flipped through his notepad. "We found your DNA on a wad of paper that was stuck in the locking mechanism of the backdoor. Why did you put it there?"

Emily shrugged her shoulders. "I wanted to sneak in and keep an eye on Simon. There are a few cracks in the plaster of the back wall. I sometimes use them to spy on Nancy. She doesn't always do things the way I want her to." Emily wrapped her arms around her neck and closed her eyes. "A lot of women got in line just to flirt with Simon. They all fantasied becoming Mrs. Simon Black. I just wanted to make sure he wasn't being overly harassed. I know how clingy some women can get."

"You could've done that from inside the store."

Emily bit her bottom lip and gently shook her head. "I didn't want Simon to think I was like the other women. I wanted him to think that I trusted him."

A smile engulfed the sergeant's face. "We thought it was something like that."

Sgt. Ryan patted her shoulder, stood up and put his notepad back into his pocket. As he looked up, he spotted Marion leaning over the edge of the balloon. "Before I leave you and go back to the others, I have to ask you one more question."

"Go ahead, ask."

"Do you see the lady leaning over the side of the balloon."

"Yeah."

"Does her wig resemble the wig the lady sitting on the wood pile wore at the book signing?"

Emily used her hand to shield the sun from her eyes

as she stared at Marion. "Yes, yes it does."

The sergeant smiled as he looked down at her and said, "Thanks for the chat. It was very helpful. I hope the next time we talk, it will be under different circumstances."

Sgt. Ryan watched Marion and Maryann lean over the side of the basket as the balloon was being tethered. As he walked towards them, the two women got out of the basket and went directly to Maryann's car. Trying not to draw attention to himself, he increased his pace to a fast walk. As Maryann started to drive off, he stepped in front of her car.

Maryann used both feet to step on the brake. Both women bounced forward, then back into their seats. Sgt. Ryan dashed over to the passenger side of the car. As Marion lowered the window, Sgt. Ryan asked her, "At the book signing, you weren't wearing a wig. What happened to it?"

Marion's eyes bulged out and held her breath. Turning away so he couldn't see her face, the embarrassed woman sharply said, "Someone stole them."

After taking a couple quick breaths, Sgt. Ryan asked her, "How many wigs did you have?"

Marion sighed and looked at him. "I had brought two with me. Someone broke into my car last Friday and stole them, along with my makeup bag. The funny thing is that I found this wig on the back seat of my car Sunday morning. My other wig plus all my makeup are still missing."

"Was your car locked?"

"I always lock my car doors. Between the wigs, makeup and the other belongings I had with me, I bet you I had over three thousand dollars worth of stuff with me."

"But only your wigs and makeup was taken?"

"Yes." Marion turned and glared at him. "Look, it's bad enough that you know I'm wearing a wig. You don't have to rub it in."

"I'm sorry. I didn't mean to."

After taking yet another deep, sighing breath, she told

him, "I couldn't find a single hairdresser that was free. I ended up doing my own hair Saturday morning, plus going through a ton of unfamiliar makeup. You can't buy the makeup I like anywhere in Canada. It'll probably take at least a month or more to get some shipped from Italy." Her hands formed fists as she continued, "It took me hours to get my hair and face to look good enough to go out in public. I really wanted to look my best for Simon."

"Where was it stolen?"

"At the campgrounds just off the highway. I went there last Friday to see Simon's agent Robert Swayze. I had heard a rumour that he was parking his mobile home there." Marion shook her head. "The rumour ended up being false."

Sgt. Ryan glanced at Maryann, then back at Marion. "You may have been set up. I think that someone wanted you there."

Marion turned and looked out the front window. "I was so frustrated. I really wanted to be the first in line, but that thief ruined everything."

Sgt. Ryan looked at the ground and told her. "I am real sorry for making you feel so uncomfortable. Please forgive me, but we need your wig. It might contain some evidence pertaining to Simon's murder."

Marion gasped, turned and glared at him. "What, in my wig?"

The sergeant looked at her. "It may still have strands of hair from the person that took it. I already have a suspect."

As Marion almost yelled out, "So you think it was Simon's killer that stole my stuff?", Maryann revved the engine to help drown out Marion's voice.

Sgt. Ryan put his head inside the car, and told her, "Yes, but we don't want anyone else to know."

Tears started to run down Marion's cheeks as she pulled off her wig and discreetly handed it to him. "Take it.

If the killer wore it, I would rather be bald than wear it."

Marion lowered her head and wrapped her arms around her face to muffle her loud, uncontrollable sobbing. Sgt. Ryan reached in and rubbed her shoulder as he softly told her, "Again, I am so sorry, but I have a job to do."

Maryann looked at him. "I'll take her back to her hotel room. I'll stay with her and make sure that she's all right."

On the way back to the station, Sgt. Ryan told Detective Douglas what he had found out. The detective looked at him. "So you figure that we will find strands of Cindy's hair inside of Marion's wig?"

"Think about it. Roger can't leave his property without having a fit. He couldn't have gone to the campground and stole Marion's stuff. I firmly believe it was a set up. For some reason, Cindy wanted to point the finger at Marion."

"Why?"

"I have no idea. At least not yet." Sgt. Ryan sat back in his seat and watched the cars travelling in the opposite direction. "There were loads of people going in and out of that campground last Friday."

"But was Cindy MacDonald one of them?"

"I'm not sure. I can't remember if the techs picked her out or not." The sergeant thought about how shockingly different Cindy appeared on her driver's licence. "But it's possible."

"But why would Cindy want to kill Simon?"

"Maybe Robert told her about Simon and Roger's agreement during some pillow talk. If he did, she might get the idea that with Simon out of the way, she could talk Robert into re-branding Roger's books and make her the next hot commodity on the writing scene. If they split Simon's share, they both could get very rich in a hurry. Twenty-five percent on top of Robert's normal commission is a lot of hush money."

"But why return the wig? Why not just destroy it?""

"In an attempt to frame Marion for the murder. She's an obsessed loner with no real alibi." The sergeant released a soft chuckle. "Hey, for a while, I even suspected her."

"We don't have a murder weapon or any concrete evidence to back up anything you suspect happened."

"Lets get the wig checked over first." After thinking a bit, the sergeant added, "Plus it wouldn't hurt to look into both Robert Swayze's and Cindy MacDonald's finances."

At the station, Detective Douglas reviewed the fuzzy video from the book store. Every time he saw anyone with hair resembling Marion's wig, he noted the time on the video. After the fourth viewing, he realized that Cindy was wearing her wide, brimmed hat when she came into the store that afternoon. *'She wasn't wearing a hat when she got her book signed.'*

Cindy disappeared from the camera's viewpoint, and later reappeared wearing the same hat as she was leaving the store. Something seemed off. He studied the before and after imagines and printed off two images. "Sergeant come over here."

When Sgt. Ryan got to his desk, the detective showed him the photos. "Something is off in these photos, but I can't quite get what it is."

The sergeant studied the pictures for a minute, looked at the detective, and told him, "Her head is larger in this one. She must've been wearing a wig in one and not the other."

With the sergeant standing next to him, Detective Douglas reviewed the scene of the suspected killer leaving through the back door wearing what looked like a wig. After reviewing the scene a half dozen more times, he scratched his head. "I am not sure, but I still think it's a man wearing a wig to help cover his face."

Sgt. Ryan used the detective's mouse to replay the

short video clip over again. "It still could be Cindy."

The detective stroked his finger across the fuzzy image's shoulders. "His shoulders are too broad?"

"She could've used some padding."

Detective Douglas snickered as he pointed out the killer's calves. "I saw Cindy's legs and those are definitely not hers."

The sergeant looked at the hazy, still image. "You are right. Cindy had a magnificent pair of dancer's calves. I don't care how bad the image is, those scrawny things are definitely not hers."

"Maybe she hired someone."

Sgt. Ryan looked at Detective Douglas and told him, "I don't think so. I think it's Robert Swayze."

"Can't be, he has an alibi. He wasn't even in town." The detective shook his head, and added, "But it is obvious that Cindy was helping whoever it was."

Sgt. Ryan rubbed the back of his neck and began to pace the floor. "Emily told me that she thought she saw Robert in the store during the time he was supposed to be in Hunter's Crossing. I know that she was well medicated, but what if she was right."

Detective Douglas looked at him. "You can't trust someone that high. She could've dreamt it."

Sgt. Ryan stopped in front of Detective Douglas, and said, "Regardless what you say, I don't think it's Roger."

"And why not? He doesn't have an alibi. Maybe he got tired of Simon." The Detective leaned back on his chair, rubbed his chin and gazed at the sergeant. "Maybe he was getting lonely and wanted something more than just a long distance, business arrangement with a man."

"So how could they even meet?"

"Maybe she found out where he lived, went for a hike and played the damsel in distress."

Sgt. Ryan shook his head. "That is a long shot at

best."

The detective grinned. "Cindy is a very beautiful woman. Someone like that could turn a man's head around. They can make a man get down on their hands and knees, and beg like a starving puppy."

"So, even with all this new information, you still actually believe it was Roger?"

Detective Douglas looked at him. "Almost from the very beginning."

"Well I think it's Robert Swayze. He had the most to lose and the most to gain. Besides, he's the one that is sleeping with Cindy."

"Maybe she's working all the angles."

The sergeant thought about Cindy's driver's licence photo some more. "You do know that she wasn't alway so glamorous. Maybe there is more to her than we can see."

"Still, you will need to prove to me that Roger isn't the killer. Without some hard evidence to convince me otherwise, I think we should be building a case against Roger Blackett." Detective Douglas smiled as he added, "Plus, you will also need to somehow nullify Robert's alibi."

"How?"

Detective Douglas shrugged his shoulders. "It's your theory." His smile turned into a wide grin. "I'm telling you, it was Roger. He is our murderer."

The sergeant went to his computer. After two and a half hours, he got up, stretched and walked over to the printer. After a half dozen pages had printed off, he grabbed them and let the printer finish printing the rest. He pulled out the third page and showed it to the detective. "I've been looking into Robert Swayze's finances. Look at how much money he had deposited into his account over the last few months. That is a lot more than he was earning."

"So maybe he won a few windfalls. He was a bit of a gambler. Look at all of his cash deductions."

"These deposits started when Roger supposedly wrote the letter about wanting to lower his percentage of the royalties. The math works out. I think Robert had found a way to redirect the difference into his pocket instead of giving it to Simon."

"So you think that Simon found out that Robert was swindling him. That could lead to motive. Unfortunately, he was nowhere near the book store."

"Well, he certainly wasn't where he said he was." Sgt. Ryan grinned as he told the detective, "I had Officer Kelly review the video footage of any police cruiser that drove by the coffee shop in Hunter's Crossing at the time Robert said he was there. She even talked to the waiters. None of them remember a man in a blue suit waiting around that afternoon. As far as we know, he could have put a few coins in the parking metre and left his car there."

Detective Douglas huffed and sighed. "Then where was he? How did he get back to Blackett Hill?"

"Remember asking the techs to review all the licence plates on Officer Kelly's dash cam video? Well they found a match to Cindy's car." With a smug smile on his face, Sgt Ryan told the detective, "To save me some time, I told Officer Kelly the time it was taken, and she was kind enough to review the footage for me. In the footage, Cindy's car was heading toward Blackett Hill, with her behind the steering wheel. A man matching Robert was sitting in the passenger seat."

The detective scratched his head. "But we watched that video a hundred times."

"Yes, but we were not looking for Cindy's car, were we?"

"You are right." Detective Douglas shook his head and looked up at the ceiling. "Officer Kelly has been a lot of help. I'll make sure she is credited for all the extra work she has done for us." He glanced at the sergeant. "Now we have a new prime suspect."

With his right hand on his hip, Sgt. Ryan leaned back in his chair and smugly told the detective, "Plus a seemingly, very willing accomplice."

Chapter Eighteen

As Sgt. Ryan started up the car, Detective Douglas phoned Dr. Deathridge. "Hello Doctor, this is Detective Douglas. I just thought I should give you a heads up, we are on our way back to Blackett Hill."

Dr. Deathridge closed her eyes, took a deep breath and asked, "So what do you want this time?"

"We had some new developments in the case, and we need a few things cleared up before we can proceed."

"So why are you calling me?"

"Because, we need some honest, clear cut answers. If you want your benefactor cleared, you need to get him ready to be questioned ASAP."

The doctor shook her head. "What's the rush?"

The detective's voice got louder. "I can't tell you, but it's vitally imperative that we get the answers right away! I will be dropping Sgt. Ryan off at the gate in about fifty minutes. He has a list of questions that we desperately need Roger to answer."

The doctor looked up at the ceiling and rubbed the back of her neck. "Roger still needs time to recuperate."

The detective sharply informed her, "Well, if he is capable of writing a new novel, he should be able to answer a few simple questions."

The doctor snapped back, "He writes to escape reality. When he is writing, Roger isn't himself anymore. He is whatever character he is writing about. Basically, in his mind, Roger Blackett doesn't exist."

Detective Douglas tried to control his frustration. "Well I need you to make him exist." After taking a deep breath, he added, "I don't even care if you have to give him some drugs, as long as he can answer our questions."

Dr. Deathridge peeked into Roger's bedroom. He was busy typing. "You are aware that if I sedate him, you can't use anything he says in court?"

"Right now, I don't care. Right now, all I want is to find Simon Black's killer."

Dr. Deathridge scratched her head, and said, "By drugging a potential witness? What is the rush?"

Detective Douglas rubbed the back of his neck. After a brief pause, he told her, "I shouldn't tell you this, but time is of the essence. I don't want my prime suspects to leave the country."

The doctor bit her bottom lip and peeked outside of the window. "Fine, but I will need a couple hours. I'll have to go back to the clinic to get the right medicine. Then, I'll need to find the right moment to properly sedate him. Roger has worked himself into an uncontrollable frenzy. It will take a while for it to get into his system, and calm him down."

"Do whatever you have to. We'll be there in about forty-five minutes. Maybe even sooner, if the sergeant can figure out how to use the gas pedal."

The doctor tried not to yell. "That's not nearly enough time."

"Fine, I'll drop Sgt. Ryan off at the gate and he can walk in. That should eat up a little more time."

"Well, I can't promise Roger will be ready for him."

"Just remember, the sooner we get answers, the sooner you are rid of me."

Sgt. Ryan pulled the car next to the police cruiser parked by the gate. As he got out, he told the detective, "I hope he is both lucid and cooperative. If not, we might hit a brick wall."

As Detective Douglas walked around the front of the car to the driver's door, he replied, "Don't fret, something always turns up. I've seen cases last for decades before someone slips up. When that happens, there will be an RCMP officer standing there with a pair of handcuffs."

The sergeant looked at him. "And sometimes cases are tossed into the unsolved pile because no solid evidence was ever found. After all, we still have no murder weapon. We don't even know what the killer used to kill Simon."

"So, we make sure that this case isn't one of those."

As the Detective drove to Blackett Hill, Sgt. Ryan slowly walked along the long, muddy driveway leading to Roger's house. The overnight rain filled in the ruts made by several sets of fresh tire tracks. When the house came into view the sergeant noticed Robert's car. Through the steamed up windows, he saw Cindy sitting in the passenger seat. They were both flipping through page after page of what the sergeant figured was Roger's new manuscript.

He walked past them and knocked on the front door. The doctor opened it and let him in without saying a word. With her forefinger pressed against her mouth, she escorted him to Roger's bedroom door. "I had to dope his coffee in order to calm him down. Any loud noise could excite him. Try to keep your voice as soft and monotone as you can."

"How..."

As Sgt. Ryan started to speak, the doctor put her finger against his lips. "Before you say a word, I should tell you that I didn't know that Roger wrote Simon Black's books."

"When did you find out?"

The doctor took a deep breath and told him, "Just before your boss called. When Robert Swayze arrived, Roger gave me a huge bundle of papers and told me to hand it to him." She turned and looked at Roger. "When I questioned him about it, he told me everything."

"But you knew that he wrote, didn't you?"

"Sure, I had encouraged him to express his feelings on paper. As an extreme introvert, Roger needed a way to vent his frustrations, and take a vacation from the pressures of the world around him." The doctor paused before adding, "Roger was fascinated with Simon Black. I thought that he was merely copying his writing style."

"Didn't you read any of his writing?"

"Sure, a couple pages here and there, but we mostly just talked about it. He has a very vivid imagination. With it, he can be anywhere in the world and never leave his house."

"Have you ever read any of Simon Black's novels?"

The doctor shook her head. "I'm to busy to read fiction. Like I said before, I thought Roger had inherited his money. I thought his writing was nothing more than a way to get out his emotions, and cope with the rest of the world."

"So he kept some secrets from you."

The doctor glanced at the sergeant and then back at Roger. "He is an extreme introvert. I should've expected it." After a brief pause, she added, "He gave me everything I ever wanted. I guess I put him on a pedestal, and overlooked the fine print. He was working his butt off trying to keep this place going, and all I saw was a scared, confused introvert."

Sgt. Ryan stretched his arm over her shoulder and rested his hand on the doorframe. Roger's chair was turned to face the window. He just sat there motionlessly staring at it. "I hope that you know that I never really thought that he was Simon's killer."

The doctor glanced at the sergeant's face. "I got that feeling. That is why I insisted that you were the one that questioned him."

Sgt. Ryan crept into the room, sat on the bed and leaned towards Roger. With the doctor sitting next to him, he asked Roger, "If you are the real writer, why were you giving Simon a larger percentage of your books' profits?"

Roger kept staring through the window as he answered, "We wanted to buy one of the Islands in the Saint Lawrence Seaway. Too many people know about this town. The people here are like me. They need to be somewhere safe. Simon was going to look after the entire transaction."

Sgt. Ryan looked at Dr. Deathridge. While shaking her head and waving her arms in front of her, she mouthed out the words, 'I didn't know anything about it.'

The sergeant turned to Roger and asked him, "Did something happen?"

"When Simon hadn't received any of the extra funds, he assumed Mrs. Green was holding on to it for him. It was months before we figured out it was gone."

"Do you know who by?"

"Not for sure." Roger lowered his head and closed his eyes. "I confronted Robert Swayze about it. At first he gave me the run around, and said it must be a booking error. When I insisted that he look into it, he started to laugh. Something came over me and I shoved him against the wall of the book store. I couldn't wait for his answer. I panicked. I couldn't breathe. I ran almost the entire way home."

Sgt. Ryan looked out the window and saw Robert in his car using a stylus to work on his tablet. "Do you think he is involved?"

"I'm not one hundred percent sure."

"But you still gave him your latest manuscript, why?"

Roger gazed at Robert. "I need that island. The seller has already got another bidder and I am still a few million short. In order to get it, I'll need a huge advance on the royalties of my next book. Robert assured me that he can make it happen."

"If you don't trust him, why don't you get another agent. I bet that there are hundreds of them that would do anything to get you to sign with them."

"That takes time. Right now, I don't have the time or energy to sieve through all of them. The closing date on the island is the end of next month. If I don't have the money by then, I'll lose both the island and the million dollar deposit I put down as security."

"You could always go to the bank and apply for a mortgage. They should know that you are good for it."

"Mrs. Green had already looked into it. I was turned

down. They told her that the money deposited in my account over the last few months barely covered my monthly expenses. They needed some proof that I can pay it off."

Sgt. Ryan looked through the window and glanced over at the trees where Simon's ashes were spread. "Why spread Simon's ashes here, when you are planning to move?"

"It was his wishes. Besides, it will take almost a year before the island is ready to be inhabited." Roger turned to look at him. "By then, the trees and vegetation would have transformed Simon's ashes into the air I breathe." Turning back and facing the window, he added, "I can't wait to inhale his essence. When I leave, I'll be taking part of him with me."

"You could have talked to his lawyers, and maybe kept his ashes in the urn."

Roger shook his head. "It's better this way. I don't want him sitting on a mantel like a conversation piece. What would happen to his ashes after I die?"

Sgt. Ryan glanced through his notes. "So why Simon? Why did you let him become the face of your novels?"

Roger smiled and slowly told the sergeant, "I am a writer. Simon's an author. The difference is one writes books, and the other has the ability to go out there and actually sell them. We were a perfect match. He wanted to prove to the world that he wasn't the same social misfit that he once was. While I just wanted something to eat. When my parents died, I had no real income. I couldn't afford to pay my bills."

"There are government services out there that are willing to help you?"

"They wanted me to sell my property, move into a town and look for work. One worker even offered to help me get a computer so I could work from home. Even she didn't fully understand the restraints of my condition. I simply can't function with other people. Even my visits with Dr. Deathridge had to be kept short."

"But you could with Simon."

"Simon was different. At first, he arranged everything. We never even had to talk, or see each other. Everything was done by mail."

"So, how did you survive before your arrangement with Simon?"

"I cut and sold lumber and firewood to pay the taxes. I had a stand at the end of my driveway with a money box. I found that most of the people here were honest. I trapped and harvested what I could to eat. When poachers and hunters began trespassing on my property. They shot everything. My traps were empty and I was left with nothing except a few rodents and a handful of ferns to eat. I was starving."

Sgt. Ryan refocused on Robert. "Do you think Robert could have killed Simon?"

Roger's facial expression changed as he turned and looked at Sgt. Ryan. With his eyebrows almost touching the top of his nose, he told the sergeant, "Why, Simon is the one that sells the books? He is the one that makes everyone rich."

Sgt. Ryan calmly answered back, "What if Simon thought that Robert had something to do with the missing money? Do you think he would confront him?"

Roger remained silent for a while before he mumbled out his answer. "I guess he might."

"What if things got violent? Robert isn't stupid. He knows how to manipulate people. Do you really think he won't have a plan in place to deal with Simon?"

"But murder? Why kill him?"

"For money. I believe he had ran up some huge gambling debts." The sergeant took a deep breath, flexed his hands and tried to remain calm. "How could you work with someone that stole money from you, and may have even killed your partner?"

Roger vigorously shook his head and tried to shake off

the effects of the drugs. He looked at the sergeant, grinned, and in a sharper tone said, "Karma can be a real bitch when she needs to be."

In a more forceful voice, the sergeant blurted out, "And so can the law."

Roger's eyes rapidly bounced around and his head started to twitch, as his brain tried to digest all the information it had just received. His left hand turned into a fist, as he angrily, spewed out, "If what you say is correct, either way, mister Robert Swayze will pay for what he has done."

Stg. Ryan smiled and told him, "And I will see to it."

Roger turned his head and looked at the doctor, than back at the sergeant. With a strange grin on his face, he told him, "Once I have gotten what I need from him, I'm willing to let karma settle things." Roger had a faint smile on his face as he added, "No one truly gets away with anything. Not here. Not in my town."

In Blackett Hill, Detective Douglas walked around the outside of the book store and forced his way through the hedge behind it. After brushing off the twigs and foliage off his clothes, he knocked on the back door of the cynical woman's house. As he knocked a second time, the short, feisty lady yelled out, "Who is it?"

"It is Detective Douglas. We spoke a while ago about the people loitering behind the book store last Saturday."

The lady opened the door. "Oh yeah, the lazy, loud mouth, do nothing cop."

The detective squared off his stance, took a deep breath and tried to control his anger, "Can you remember someone wearing a dark wig that day. It would have been rather late."

"Was it a man or a woman?"

Surprised by the response, the detective shrugged his shoulders, and said, "Either or."

The woman looked down at the ground and shook her head. "That was a while ago. I seem to recall a funny looking man with something on his head."

The detective rocked his head back and forth. "Why do you say funny?"

The lady looked up at him. "He was wearing a garbage bag over his jacket and it wasn't even raining at the time. How funny is that?"

"Why didn't you tell me this before?"

"I just thought my eyes were playing tricks on me." She spotted another piece of trash stuck in a bush. While pointing at it, she said, "I was a bit frazzled by all the mess. I initially thought it was Nancy putting out the trash, but the fool forgot to take it with her. The poor girl isn't the brightest bulb on the planet."

"But you said man, not woman?"

"That's right." She stared into the detectives face. "He was much too tall, and his shoulders were to wide to be Nancy. I don't know what I was thinking. Like I said, I was completely frazzled at the time."

"Did you see what he had on his feet or legs?"

"No, I was bent down picking up some garbage at the time. The hedge was blocking my view. I only saw him from his waist up."

"So, you didn't see his face at all?"

"Sorry." The lady shook her head and forced herself to smile. "He turned and walked away too fast to get a look."

"So you wouldn't be able to identify him?"

"No way. Basically, all I saw was a man wearing a dark garbage bag, with some dark shaggy thing over his head."

Detective Douglas took out his phone and found a short video of Roger. He held his phone in front of her and said, "Does this man look anything like the man you saw?"

The woman shook her head. "I don't think so. Like I

said, I didn't get a good look at him."

The detective flipped to another video and repeated his question. "Does this man look anything like the man you saw?"

The woman froze. "That could be him. They both walked in the same smug fashion. You know, like a cocky young hoodlum or a sleazy politician."

Two small, rain drops fell on Detective Douglas's phone as he paused the video of Robert and Cindy walking to the porch. Ignoring the light drizzle, he released a long, loud sigh. He smiled at the stunned woman and told her, "Thanks for the information. It really helps our case."

"At least this time, you are actually making an effort to find the real felon."

The detective froze for a second. "What do you mean?"

"You don't remember me do you? Well, I'll never forget you." The woman stormed back into her house and slammed the door shut.

The stunned detective heard her lock the door. "I know I should know her, but from where."

Sgt. Ryan opened the door and saw beads of water covering Robert Swayze's car. He pulled his coat partly over his head before stepping outside. As he walked around Robert's car, he stopped beside it to turn up his coat's collar.

As he glanced through the driver's window, he saw Robert insert the stylus end of his pen into a clip on the top of his tablet like an antenna. Robert turned to him, smiled and nodded his head, as he folded the stylus down the side of the tablet. The sergeant watched as a second clip circled around the head of the pen and snugly encapsulated it.

Almost halfway down the driveway, Sgt. Ryan heard a car creeping up behind him. He turned around and saw Dr. Deathridge's head sticking out the driver's side window. As their eyes met, she yelled out, "Need a lift to the end of the driveway?"

The sergeant yelled back, "Sure."

When the doctor dropped Sgt. Ryan off at the gate, he saw the police officer was sitting in his car. After thanking the doctor for the ride, he pulled up his coat and ran to the passenger side of the police cruiser. By the time he got inside, the doctor's car was out of sight.

While waiting for Detective Douglas to return, Sgt. Ryan jotted down some notes about the interview. He rolled his pen between his fingers and thought about Robert's stylus. It was different. It had a pen at one end and a rubber knob at the other. He thought about how easily the rubber end snapped into the hinged clip. *'You would never have to worry about the rubber coming off and marking up the screen with that stylus.'*

Then he recalled seeing grey stress marks around the pin that attached the black clip to the corner of the tablet. It took him less then a minute to come up to the conclusion, "That's the murder weapon. He used his tablet to push it into Simon's brain. He didn't use a novelty pen, he used his stylus."

The officer turned and looked at him. "What are you talking about?"

Sgt. Ryan stared at him and said, "We never identified the murder weapon. I think I know what it was."

As the officer repositioned himself to talk to the sergeant, Robert drove through the gateway. Sgt. Ryan pointed at Robert's car as it turned onto the road, and blurted out, "And it is in that car!"

The officer repositioned himself behind the steering wheel and turned on the ignition. As he was about to turn on the flashers, Sgt. Ryan said, "Stop, we'll need a warrant."

The stunned officer glared at him, and said, "Are you sure? We can easily catch up to them?"

Sgt. Ryan shook his head. "If he suspects that we

know what the murder weapon is, he could toss it out the window and we may never find it." With a twisted smile on his face, the sergeant added, "Besides, we could easily arrange for it to be confiscated at the border. The border guards could examine it, and confirm my suspicion, without them even knowing that they are under investigation."

Chapter Nineteen

The drizzle had turned into a light rain as Robert drove down the narrow two lane road towards the highway. He reached over and gently rubbed Cindy's thigh as he approached a long, right bend. To his right was a chiselled out rock face and to his left was a deep ravine with a raging river below.

After releasing a sigh, Cindy turned and looked at him. "That didn't quite go as planned."

Robert smiled and told her, "At least I got him to sign a very generous book deal. That alone will make us rich."

Cindy bit her bottom lip and stared out the side window. As she brushed his hand away from her thigh, she told him, "It's just that I was expecting so much more."

As Robert continued around the turn, the four-way flashers of a parked car in the oncoming lane redirected his attention. Suddenly, a woman standing in the middle of the right lane came into view. Wearing a bright orange jacket, she frantically waved her hands in the air to get his attention.

The woman seemed to panic and ran towards the parked car. Trying to avoid hitting her, Robert swerved towards some greenery on the right of the road. It wasn't a bush. It was just some vines clinging to the side of a large boulder.

As the front passenger corner of the car hit it, Cindy lunged forward. Her seatbelt whipped her head backwards, and smashed it against the passenger side window. The impact caused blood to gush out of her nose, and a large gash above her right eye.

Robert lost control of the car as it's rear end began to spin around. It's bumper narrowly missed the parked car as it crossed lanes.

The car spun towards a badly eroded section of the shoulder. After spinning in a complete circle, the rear driver's side of the car struck the poorly maintained, guard rail with enough force that it snapped off four support posts. The railing curled upwards as the rear of the car slid into the washed out gap beneath it.

The back three-quarters of the driver's side of the car was leaning over the edge. The twisted guard rail clung to the front passenger corner of the car. Robert unbuckled his seatbelt, grabbed his tablet and leaned over Cindy's comatose body. After pushing the passenger door open as far as it would go, he stretched out his left arm and yelled out, "Lend me a hand."

Dr. Deathridge walked over to him. With a wide grin on her face, she told him, "Why should I?"

As the car started to slide under the twisted guardrail, Robert yelled out, "Come on! You are a doctor. You have to help me!"

The doctor kneeled down and looked at him. "Karma is a bitch, and guess what, I'm Karma. Everyone around here knows better than screwing with the residents of Blackett Hill. I guess people like you just have to learn the hard way."

Robert flung his tablet onto the shoulder of the road. Using both hands, he frantically crawled over Cindy's limp, slumped-over body. He reached out and grabbed the bottom lip of the guard rail with his left hand, and a clump of tall grass with his right.

The rock that was bracing the rear, passenger wheel gave way and the car jolted clockwise. Robert was forced to release the grass and twisted his body around the passenger door. Cindy began to moan as he used her head as a foot hold. As soon as he flipped back onto his stomach, he grabbed a clump of weeds with his right hand and yelled out, "Come on, you got to help me. I'll make it worth your while."

The doctor stood up and started to laugh. "I'm not like Simon, or even Roger. And I'm definitely nothing like that floosie you are so willing to sacrifice."

The loud snap of another post made Robert looked

back at the car. He heard Cindy scream as it started to roll down the ravine. Her screams stopped as it hit a boulder, flipped end over end in the air and landed right side up on the river bank. He turned to the doctor and yelled out, "I'll give you anything you want."

"How about what you took from Simon Black?" Dr. Deathridge stretched out her leg and pressed the smooth, wet, leather sole of her shoe against the exposed tip of his thumb.

The pain ran up Robert's arm and caused him to clamp his jaw shut. While he clung onto the railing, he tightened his grip on the clump of damp weeds, and desperately tried to find some footing.

As the doctor twisted her foot, his thumb initially felt like it was burning, then turned cold. She grinned and stared at him. "Do you know that watching justice being served can be very rewarding? Trust me, it is."

As soon as she took her foot away, Robert's numb thumb slid away from the railing, along with his fingers. He scrambled to get a hold of anything he could. The fingers of his left hand clawed into the damp ground and grabbed a hold of several thin, string-like roots of a nearby spruce tree. He watched in horror as the long, shallow roots popped out of the ground. He slipped sideways but managed to hang onto the four, unearthed roots. Using both hands, he used them to climb up the embankment.

As he reached for the guard rail, he looked up and saw the sadistic grin on the doctor's face. The rain made her hair shimmer. With water dripping off her nose and chin, she tilted her head to the side and told him, "Where do you think you are going?"

He felt one of the roots break. Robert's jaw hung open as he watched the others rapidly follow suit. When the last root snapped, Dr. Deathridge smiled as he tumbled backwards over the side of the ravine. The doctor started to chuckle as his screams echoed in the ravine below her.

She continued to laugh as she ran over to a solid part of the guard rail, and peered over the edge. She made it just in time to see Robert's body bounce off a boulder and splash into the river.

The doctor smiled as she slowly danced her way back to her car to report an accident. She left her four-way flashers on as she parked her car onto the shoulder of the road. While listening to some soothing, meditation music, she closed her eyes and calmly waited for the police to respond.

A wailing siren caused the doctor to opened her eyes and scramble out of the car. She frantically used both of her arms to wave Sgt. Ryan and Detective Douglas to stop.

While the detective was getting out of the car, she ran over to him and almost screamed out, "I was heading back to Roger's house when I noticed the curled up, guard rail. The posts weren't snapped like that when I initially drove by, so I stopped to check it out." Pointing to the eroded gap under the turned up guard rail, she added, "The car must have really creamed the railing and slid under it."

As Sgt. Ryan put on his reflective vest, he asked her, "What caused you to turn around and go back?"

Dr. Deathridge used her hand to shield her eyes from the rain. "I got a message from Mrs. Green saying that Roger needed me."

Detective Douglas put on his reflective vest as he walked over to the twisted guard rail. In the mud, the only tracks he initially saw were that of the cars. As he walked along the shoulder to get a better view of the ravine, he spotted what remained of the doctor's nearly washed out footprints. Looking down, he saw an upright car halfway in the river. The current was rocking it back and forth, inching it further and further into the water.

Sgt. Ryan grabbed a pair of binoculars from the glove

compartment of their car and used them to inspect the wreckage. The passenger door had been ripped off, and a woman's body was draped halfway out of the car. From what he could see of the licence plate, he deduced, "That's definitely Robert Swayze's car. That means the woman in the passenger seat is probably Cindy MacDonald."

Detective Douglas grinned and shook his head. "I guess Robert was in a bit of a hurry to leave the country."

Sgt. Ryan glanced at the detective. "The driver's door is shut, but no one is in the driver's seat."

Detective Douglas noticed the pulled out roots and dug up vegetation. "I think the coward must have crawled out. The weasel never even tried to save her."

The sergeant leaned over the railing, and studied the area where Robert had tried to climb out. "I don't think he made it. If he had, we would've seen some evidence of it along the railing and the shoulder of the road."

"You are probably right. Even the doctor left some footprints behind." Detective Douglas sighed and as he looked down at the fast flowing river. "I'm sure his body will eventually pop up somewhere."

After he set up some flares to warn any oncoming traffic, the sergeant inspected the faint skid marks on the damp road. Detective Douglas pointed to the paint on the boulder, and told him, "Something must've distracted him. He barely had time to hit the brakes before he clipped that boulder."

"Could have been an animal."

The detective shrugged his shoulders. "I don't see him as an animal lover. Maybe it was another car, or a small herd of deer. Something big enough to actually scare him."

"If it was a herd of deer, he didn't hit any of them."

Squatting down, the detective studied the skid marks. "This rain is going to make it hard to properly assess the scene. By the way the rubber scraped off his tires, I would say that the car flung around in a complete circle and smashed into the guard rail."

The doctor stood next to her car and smiled. "Karma can be a real bitch."

Sgt. Ryan slowly rocked his head back and forth. "In this case, you might be right."

When he looked over at the doctor, he noticed something under her car. "Can you pull your car ahead a bit?"

"Sure."

The sergeant guided the doctor ahead. Then he went behind her car, squatted, and looked at Robert's muddy tablet. Despite the doctor driving over it, and squashing it into the mud, it appeared in relatively good shape. The hinged stylus was swung around and resembled a radio antenna. He waved the detective over and pointed at the tablet. "I firmly believe that, that's your murder weapon."

Detective Douglas looked down at the tablet. "So you believe that he just used the tablet like a handle to push it in."

"Like a lot of people, he just used the pen as a stylus. That is why there was still wax covering the end of the ink cartridge." Sgt. Ryan smiled and added, "Remember the rectangular bruises on Simon's chest. I'll bet the corners of that tablet will match them."

"I think you nailed it bang on." Detective Douglas saw Dr. Deathridge looking over the edge of the ravine and shook his head. "I guess Roger will never get his island."

Dr. Deathridge turned around and smiled. "Why not? Robert had emailed Roger's manuscript to his publishing house before he left, and the paperwork is all signed. That was the message that Mrs. Green had sent me. That's why I decided to turn around."

"But who is going to sell the books? Simon is dead and so is Cindy."

The doctor smiled. "The book will be released in

Simon's name. A book from the grave will sell itself. Roger will make a small fortune."

Detective Douglas rubbed his chin. "We thought that Robert was going to release it under Cindy's name."

The sun broke through the dark rain clouds as the doctor started to laugh. "That is what Robert Swayze wanted to do, but Roger wouldn't agree to it. That was probably why he left in such a huff."

"But Roger was drugged up? Would his signatures be even legal?"

The doctor stepped toward the detective and grinned. "I gave him a stimulant to counteract the drug I gave him. Besides, under the circumstances, I don't think anyone is going to make a fuss."

The drive back to English Lookout was quiet. The smug look on the doctor's face haunted Detective Douglas as he stared out the car window. Shortly after Sgt. Ryan turned onto the highway and pointed the car south, the rain had completely stopped. As they approached English Lookout, everything appeared completely dry. It looked as if they never got any rain at all.

Sgt. Ryan made a detour past Detective Douglas's house. Two sets of scaffolding were set up outside of it. As they got closer, they noticed a pile of garbage bags and luggage on the lawn. Detective Douglas saw the pile and yelled out, "Pull in."

The sergeant stepped on the brake, backed up, and drove into the driveway. Detective Douglas opened his door before the car even came to a stop.

Seeing her husband approach the door, Mrs. Douglas stepped outside with some pamphlets in her hand. "Well, since you are never here, and the painter's were, I thought I'd get the outside painted."

Detective Douglas put his hands on his hips. "So what colour this time?"

"Pink, I maybe colour blind, but there is something about the colour pink that I like."

Detective Douglas yelled out, "Well I don't, and I never will."

His wife smiled and released a soft, defiant chuckle. "I know. That's why I packed all your stuff." Pointing to the bags on the lawn, she shook her head and added, "I've tried and tried. I even asked the sergeant for help."

Detective Douglas glared at his wife as he barked out, "That was really underhanded of you. A real wife doesn't do stuff like that behind her husbands back."

Rocking her head back and forth, she yelled back, "You are aware that everything doesn't always have to be your way, all the time. I'm a person too." In a calmer voice, she added, "I want to know what it is like to have things my way for a change."

As the detective stared at her with his mouth open, Mrs. Douglas turned to the painters. "So what do you think you are doing. Get to work."

Detective Douglas screamed out, "Stop! Just stop everything!"

Mrs. Douglas walked over to him and handed him the pamphlets in her hand. "Take these. You might need some reading material in whatever hotel room you will be staying at tonight."

He looked at the pamphlets, 'Understanding Abusive Behaviour', and 'Escaping an Abusive Relationship'. While looking at his wife, he mumbled, "So our marriage is over, just like that?"

"Yep." Turning to the painters, she yelled, "I hired you to paint, so get painting."

Detective looked at the pamphlets again. His face began to scrunch up as he remembered where he had seen them. "That dam meddling doctor."

Sgt. Ryan watched the detective pound his fists

against his forehead, as the painters began to paint over the white siding. As the fresh, pink paint glistened in the sunlight, the sergeant couldn't help but smile. "I guess karma really is a bitch."

The End

Lightning Source UK Ltd.
Milton Keynes UK
UKHW012048080321
380016UK00017B/1978/J